Months after she had been injured in an horrific car crash Marie MacSweeney wrote up her experiences of the event and its immediate aftermath in an article which was published in the Sunday Independent. Among the many responses was a letter from poet, Pat Ingoldsby. He explained how moved he was when reading the article. "If you are not already a writer," he wrote to Marie, "you sure as hell should be." It was many years however, before she was free to take her writing seriously. And today, among the exciting stories in this collection are some which have been chosen for publication or as prize winners by John Boland, Roddy Doyle, Ita Daly, James Plunkett, J.P. Dunleavy, Brian Leydon, David Marcus and Peter Fallon.

Marie MacSweeney grew up in Dublin, one of five children of Kerry parents. She also lived in Wales and in County Meath before moving to Drogheda. She is a member of the Meath, Louth and Kerry Archaeological and Historical Societies. She tutors in Creative Writing and is an occasional broadcaster. She has three grown-up sons.

GW00976010

Marie MacSweeney

OUR ORDINARY WORLD
AND OTHER STORIES

To Betty

Warmest Wishes

Marie MacSweeney

June 2004

Printed in Victoria, Canada

Note for Librarians: a cataloguing record for this book that includes Dewey Classification and US Library of Congress numbers is available from the National Library of Canada. The complete cataloguing record can be obtained from the National Library's online database at:
www.nlc-bnc.ca/amicus/index-e.html
ISBN 1-4120-2095-6

TRAFFORD

This book was published on-demand in cooperation with Trafford Publishing.
On-demand publishing is a unique process and service of making a book available for retail sale to the public taking advantage of on-demand manufacturing and Internet marketing. On-demand publishing includes promotions, retail sales, manufacturing, order fulfilment, accounting and collecting royalties on behalf of the author.

Suite 6E, 2333 Government St., Victoria, B.C. V8T 4P4, CANADA
Phone 250-383-6864   Toll-free 1-888-232-4444 (Canada & US)
Fax 250-383-6804   E-mail sales@trafford.com   Web site www.trafford.com
TRAFFORD PUBLISHING IS A DIVISION OF TRAFFORD HOLDINGS LTD.
Trafford Catalogue #04-0019   www.trafford.com/robots/04-0019.html

10   9   8   7   6   5   4   3   2

This book is dedicated to my sons
Noel, Eoghan and Ciaran Cosgrave
And to Eleonora, Helen and Simone –
the women in their lives
- with love.

ACKNOWLEDGEMENTS

Some of these stories have been published or
broadcast by The Sunday Tribune,
The Connaught Tribune,
The Meath Chronicle,
The Drogheda Independent,
The Fingal Independent,
STET
Drumlin,
R.T.E. Radio One,
The Stranger & Other Stories - Fish Collection,
Phoenix Irish Short Stories 1998
edited by David Marcus,
Splinters 3,
The Edgeworth Papers, Volumes 3 & 5,
Cork Literary Review,
The Waterford Review, Volume 6,
Extended Wings 4.
Here's Me Bus (New York).

CONTENTS

STRANGERS AND BARBED WIRE FRIENDS

Immediately I was introduced to her I was drawn to Lise-Ann Hinds. Opposites attract, the wise ones say, and indeed she was the polar opposite of me in every conceivable way. Physically she was fluid and loose limbed while I held myself together for fear something might shatter me. I was also fatter, more tense and, compared to her, exceedingly timid. I thought I had the edge on her in some ways though, intellectually I suppose, and in my knowledge of art and other cultural matters. But she surprised me one day by phoning to ask if I'd be interested in attending a lecture on Gauguin in Belfast early the following week. Truth is I never suspected she knew about Gauguin at all.

"Lise-Ann, I'd love to," I stammered.

"Oh good," she said, "he's one of my absolute favourites. There are a few things I'd like to go over with you, especially in his earlier works."

"Of course," I said, not quite knowing how to evaluate this new dimension of our relationship. "I'll look forward to that."

"Half eleven then, next Monday," she beamed at me down the line, "see you then."

I hurried the coat-trailing week towards Monday. The shop was busy enough, with a good throughflow of customers and lots of new merchandise to price and to hang. I closed up early on Friday and set out for the library. The traffic was bad, as was usual at the beginning of the weekend, and I bit my nails to shreds while I was waiting. In the library I quickly located some books on the life and works of Gauguin. I knew, of course, that the nineteenth century French painter had been taken, while still a child, to Peru. I was aware of the fact that when he was thirty something years old he had packed in his job at the Paris Stock Exchange and become an itinerant painter especially bewitched by the islands and islanders of Tahiti. I knew also the dazzling splash and spray of his work. But all this was not enough if I were to be adequate to Lise-Ann's demands. I'd have to read up some more.

I was in business with Susan. We ran a boutique together. She's fifty and single and was in the rag trade in England until some Italian importer wiped her eye. I'd needed to get something going for myself and was glad when she suggested that we might run a shop together. It was agreed that she'd handle the buying end and that I'd keep the accounts. Both of us would spend time in the shop, on a week on week off basis, and be available to our customers. My husband had absconded about six months earlier and left me with lots of time on my hands so this arrangement suited me. I had no idea where Danny was. It was reported to me on many humiliating occasions that he was still in the locality but I had not seen or heard from him since the day he disappeared with the money I'd stashed away in a 'safe place' in case I needed to make a quick getaway. He never beat me, but l was mortally afraid of him.

On Monday I rose early. I read and reread the important passages of the book on Gauguin in preparation for any questions Lise-Ann might ask. I was at the main entrance of the lecture hall at half past eleven, as she had suggested. Winter lingered, though it was late spring. The wind blew in directly from the north and brought with it a hint of rain. I shivered slightly and had to stamp the ground to keep warm. About ten minutes later Lise-Ann flounced up the steps towards me, her golden hair a gleaming frame about her head, her eyes eager and alert.

"How are you, Eileen?" she asked, smiling.

"I'm fine," I told her, "just fine."

"The lecture begins at twelve," she said then, "let's have a cup of coffee while we're waiting."

Our visit to the gallery was satisfactory. Lise-Ann turned to me for opinions on many aspects of Gauguin's work but particularly on the Brittany period. This was good. It narrowed the gap between us. There were times, you see, when I wondered what Lise-Ann saw in me and why she was my friend. She was altogether more vivacious and extrovert and I thought she must have found me very dull indeed. The Gauguin visit gave me a chance to show off and to consolidate our friendship.

It upset me terribly when she introduced Claire to the scene. I'd have been happy to encircle our developing friendship with barbed wire and to keep out all newcomers. But Claire was in Lise-Ann's house on one of the evenings I'd been invited round.

"Eileen," Lise-Ann said as she ushered me into the lounge, "meet Claire."

Edging slowly across salmon deep-pile I reluctantly placed my hand in Claires. It was obvious she was expecting me.

"Claire is an old friend," Lise-Ann said to me. "We've known each other since we were at school together in the seventies." They smiled in tandem towards me and I was jealous and afraid.

"Delighted to meet you," I lied.

"Me too," Claire murmured. She was large, in her thirties, and was attractive in a dark and brooding sort of way. I did not like her at all.

"Sit down you two," Lise-Ann instructed. "You can chat together while I get supper. I won't be long." Claire lowered her ample frame into a deep armchair and indicated another one for me. Already I was at a disadvantage, schoolgirl-like being told what to do.

"Annie tells me you two go to art galleries and things," she said. The familiar 'Annie' unsettled me.

"Well," I began to stutter, "we don't actually ..."

"I wouldn't know a Rembrandt from a rough sketch," she interrupted. Her admission was articulated as a position of superiority. I detected the advantage in her voice.

"Lise-Ann likes Gauguin," I said foolishly.

"She likes what?"

"Gauguin. The French painter Eugene Henri Paul Gauguin. She likes his work."

"Is that a fact now?" Her tone dismissed my confidence as insignificant.

Inside the dining room we found the table laden with all manner of mouthwatering things. Over supper the two of them discussed mutual friends and exuded me. At half past ten I made my excuses and left. It was raining as I made my way home and I allowed the rain to filter through my hair and to coast slowly down my face. It would, perhaps, clear away the confusion that was enveloping me. From that day forward the only way I could meet up with Lise-Ann was to suffer Claire. Usually it was just for a mid-morning coffee on one of my days off or for the occasional shopping trip to the city. During these outings Claire chatted away to me but there was a critical distance in her tone which invalidated her protestations of friendship. And anyway, I was not at all ready to be friends.

On an early summer day Lise-Ann suggested a seaside picnic. When I arrived for our usual morning get together she and Claire had a picnic basket prepared and were ready to leave. The whole thing came as a surprise to me.

"We'll use my car," Claire said. "It's more comfortable for three."

We set up the picnic at a spot where a river enters the sea. An onshore breeze came in clean and cold from the east, and the dried vegetation clinging to the small rocks nearby reminded me of the frail, thin-haired heads of old ladies. I ate reluctantly, entering unenthusiastically into a conversation about the individual qualities of Lise-Ann's collection of exotic houseplants.

"Where's your husband, Eileen?" Claire suddenly asked.

I'd never discussed Danny with her and her question startled me. "I've no idea," I replied, resenting her enquiry, "no idea at all."

A few weeks later Lise-Ann prepared another picnic. This time we went to a forest. Two men hung about all the time we were there, but when I mentioned how disturbed I was to see them stalk us like that Lise-Ann and Claire dismissed my fears as nonsense.

"You've been on your own too long," Lise-Ann scoffed. "If you're sure your Danny's gone for good you should get yourself another man."

Sometimes you get caught in other people's images of you. That's what happened when I agreed to meet Lise-Ann and Claire at the Leisure Centre.

"You're such a sport," Lise-Ann prattled as she persuaded me to teach her how to swim. The Leisure Centre was three miles outside the town and Claire picked me up and drove me there.

"Do you swim well?" she asked as she drove.

"They say l do," I answered.

"I can only do the breast stroke," she offered. "Which stroke do you prefer?"

"I like the front crawl best, I suppose," I said, "or the butterfly. It really depends on my mood."
She laughed. "Even on my best stroke," she blustered, "I'm terrible. I can only do one width."

The pool was almost empty. Evening sunlight burst through the heavy glass panels and peppered the water with tiny shards of silver. Lise-Ann looked stunning in a scarlet swimsuit.

"Have you brought a cap?" I asked her.

"Oh, do I need one?"

"If you want to learn to swim property you'll have to put your head right down into the water. A cap is essential."

"I'll bring one next time', she said, smiling. "What do I do now?"
While Claire swam an indifferent breaststroke around the edge of the pool I began a basic routine with Lise-Ann. She was extremely receptive to my coaching.

"You're good," I encouraged. "Very good. You'll make a swimmer yet."

"Will I really?" She seemed genuinely pleased. And it pleased me greatly to see her pleased.

"Oh yes," I told her. "You're a natural. I think you'll do very well indeed."

On the way home Claire drove very slowly. Neither she nor Lise-Ann spoke, and I was too heavily involved in my tiny triumph to notice their mood. About half a mile down the leafy lane we were travelling Claire suddenly brought the car to a stop. Lise-Ann jumped out and opened the back door so that a man who had emerged from the ditch could sit in beside me. Instantly I recognised him as one of the pair who had watched while we picnicked in the woods.

"So this is Danny's lass?" he asked.

"Yes," Lise-Ann said.

He turned to Claire. "She wouldn't tell?" he demanded, "you got nothing out of her?"

"No. Nothing at all," Claire said.

"We'll soon alter that." He spoke to her while smiling at me. I saw the smile spread slowly across his face but his eyes were cold. I began to scream. Lise-Ann quickly opened her bag and drew out a solid wedge of cotton wool. The man grabbed it from her, sprinkled something over it and held it firmly over my mouth and nose. I struggled in vain for a few seconds, but the world gradually spun away from me into the terrible darkness of outer space.

I sat shivering in a damp place. Above me I smelt the rancid odour of decomposing thatch. My hands were tied behind my back, my ankles bound together and a blindfold covered my eyes. I heard a brief, whispered conversation nearby and then someone entered the room.

"Where's Danny?" the voice demanded.

"I don't know," I told him. "You must believe me, I don't know."

"Really? Why should I believe YOU?" The owner of the voice fumbled with the blindfold and it was quickly removed. Two green eyes stared at me from out of a black mask. Odd, but the hen-brown, speckled centre of the pupils reminded me of my Danny and how his eyes had laughed along with him - all those years ago.

"My husband's gone almost a year," I stammered. "I've no idea where he is."

The man knelt in front of me and removed the tight cord which was around my ankles. "Really?"

"I haven't heard from him at all," I elaborated. "I tried really hard to trace him but got nowhere with the search. As far as I'm concerned I'm a deserted wife." The information tumbled out in an incoherent rush. My questioner winked at me.

"Really?" he persisted. He screwed his mouth into a lop-sided smile. My stomach lurched at the trice-repeated query and how he smiled when he spoke to me. I was relieved when he finally left the room. Later, on what sounded like a small, battery-operated radio nearby, I heard that the police were searching for me. My captors laughed at this, telling themselves how well concealed I was and how utterly impossible it would be for anyone to find me until they were finished with me.

Claire arrived each day at eleven. She sat opposite as he questioned me. She muffled my screams when he beat me. She helped hold my head under water when frustration drove him to pretend to drown me. But she never spoke.

"We're sick of you playing the innocent," Lise-Ann said when she arrived on the sixth day. I cried openly. I'd hoped that what was happening was happening in spite of her. I'd convinced myself that she was an unwilling dupe in Claire's scheme. For comfort I took to remembering the good times we two had together and I told myself that if I ever got out of that place in one piece I'd search for Lise-Ann. I thought she might be a prisoner too. Sometimes I even imagined I heard the small, suffocated weeping of a brutalized woman in the room next to me.

"Cut out the shit," she barked at me, "where's Danny? Tell us where Danny is and we'll let you go."

"I don't know where Danny is." Fear transformed that statement into a scream.

"Come on. No one believes Danny left his little love nest without good reason. He's away on a job, isn't he? Admit it, bitch. That husband of yours is away on a job and you know where."

"On a job," I repeated, knowing in my heart that my husband was capable of all kinds of terrible things.

She laughed at me. I recalled how she laughed the evening she first swam, the same evening she had arranged for my capture, or so it now seemed.

"You don't think I'm a f, f, f, Fenian?" I asked, faltering over the familiar word.

"As good as," she replied. "Fucking one and then protecting him when all we want is to give him his due. But believe me, Eileen dear, he will get his due."

I was there for about ten days when there was a sudden commotion nearby and I heard the high-pitched whine of a helicopter in the sky. They threw open the door of my room.

"Get on your feet, bitch," the man ordered. His voice trembled slightly as he pushed me to the door.

"Where's Annie?" I heard Claire shout above the noise. "She went out to the loo a few minutes ago. Where is she?"

"How would I know?" the man yelled. "It's up to her to get herself back inside." He flung me out into the open as the helicopter landed. I saw Danny jump from its door.

"I didn't think he'd come like this," the man mumbled to himself, "not out of the bloody sky." Suddenly Claire, standing directly behind me, drew a sharp breath. "He's got her," she howled. "Look, he's got Annie."

Danny had pounced on Lise-Ann as she attempted to make her way back into the cottage. He pushed her face into the ground and kicked her head. Hearing her shrill, animal scream over the noise of the endlessly rotating blades I broke free and ran towards her.

"Leave her alone," I yelled at Danny. "Don't do that, you bastard. Leave her be." Almost immediately he spun around and aimed his gun at me. There was a single, loud crack. I think I saw Lise-Ann crawl away from Danny as I collapsed onto the grass.

She's just come to visit me. She has a bad scar on the side of her face where Danny kicked her with his hob-nailed boots. Her speech is a little slow, and somewhat slurred - I think it's because of the medication she's taking. She said she'll help out when I go home. My wheelchair will need some getting used to and she's promised to be there. I enquired about Danny and Claire. Their man, Wally, shot Danny dead. Wally and Claire were sent to prison for a total of twenty-eight years. Lise-Ann was deemed to have acted under duress and was put on probation. She was ordered to do community service.

I closed my eyes as she left the ward, hearing only the clip, clip, clip of her elegant high heels down the long hospital corridor towards her home. One whole year. Me - and my wheelchair - and Lise-Ann. Community service, she'd said.

LEARNING FROM FELIX

Mother wrote me several pieces of sadness in one short letter. Her best cow strayed onto a busy road and was hit by a car. The poor beast suffered a broken hip and had to be put down. The warm weather caused her well to run dry and she had to spend hundreds of pounds drilling deeper for the elixir of life. A friend moved over a hundred miles away and left her without a soul to talk trouble with. And my father was dying. She presented this news casually, almost as if it had the same status as her other offerings. "Your father," she wrote, "has a tumor. He could fight it but he has refused to do so. He's turning away from life."

I visited soon afterward. It was hard for me to imagine him brought so low, remembering how superior he always seemed, to mother, to the neighbours, to the 'ordinary' parishioners, and dare I say it, even to God himself. After he first beat me (I'd accidentally sat on a slice of buttered toast) my mother had to spend many hours stroking the horror away from me. And in the years that followed I automatically slipped back to the consolations she offered whenever the occasion required. But there came a day when she turned away. I was sixteen, and had come joyously home from school with my Group Certificate results in my fist. After scrutinizing it for a few seconds my father screwed the result sheet into a ball and tossed it onto the fire. As I watched the leaping flames take away the news of my seven honours and my one failure they also devoured a part of me. And when I brought my shivering spirit to my mother she backed away. "He doesn't really mean it," she said. "He's ambitious for you, that's all."

Soon after that my father employed a man to give me grinds in Leaving Certificate Mathematics. Greasy-haired, and with revoltingly dirty fingernails, Mr. Breslin cycled ten miles over the mountain to our house. My parents fussed over him, taking him into the front room and serving him cakes and tea from our best china before our lessons began. He told them I was 'weak' where maths was concerned and would need at least five hours tutoring each week if I was to have even the remotest chance of picking up an honour in the subject later on. I didn't like him. He lectured me incessantly about how 'good' my parents were, how my father had such 'tremendous' standing in the community, and how 'generous' it was of him to be planning a university education for me when he himself was forced to leave school at the tender age of twelve.

"You see what a lucky girl you are?" he'd say, his hands hunting my knee or groin. If I smiled a polite 'yes' he'd eventually move away.

My father's high standing in the parish was beyond dispute. He went to Mass each day and to the altar too. He sang lead baritone in the church choir. And he was the one who headed up the local charity. In our parish it was unusual for a farmer to be so honoured, but my father's reputation for holiness, aptitude for figures and general good name meant that such a post would inevitably be his. When it finally happened, he plunged into the activities with such enthusiasm and vigor that he withdrew from farming altogether and left my mother to run the place with the help of a hired man called Andy.

I sometime accompanied my father on his charity visits, when he'd be welcomed with open arms and hearts into the homes of the poor. He'd stay and chat with them, probing relentlessly until he was sure he knew enough about their lives to judge their need. I was frequently uneasy about these activities, sitting at many a kitchen table with stale biscuits and tea before me, watching him smile a million smiles, but knowing what would inevitably happen when he left the house. He'd fling certain words about us as we hurried home, words like 'ignorance' and 'drunkenness' and 'sloth'. He'd remind me of the importance of education, dedication and hard work. Later he'd talk with the committee and together they'd determine if money or other help might be offered. I liked Mr. Moriarty more because he sometimes slipped a few bars of chocolate or even a bunch of flowers from his own garden into the donations that were made. And his help seemed to be offered without judgement. My father scoffed at this 'softness', insisting that Moriarty was setting a bad example for the rest of the committee. Eventually he called for him to be expelled. When, years later, I was fighting hard to avoid disintegration, I'd imagine myself as a child running into Mr. Moriarty's smiling arms. It was like he was the Daddy I had always hoped to have.

My own father shrieked with rage when I told him I was not going to university to make a clever girl's Daddy out of him. My mother stood behind him, watching his loaded words hurtle in my direction.

"Ungrateful bitch." "Lazy whore." "Selfish."
"Sad." "Sinful girl." And I'd be sorry. I surely would. I fled the house that evening, my father's frenzied litany ringing in my ears and vowing never to return. Three days later the police found me in the forest, in the woodsman's hut, and the only words I uttered were geometric formulae, they said.

My parent visits to the hospital blended into one precise experience – panic. I asked the nurses not to let him in, but they must have forgotten my request. When he came I tried to concentrate on his presence there at that particular time, but all I saw was his neediness crouched behind me in the evenings as I studied maths, his heavy breathing playing around the back of my neck. I think I forgot who I was for a while, and only remembered when the matron called out my name. I had been found wandering naked in the grounds and, with a red blanket thrown about me, had been led back to her.

"Why?" she asked simply, and all I could do by way of response was to cry. She told me that she had once swum naked in a river near her home in order to be completely herself. I understood how this might be.

"Did your father ask you what you want to do with your life?" a doctor asked.

"No."

"But you must have told him."

"I tried, but he wouldn't listen."

"And your mother? Did she not put in a word for you?"

"Only when I was very small."

He nodded.

"But she grew weary," I continued. "Totally weary of trying to protect me – and of struggling to get through to him."

I left the hospital after several weeks and headed for Dublin. With my good Leaving Certificate results it was easy for me to get into the Civil Service and easy for me to stay there. I climbed the ladder – if he'd seen my dexterity my father might have been a little proud of me – and became a 'boss' to many staff. I acquired a mortgage, an apartment and a kitten, in that order. I named the kitten Felix. He was black, except for a daring slash of grey fur across his right side, and he looked at me as though he owned my very soul. Sometimes he'd gather himself into a ball on my lap, sleep for a while, and then unfurl his dreams before me as he woke. That's how I imagined it anyway, as he stretched out his delicate limbs and purred loudly. I had my own dreams too, I told him, but lost them in a forest a long time ago. Now, whenever I slept, there were other forces tearing my world apart. I believe the little fellow knew this was happening. When I woke screaming I'd find him sitting beside me, almost as though he was urging me to defy the darkness. I'd touch him, his soft fur, his reassuring warmth, his serene green little eyes, and be a little healed of the terror of the night.

My father lingered on for several months. Mother took to phoning me quite often. She'd begin by charting the progress of the village, filling me in on the minutiae of our neighbour's lives and waiting for me to ask about my father. When this did not happen she'd introduce the subject.

"He'd like to see you again," she'd plead, "can't you come home?"

I'd hum and haw and leave her without an acquiescence or refusal. I felt guilty about doing this, of course, but reminded myself that she had stood aside for years and watched him scrape away my soul.

"You forget he's only got you," she once reminded me when we were having coffee together in a café in the city. "All his hopes were bound up with you."

"I'm not likely to forget there's only me," I retorted. "But his hopes were for him, not for me. He had no hopes for me."

She spooned some multi-coloured sugar into my decaffeinated coffee. "Jenny, too much remembering is dangerous," she said slowly. "It's as dangerous as too much forgetting, you know."

I tried to forget about them both when I went to the Canaries at Christmas. Two weeks in the sun. Blue skies, which were certain to banish all traces of grey death. Good food. Some slight flirtation, perhaps. And walks into the sand dunes, and the enormity of feeling lost among such tiny gathered fragments as make a desert. And the pleasures of the pool, and the healing of sea water. The holiday slipped quietly away as I had planned and I scarcely thought of my father slowly dying over fifteen hundred miles away or of my mother insisting that he needed me. But I often thought of Felix. I missed him badly and hoped he had not been too upset when I handed him over to my neighbours for the duration of the break. I couldn't wait to see him again, and the first thing I did when I arrived at the apartment block was to knock at his minder's door. Barry's solemn face alarmed me.

"Come in," he said, "I'm afraid there's been a ...."

"What's the matter," I interrupted,"is Felix all right?"

"Yes and no," he replied enigmatically. "Come inside and I'll explain."

I sat on the cold edge of Barry's beige leather suite while he explained that a larger Tom who'd wandered into the area had bullied Felix. He said he'd disappeared for a few days but was now back - but had got himself stuck high in a tree and was afraid to come down.

"I got a ladder out," Barry assured me. "But I couldn't reach him. Then I called this friend of mine who's a vet and he came round and advised me to leave him alone. He said Felix would make his way down in his own time."

"That's ridiculous," I said. "Doesn't the Fire Brigade rescue cats?"

"Seems it's rarely necessary," Barry said patiently. I left my luggage on Barry's doorstep and ran into the grounds, soon hearing the weak but unmistakable sound of Felix's crying. I looked up and saw him precariously wedged between two branches.

"Here, puss, puss," I called, but he did not budge.

"He seems to have come down a bit. I'll get the ladder again if you like," Barry suggested. I'd hardly noticed that he was at my side.

"Please do," I said, and in no time at all I was climbing and calling out in my most persuasive tone to the little fellow above. But just as I was about to make a grab for him he jumped sideways to another tree and from there towards a high wall which borders the street. A sudden screech of brakes was the only sound I heard as Barry led me away from the ladder.

Barry's wife helped me to get settled back in. She even unpacked my suitcases, putting my laundry into the washing machine and hanging the rest of the stuff on hangers. On the bed she laid out the few gifts I'd brought home, among them a dazzling red studded collar for Felix. By the time Barry joined us I was bawling my eyes out.

"He didn't suffer," he told me. "died instantly. Not a mark,""

"But the vet said he'd come down in his own time," I said. "I should have waited."

"Don't blame yourself," he said. "It might have happened anyway."

"No. It's my fault," I wailed. "I should have waited. I insisted on trying to rescue him and I was wrong."

"You did what you thought best," Barry's wife soothed. "We all try to do that. Sometimes we get it wrong. But it doesn't cancel out our good intentions, does it?"

Barry touched me on the elbow. "You've had a long journey," he said. "You should rest now. In the morning I'll show you where I've buried the little chap."

Early next morning the phone rang. It was my mother.

"Oh, thank goodness you're home," she said breathlessly, "your father's bad. It's nearly over."

"I'll come straight away," I said. "Expect me in about three and a half hours – and don't fuss."

"What about your little cat?," she asked, half weeping. "Who'll mind him for you this time?"

"I won't need anyone to mind him any more," I told her. "He died yesterday. I was trying to rescue him from a tree and he jumped out in front of a car."

"Oh what a shame," she said.

"I blame myself," I explained, "I was told he'd make his own way down in his own time but I though I knew what was best for him."

I heard a long sigh from the other end of the line.

"Are you there, Mother?," I asked.

"I'm here, love, " she said. "And you must forgive yourself, you know. You set out to help that cat. You do realize that, don't you?"

The day was a bright mixture of drizzle and sun. When I arrived at the house the blue tiled roof was luminous and bright against the sky. A small kitten, which had been sitting on one of the front windowsills, fled to the back of the house as I pulled my car into the driveway. Mother met me at the door. There was an air of quiet confidence about her, as though she had been to all the foreign places ever known and had arrived safely back to where she belonged. As soon as I embraced her she broke down. I held her in my arms for a long time, feeling so many emotions that my head spun and my heart heaved with the burden of it all.

When we went into the my father's room I was surprised at how bright it was, with fresh chintz curtains on the window, flowers on a table near the door and a gentle breeze from the slightly opened window carrying in faint traces of pine from the woods. My father lay dozing under a light duvet. I sat on the edge of the bed and took his hand.

"Is he conscious?" I asked my mother, and just as

she began to shake her head I felt his fist tighten over mine.

"I'm home, father," I said. This is me – Jenny – I'm home." His eyelids flickered.

"Are you in pain?" I asked. There was no response.

"I've been on holiday," I told him. "To the Canary Islands. Out in the Atlantic Ocean off the coast of Africa. I'm as brown as a berry now, aren't I mother?"

He opened his eyes for a moment and closed them again.

"You know my little cat, Daddy," I said, and I saw him smile. "You've heard about him. Felix was his name. I'm afraid he died yesterday."

Large tears began to trickle down my father's yellowed cheeks. I attempted to dry them with a tissue but my mother motioned me to leave him be.

"Sorry. I didn't realize that Felix's death would upset him so much," I whispered to her. "Otherwise I wouldn't have mentioned it at all."

"It's not that," she said, smiling. "Don't you realize that it's over seventeen years since you called your father 'Daddy'?"

And so it was. It was me who was crying now, sobbing and stumbling blindly as I approached my father once again.

"Daddy," I said. "I'm truly, truly sorry for ….."

My mind searched frantically for a simple way of describing disappointment, confusion, loneliness, loss, fear - all the emotions I now realized we had both experienced over the years. But he forestalled me.

"For our lives? Don't be, Jenny," he said simply.

"I'm not."

I nodded and he smiled back at me.

Later I moved to the window. Wind ruffled the sheets on the clothesline outside. Beyond the garden fence ewes with lambs at foot grazed quietly, and in the distance was the forest I'd known since I was a child. A trace of crimson smeared the low sky.

"I don't like the sun going down," I said out loud, and immediately wondered what angel it was, or what demon had put those words into my mouth.

"The sun only seems to go down, Jenny," my mother said softly.

She was sitting in a chair beside my father's bed, bending sideways, her head resting on the pillow next to his. I crept softly from the room. Two hours later, when I returned to call her for tea, she was dozing beside him, and he lay, like a lovingly protected child, with his dead head cradled in her arms.

LACERATION

See this. The little girl skips along the old road. She holds the wooden handles of her rope awkwardly. You can tell it's a new rope and that she's learning how to dance it over her head and thread it under her feet for the very first time. She has brown hair plaited down her back, and the plait swings towards the May sun each time she jumps. See that her eyes are shining, how delighted she is to do a new and unfamiliar thing. And when her shoelaces come undone because she hops about so much she stoops down and quickly ties them up again. While she fingers the wayward laces into tight bows the skipping rope lies beside her in the soft grass. The boy is in the ditch, watching.

He steps out in front of her at the bridge.

"Hello," he says, standing his ground. The stance is confident but he is afraid. She is more interesting than ever now, damp and gleaming with exertion. She might push him away, or ignore him. "I was watching you," he continues, his voice suddenly fine and spidery. "Back there in the ditch when you tied your laces I was watching you."

"Why?" She regards him calmly.

Instantly he thinks of several reasons he might tender. But he tells the truth. "Because I like you."

"My name's Mandy," she says. "What's yours?"

Mandy is just right, he tells himself. "It's Cornelius," he explains, "but they call me Con."

A wee giggle escapes the girl. He is embarrassed and turns away.

"Mine's really Amanda," she quickly offers. He notices that she regrets her amusement so he turns

31

his face towards her once again. They begin to walk together to the town.

See how they gather in the evening in the big house. It's chilly now so a fire is lit. Amanda watches the sparks escape into the dark tunnel of the chimney. Her mind races ahead, preparing them a way.

"Stop dreaming Amanda." It's her mother come into the room with some embroidery in her hands.

"Have you not got a book to read or something else to do, dear? Don't idle."
The girl leafs carelessly through a book she has taken from a shelf. It's obvious her mind is elsewhere. On the back stairs, on the way to the kitchen for her bedtime snack, she overhears a conversation.

"Don't know why he ever went across the street to them," she hears her grandfather mutter.

"He should know you can't trust them," her father observes. "I know. I tried. Remember Daly?"

"Of course I remember Daly." Her grandfather sounds cross because her Daddy judges his memory to be poor.

"He never admitted the theft," her father continues. "but he did it. I'm sure he did. There's no other explanation. They always bite the hand that feeds them, that's what they do."

"Well, the Rev. Mr. Harris is finally gone from here now." The statement is so cold that Amanda huddles up inside her sweater as she faces it.

"Where to?"

"England, I suppose. Or Scotland," her grandfather says. "Does it matter? He betrayed us by wandering into their church last Christmas. We made it clear then we didn't like it, and now he knows."

"Said they were our brothers and our sisters. I can

see him now, perched up there, smiling down at us and asking us to love all our brothers and our sisters."

Amanda doesn't like the way her Daddy's lovely voice becomes sour. He must be very frightened, she thinks, to speak like that. It isn't good when her Daddy is afraid. Now that fear is re-generated she cannot be on her own. She knocks lightly on the kitchen door and enters.

"Ah, Mandy, my love." Her grandfather opens up his arms and draws her towards him. She loves the close-up smell of her grandfather, a mixture of snuff, horse and tobacco. And he is the only one to call her Mandy. She likes that.

"What did you do with yourself today?" he asks, as he releases her to a chair. "Did you play with my rope?"

Last week her grandfather brought the rope home from Germany.

"Yes," she says. "It was a bit tricky at first, but I got used to it."

"Is that so?"

"Yes," she explains earnestly. "In the beginning the rope tripped me and sometimes it hit my face or my arms. When I did this" - and she stands up in the centre of the kitchen and hops - "it was sometimes too late and the rope twisted round my ankles. But after a while," she adds," I got it right."

"You're a great girl," her Daddy praises. He places a cup of steaming cocoa in front of her. "I'm sure you are a tremendous skipper already."

"Con said that I am," Amanda is eager to confide.

"Who?"

"Con." She draws back a little now.

"Who's Con?"

She wonders why her Daddy holds the name out on

a pair of tongs like that.

"Just a boy. He watched me skipping," she says. The two men toss the name between them for a short time. Amanda eyes each of them in turn.

"You mustn't speak to that boy again," her father finally commands.

"But Daddy, he's my friend."

"Friend, indeed. They're all the same. Now you listen to me, Amanda. Do as I say. Don't speak to that boy again."

Hear the music. It begins in a small place. She knows why it is and where. Con told her all about it yesterday. 'May Procession' he called it.

"What's a 'procession'?" she enquired.

"People walk along the streets," he said. It was a matter-of-fact answer.

"They always do that," she said, dismissing his explanation as a nonsense.

"I mean they get together in the church and they pray and then they go along the streets singing hymns."

"Why do they do that, Con?"

"'Cos Our Lady likes it!"

"Which lady?"

"Ah, yea know. God's mammy, Mary."

"Oh. I see."

"Have you never seen the May Procession? Did you never dress up in white stuff and go too?" he asked, his eyes smiling.

"No" she said candidly. "I didn't."

"Want to come tomorrow then?" he invited.

"Can I?"

"Sure you can. You're my friend. You can walk with me."

This dress will do well. See its creamy textures, how

it is not a coloured dress or even a white one. Mandy takes it from the trunk. She removes wrapping tissue and shakes it out. She holds it to her front and regards herself in the full-length mirror of her wardrobe. Con said the girls wear "white, fluffy things." The boys put on their best dark suits.

See the girl step into this old dress, pulling the belt around her waist and fixing it at the back. See her try on a pair of pale blue shoes. Now that her mother's old trunk has been opened the air is filtered through the lavender scent of newly unpacked things. A voice reverberates through the scented air.

"Amanda," her mother calls.

"Coming, Mummy." She quickly stuffs the shoes and dress under her blanket and goes down to lunch.

Touch the taffeta as it surges over her. She draws the dress close and creeps out along the back hall. She subdues its movement until she is some distance away from the house. Then she allows it its proper freedom, and it carries her on lightness, a rush of May evening air, to Con. She sees him enter the church ahead of her. Soon she is sitting beside him. The church organ swells into an authoritative statement and the people stand up. She looks at the loveliness of the other girls and is certain that she too is lovely. But she wishes the blue shoes did not pinch at the heels.

"This is where we kneel down," Con whispers, a little bit awkward now that this girl from 'the other side' is here with him. She quickly mimics him. The man who is speaking wears long white and gold robes. Mandy knows that he is a priest, and that he is reciting some prayers. She does not speak any prayers but smiles at Con who is close to her. He seems glad that she does this.

Smell the rose petals, how they bleed in a mysterious surge on the sheet outside. Mandy is bewitched. She walks beside Con through crushed roses, and their fragrance triumphs. The music follows them along their path. It is feeling a way with them. Ahead of them, in the market place, the priest has climbed onto a raised platform. He also is singing. The people close in around him in row upon row of concentric circles. Mandy knows that she will soon be among them.

"We have a sort of Benediction over there," Con informs her.

"What's that like?" she asks.

"It's kinda quiet," he replies, "at least some of it The bells ring and everyone stays still." He drops his voice to a whisper. "Then," he continues, "the priest says a litany -that's all the names we call God's mother - and everybody says "Pray for us" every time he calls out a name."

Taste her excitement, how the young girl tingles inside this mysterious drama. A cloud of incense floats towards her. Con does not like the scent, but she does. There are more crushed roses here. The ground is a pink, yellow and orange tapestry and she kneels on the colours spread out below her.

"Morning Star."

"Pray for Us."

"Gate of Heaven."

"Pray for Us."

She holds the boy's hand. "Pray for us." "Pray for us." "Pray for us." An abrupt noise from a corner of the gathered congregation causes the priest to hesitate and then to cease his pleading. As if a cleaver had been applied to it, the crowd parts sharply. The ugly wound opens up to the probing stride of an angry man. He is approaching Amanda. Con stands in front of her. He is twelve years old. He is a big enough lad but he is a hundred years too small. He cannot hide her. She runs away.

There are no roses spread along the road which leads westwards from the town. Amanda is still running. The prayers begin again, and she hears them in pursuit of her. Somewhere out there too is a man. He carries a rope in his right hand. Her heart beats far too fast and she feels sick. She wonders if his fear is the same fear that she now feels. As she crosses the bridge her cramped blue shoes slip on the shiny surface. She is on her knees again. She bleeds. Gravel becomes embedded in one knee. The cut is deep and dirty and is almost two inches long.

Within seconds Amanda rises. She sits in the blood-stained cream taffeta dress. She sits in the ditch and cries. She is a very small child. She sits and waits. See her wait for her Daddy.

HOME SWEET HOME

Everything in life has a context and it is only in that context that it is fully understood. In this case my specific learning context was 'home'. Three weeks ago I returned from Capetown for my mother's funeral. The initial phone call, which told me that mother was ill, was followed within days by the news that she had died. At eighty nine, going on ninety, we could not be angry at her death but only sad at the closing of an era, and the loss of the most robust link in a family that had been, however scattered, very strong.

As her last born - my mother became pregnant for the final time at the age of forty-five - I could not have known her as well as the others. Half of her life had been lived before I arrived. When this fact first dawned on me I felt deprived. There were, of course, many photos to show what she had been like when she was twenty, thirty, forty, forty-four. Flicking through an album I saw her, side by side with my handsome father, proudly cradling their first born child. That was my brother, Tim. He died soon after the photograph was taken. It was several years before another baby was born, and that child's eagerly awaited birth was celebrated in a mini album of its own picturing my mother, aged twenty-nine, and looking rather vague and troubled, my father, then thirty-six, proud as any new father had a right to be, and my sister, Sylvia in all sorts of cutie poses. I asked my mother if she had been unhappy when those photos were taken and she told me that she was remembering her first child. Her tone vetoed any further discussion.

It was Sylvia who rang when mother became ill. Between strangled sobs and stifled sighs she delivered her news. We talked for a while about our brothers, Vinnie and Simon. Simon was in Belfast and Vinnie just down the road in County Wexford. It would, Sylvia figured, be no problem for them to come home in a hurry if they were needed. Mother was old, but a fighter, and we both thought she'd pull through.

After Sylvia's phone call I went walking in a nearby park. I thought I heard my mother shuffle beside me as she'd done when she'd visited with me five years earlier. It was autumn, and there were sunflowers growing beside the park keeper's cottage. Mother talked about the sunflowers she'd cultivated in the greenhouse in her back garden, explaining that she had to slide down a few of the panels in the glass roof in order to let them grow to their full height. She's won a national competition for them that year. I thought of telling her of the stunning acres of sunflowers I had seen when I was on holidays in Umbria, but desisted. Her few straggling winners, rising above a greenhouse roof, would suddenly be dwarfed.

"We should never stop things from growing, Valerie," she said then. "We should always help nature in her highest endeavours." There was a tremor in her voice which sat uneasily with her preachy tone. But I dismissed it as unimportant. She was, after all, a very old woman visiting a far-from-home city and recounting a recent triumph to an emigrant daughter.

Vinnie was her favourite. We all knew that. Even he acknowledged the fact on one occasion, an embarrassed but somewhat smug smile on his face. We had come together to celebrate mother's eightieth birthday. It was a small party in a private room in a local hotel, ourselves, a few friends and an old fashioned pianist rattling out some ancient tunes on a honky-tonk piano. Several people commented on how well mother looked "for eighty". They congratulated us on having cared for her so thoroughly.

"It's our Sylvia who does all the caring," Simon said. His vowels had broadened out, Belfast style.

"She's the one who deserves the credit. Myself and Valerie and Vinnie just write - and visit occasionally - but it's Sylvia who does all the hard work."

Simon was laughing, but I noticed a tiny vein arch and throb in Sylvia's neck.

"But he gets all the credit," she hissed, glaring at Vinnie. "He's her treasured golden boy."

"What do you mean?" Simon asked awkwardly.

"Mother would be lost without you. Hasn't she said so often enough?"

Simon's wife frowned, furiously elbowing him to shut up.

"No she hasn't, as a matter of fact," Sylvia snapped. "Not to me anyway. But she talks about HIM non-stop. Ring Vinnie for me, darling. Is there a letter from Vinnie, darling? Would you go and post this parcel I've made up for Vinnie, darling?"

Vinnie put a conspiratorial finger to pursed lips.

"That was our secret," he said to Sylvia, "mother's and mine. Now you've gone and let the cat out of the bag."

"I don't find it at all funny," Sylvia said. "I can't see why..." she continued on, but stopped short when she saw mother reappear at the door.

"Don't be such a sour-puss," Vinnie mumbled under his breath. "This is supposed to be a party, you know."

Maybe we were afraid of a similar confrontation after mother's death. I certainly was. On my first day back home I walked the neighbourhood for hours rather than sit in with them. But when I returned they were still discussing our family life.

"Do you remember the time I fell into the canal?" Simon asked. "Mother didn't know anything about it until a year later."

"Yeah," said Vinnie. "I remember. Who told her anyway?"

"I did it myself," Simon said. "She seemed kind of sad one day and I thought I'd give her a laugh."

Sylvia arched her black eyebrows. "Give her a laugh," she mimicked. "You told mother you fell into the canal to give her a laugh?"

"I was only twelve," Simon reminded her. "I wasn't exactly a fountain of wisdom when I was twelve. Were you?"

Before Sylvia had time to reply I introduced my own agenda.

"She did seem to be preoccupied a lot of the time," I ventured. There was a sharp intake of breath. They were keeping something from me, I thought, an alarming history that happened before I was born, which they dared not utter in my presence. I fought down the paranoia as the conversation turned to childhood outings to the seaside and to the zoo and to examination of the day we all visited a Norman

Castle in County Meath.

Vinnie almost had an accident that day. While our parents set out the picnic we children wandered around. It was only when the meal was ready and my mother yelled for us to come that we noticed Vinnie stranded on a ledge about twenty feet above ground. He'd attempted to scale the castle walls and had lost his nerve. While mother made calm, soothing noises underneath the ledge father ran to the nearest house and returned with a long ladder. He set the ladder against the wall and climbed up. When he was directly behind Vinnie he gently prodded the terrified boy into moving. Trembling uncontrollably, Vinnie made the slow descent to the ground, where mother immediately took him into her arms. For a while there seemed to be no one there but this mother and her adventurer son clinging tightly to each other, sobbing away their pent-up distress. Father marshalled the rest of us back to where the food was laid out.

"She never talked about it afterwards," Simon said.

"Not even to me," Vinnie added.

I was curious. "Maybe she wrote about it in her diary that night," I suggested. Mother had been a great one for recording the details of her life, and there were decades of diaries stashed away in a trunk in the spare room.

"But they were private," Simon protested. "Even father never read them."

"They're still there", Sylvia said. "If mother didn't mean us to see them at some stage she'd have destroyed them by now, wouldn't she? What year was it, Vinnie?"

"1959," he said. "It was my birthday. I was sixteen."

Sylvia hurried away and returned with a box containing all mother's diaries for the 50's. Her fingers ran along the spines like those of a blind woman reading Braille. There was something unnerving, almost practised, about that skill. The entry for August 2nd. read:-

"Picnic at Trim Castle. Vinnie put the heart cross-ways in me. He climbed onto a ledge and couldn't get down. It was a drop of over twenty feet. If he'd fallen he might have died. Tom borrowed a ladder and helped him down. I forgot to thank poor Tom. I was so worried about the whole thing. What would I have told Richard if anything had happened to his son? I don't think I could face his anger again. And to lose the only remaining link...... it is unthinkable."

It was dusk. Slivers of pink light filtered into the room. It seemed as though Vinnie's surprise, Sylvia's rage and my confusion were trapped in the dark spaces between us. Only Simon spoke. "It's late," he whispered, "and we have a busy day tomorrow. Let's get the funeral over with first."

On my way back to Capetown I negotiated airports and aircraft without getting bogged down in the type of casual conversation such places engender. Neither was I drawn to more serious stuff - specifically to the possibility of opening up my heart and mind to a stranger whom I would never encounter again. Far too much had happened in recent weeks. It had emerged that Vinnie had no idea, no idea at all. He was aware that he was mother's favourite but she'd never told him why. Sylvia knew. She denied any knowledge, of course, admitting only that she suspected that mother's affections were not truly centred on our father. Simon was shattered by the clear evidence that his mother had had a lover and that Vinnie was that lover's child. Each of us speculated about whether or not our father had raised Vinnie without knowing that he was not his natural son. And poor Vinnie was devastated. As far as he was concerned his entire, warm, boisterous childhood lay in ruins around him.

Nothing I might have done or said could have comforted either of my brothers. For this reason - and because I did not trust Sylvia - I told no one about the small package a nurse had found clasped in my dying mother's hand. It had lain in my bag until now, a sealed blue envelope marked "Valerie". I opened it carefully and found an old sheet of paper inside. There was a name - Nurse Swan - written in an immature but unmistakable version of my mother's handwriting and the message:-
"Went to her last week. Richard does not know. He'll be angry when I tell him. But all hell would break out at home if my parents found out. I have this strange feeling that it would have been a boy. In my head I had already called him 'Sam'.
Vinnie's aborted elder brother? I folded the note carefully and returned it to its envelope.

Africa below. A continent of contrasts. A land of great light and terrible darkness. A place in which I have experienced both singing and sorrow. Maybe mother intuitively understood that such had been my life. Maybe that is why she left the old note and the old news to me. The pilot announced that he was preparing to land. As we lost height crystals of ice on

the aircraft window began to dissolve. I shivered.
"I was," mother once told me," remembering my
first child." The terrible context of her sadness had
at last become evident. And its occasional song.

The official stared at me. I could see her bring out her mental smileometer, attempting to ascertain if there might be a hidden trace of humour on my face.

"I'm not a wife," I reiterated. "I haven't been a wife for quite a while now. And although I'm very glad to have a house, I wouldn't fancy being married to one."

"What will I put down under "occupation"?" she demanded.

"Leave it blank," I said. "That's what I would do if I were you."

"I've got to fill in answers to all the questions on this form." She smiled at me, begging me to understand her onerous bureaucratic duty and to co-operate as fully as I could.

"You could put me down under "unemployed" I think."

"May I have your card?"
It was my turn to be perplexed.

"Your UB card please?" she elaborated, her patience beginning to thin.

"UB?"

"Yes", she spat out. "Your Unemployment Benefit Card."

"I don't have one."

"UA then." I had become a tedious burden, I could tell.

"Your Assistance card. May I have it now please?" She thought that because I said I was unemployed I should have a card to carry around designating me as such for all the world to see.

"No, you've misunderstood," I told her politely.

"I am unemployed, but I don't have a dole card.

I've managed on my savings so far. I've never been on the dole."

"Then I can't enter "unemployed" for you," she wailed, glancing apprehensively at the rapidly forming queue behind me. I noticed that the woman two down was elderly and on crutches.

"Ok, Ok," I said, relenting. "Ok, be my guest. Write in whatever you want. I don't mind."
I did mind, of course. But there was little else I could do. I watched the woman quickly scribble something down. She was in charge again.

"The neutron star is as massive as the sun. And it is so dense that a pinhead of its material contains a million tonnes of matter."
I was reading a scientific magazine, but my mind wheeled, at this critical point, from the stars right down to planet earth. It was the pinhead image that did it, grounded me right beside the ancient Church Father, Thomas Aquinas. You see, it was he who suggested that dozens of angels could dance on the head of a pin. Wasn't he imaginative? And did he not possess extensive powers of observation? My friend Dorothy told me all about this.

"Just because you can't see them is no reason to dismiss them," she'd said in response to my raised eyebrows.

"Oh, I'm not. I'm not." I wanted to be kind to her concerns. "It's just that they are rather insubstantial, are they not?" With my left arm I made a swinging movement between us, as if to slay all the imaginary angels squatting there. None fell. And she was not impressed.

"Thomas Aquinas was a great teacher. He was making a profoundly spiritual observation when he said that forty angels could sit on the head of a pin." It seemed that this was her summary, her high-powered precis, her entire presentation.

"Did he see them there?" The question might have appeared slightly offensive and smart-alecky, but I did not intend it to be. My multi-directional enquiries could not be adequately answered by her one-eyed words. Better narrow it down, I thought, to a slimline, tangible thing.

"What do you mean?" Dorothy squeaked. She was offended, but I would not backtrack.

"Well, I was only asking if he had any empirical evidence for his assertion."

She hesitated and immediately I took advantage. "I mean," I added, "when and where did this Aquinas chap observe forty angels cavorting together on the head of a pin?"

It was then that she told me it wasn't that kind of knowledge at all.

"St Thomas Aquinas," she enunciated carefully, as an obvious antidote to my disrespect, "St. Thomas Aquinas was a theologian and not a mathematician."

"What's an angel?" I asked then, deciding to try another angle, becoming more awkward now.

"Neither man nor God," she said.

"Good," I retorted. "You've just told me what an angel is not. Now tell me what it is."

"A Spiritual Entity," she creaked, once more unsure of herself.

"Ah, yes, but then, so are we."

"But we are human."

"So what?"

"Angels are not."

"Nor animal?"

"No, of course, not animal."

I was determined to press ahead. "In what particular form do they exist?" I enquired. "I need to know."

"Incorporeal form," she told me. "They are spirits. They exist without a body."

"Ah." I was inspired again. "Aha, now you've admitted it."

"Admitted what?" she blustered. I think she was beginning to regret the entire conversation.

"Admitted that this Thomas Aquinas guy was a chancer."

"I have done no such thing," she said, using her Senior Infants voice against me. Maybe this was how she saw me, as an intractable six-year-old.

"But you have just stated that angels have no bodies."

"Yes."

"How then," I flung at her, "could Thomas Aquinas, or any other divine, have counted them together on the head of a pin?"

I was not reconciled – and that brings me to another negative aspect of Dorothy's personality – her preachy manner, ultra smug, in fact. It was all right for a state-sponsored, twice-pensioned National Teacher to say "be reconciled to your lot", but she never agonised each morning over what to do with her day. She wouldn't have me do it either.

"If you try to kill time," she once quoted, "you will damage eternity."

Actually, I agreed with that pronouncement – as an abstract statement, that it. But it did not apply to me. I'd had sufficient difficulty coping with this realm and did not concern myself too much with "eternity". And as for "killing time", if it appeared that way to Dorothy, it was because she did not appreciate the romance of my struggle to learn

Russian or the integrity of my striving to invent something cheap, wholesome and desirable for the peoples of the world. That reminds me. I could have answered 'inventor' to that officious clerk yesterday. It would have sounded impressive. It would have been legitimate. I am an inventor. I made an integrated series of disposable household items once. I mustn't say what they are because I have not yet taken out a patent and I'm certain they'd be popular if ever I managed to get them off the drawing board and into the nation's kitchens. If the important people could see working models they'd be impressed. I don't know why I forgot to say that I was an inventor. On the other hand, I might have told her that I was a student of Russian. That would have made her come down hard on her already hard-bitten nails. But it also is true. I have courted it all for years, the magic of St. Cyril's alphabet, the chunky and soft sounds, the challenge, the chat. One night during class I'd even dared write a note in Cyrillic script to fellow-student, Darragh:

YA OCHEN LUBIO VASH, TAVARISH TALOUR
(I LOVE YOU VERY MUCH, COMRADE TAYLOR)

I'd written, forcing each character slowly and lovingly out with critical reference to the Standard Cyrillic outlines in the textbook before me. I was pleased to receive a prompt reply. A note swiftly stuffed into my fist as I left that night said simply:

SPASIBA YALINA. KHARASHO

Darragh had thanked me very much. But he never returned to that class again. Maybe I had frightened him. Maybe he had gone off to Russia. I don't know.

I drifted, seated, and lolling gently on the garden swing, the spring juices of the earth a blend of perfumes about me. If a bud, despite everything that here and now is evil, grew into a leaf, I would know. And I would call it a leaf – simply a leaf. It was essential to be able to identify things. When my daughter was smaller I taught her to recognise animals. In her little room I'd posted cut-outs on the wall, and I would lead her around to each one and she'd exclaim, cat, cow, dog, chicken, horse, donkey, fox. I added a second dog later. It was a different breed and smaller and lighter in colour and I wondered what she would say when she first saw it. She said dog, dog, lovely new dog.

"Are you single?"
"No."
"Married or widowed?"
"No."
He frowned at me.
"I told the girl she could put down whatever she liked." I was getting careless now.
He regarded me with contempt. "She has not got the authority to do that," he declared.
"Oh."
"You see, Missus," he advised, "I'm going to…"
"I'm not a Missus," I pointed out, interrupting him.
"Well, Miss…"
But I darted in again. "Nor am I a Miss," I said.
He produced an extremely audible, almost primal sigh which made the people in the office fix their eyes directly on me.
"It's Ms," I told him, "Ms."

"Ms! What's that then?" He clamped his upper lip firmly down over his lower one and his canines showed. He reminded me of Bugs Bunny. I had to strangle a smile.

"Oh," he said, "it's funny, is it? Tell me then, what is this amusing Ms?"

"It's not amusing," I told him, assuming an ultra-serious demeanour. "Ms is just like Mr. It's been in use for several years now. It's a description of a female adult."

"Not in my book, it's not."

"What exactly is in your book?" I flared.

"It's not on the form, Missus," he said. "On the form it says Mr, Mrs, Miss, clear as day. Now if you are not a M I S T E R," – he spelled out the long version of the word – "if you are not a Mister, then clearly you must be a Mrs or a Miss." He eyed me for feedback. I believe he was taking pleasure. I saw him enter the word "Mrs" beside my name. Then he drew a clear sheet of blotting paper over the entry and damped it down. This time there was no indecision. Obviously he had the authority required to do that.

That evening I needed to relax. I chose a bubble bath. When I had drawn a full quota of water and added a generous tumbler of bubble-making stuff, I pulled my head right down to the water to hear each individual bubble pop and crack. It was like an orchestra tuning up. And as the music subsided, the colour spread, rainbows captured in every conceivable shape. But these, too, proved to be ephemeral and they disappeared as I moved about and inadvertently doused them down. I drew my shoulders on to the plastic pillow and automatically my legs floated. I lifted one leg from the water and it felt unusually heavy. I quickly restored it to that comfortable, liquid surface again. Is it not easy to believe, I asked myself, that water was our first world and that I was once – in the ocean – once – billions of years ago – no, not me – but a very remote and tiny ancestor – an amoeba – a blob – a single-celled piece of cosmic plasma – feeding – replicating – budding – branching? They are still there in the ocean, the identical descendants of our common ancestors. We made a different journey, that's all. The phone rang. I heard Dorothy attend to it.

"Are you dry?" she yelled through the door.

"No. Who is it?"

"It's Aoife."

Aoife is my daughter. She's studying anthropology at a college in the States. She must be phoning to say what her plans are.

"You talk to her," I said to Dorothy. "Find out her schedule or ask her if I should ring her tomorrow." Dorothy returned to the phone.

I am splashing now. I'm seven again. I watch the fine spray from the shower target my thigh. I observe what happens when I put a fist over the shower head, the tingling in my hand, the over-spill as the pressure builds up.

"Aoife's off to Mexico tomorrow," Dorothy reported back at the bathroom door. "She says she's going there with another girl and some chaps. Field study, she calls it." There was a faint drone of disapproval in her voice. "She says not to ring. In a week or two, when she's settled in Mexico City, she'll ring you."

It's not always easy to appreciate other people's

worries, to enter other people's worlds. At breakfast next morning Dorothy was pensive and tense. She held up two forks to me, and several spoons and knives.

"Why," she asked, "is it only the tips of forks that corrode and not the spoons and knives as well?"

If this had been a serious question I suppose I would have attempted to answer it. But it wasn't. It wasn't a fun question either. It was a diversion, that's all. It was D-Day for Dorothy. At 10.30 a.m. she would have her final interview for the post of Principal of her small, five-teacher school. At thirty-seven (she's two years younger than me) and the longest serving and most experienced member of the staff, it was obvious she would have no difficulty at all. She was acceptable in other ways too. She knew her place. And she also knew the place of Augustine and Aquinas. Indeed, I reminded myself, she was familiar with the intricacies of Aquinas's speculation on the antics of angels gathered together on the head of a pin.

There was a red-haired man in front of me in the grey, public office that day. He, too, was registering for temporary work. Before ten o'clock, when the queue began to flow towards the various hatches, he sat by me. I was reading. I always bring my own reading material to waiting rooms. I am currently intrigued by the coastal counties of the west.

"Kerry is a bizarre place, behind time in a real sense, for here, in the most westerly land in Europe, the mean time of Greenwich in summer is out of place with the reality of Kerry by one hour and forty minutes"

This had never occurred to me before. I read it and

was appalled. Could County Kerry not be itself? Why did this wild and wonderful place have to be standardised like that? The man beside me was looking over my shoulder at a beautiful colour-spread of altocumulus clouds over Brandon Bay. His long, red hair tumbled down his shoulders and almost touched my face. I restrained myself admirably, for truthfully, I would love to have filtered that hair through the fingers of both hands.

"Fantastic-looking place." He grinned at me and with a quick lick of his tongue cleaned the roots of his beard. He must have noticed that there was some butter there.

"It's in Kerry." I replied.

"I lived in Kerry for sixteen months," he confided.

"Oh, really." He was a real Dub. "Which part?" I enquired.

"Beyond Dingle. I worked and lived there for sixteen months."

"What are you?" I asked and immediately regretted the question.

"A thinker," he replied, nonplussed.

"I mean, what did you do there?" I quickly realised I had compounded my folly.

"I philosophised," he said. He was smiling, no, maybe laughing at me.

"Except for the two weeks," he added enigmatically, "when I was without my bicycle."

"Oh," I said. It was all I could manage.

"You see," he explained, "my bicycle was buckled in a little accident."

I'd lost the drift of the conversation and was no longer in control. I decided to keep my mouth shut, and he obligingly ploughed ahead.

"It took twelve days to get a new front fork down

from Dublin," he continued. "While I was waiting for it, I had to walk."

I nodded.

"I didn't do well with the thinking then." He was smiling to himself, recalling some special aspect of the past.

"You see," he said, drifting back to me, "I'm lost without my bike. The pedals operate my brain. When I walk on the soles of my feet it cuts off the circulation to my head." He relaxed, assuming that I had understood, that everything was now crystal clear.

"What are you looking for?" I asked. "I mean what type of work are you offering to engage in?"

"Philosophy, of course," he replied. "It goes without saying."

"Anything else?" I asked, tentatively. I was beginning to see things his way, to open up to his world.

"Well, I can make currachs."

"Oh," I interrupted. "Did you learn that in Dingle?"

"No, I never learned."

He noticed my surprise. "But I did make several currachs while I was there."

"I don't understand. That's skilled work. Surely you'd need to learn from somebody, be an apprentice or something?" I probed.

"I didn't," the red-haired man volunteered. "One night I dreamed I was making a currach, step by step I dreamed I was making the entire thing, and from that day on I was constructing currachs with the native men."

"That's extraordinary." I did, incredibly I did believe him.

"What have you put down under "Personal Work

56

History"?" I asked. I felt I had known this man for a thousand years.

"Just thinker/boat builder, darlin'," he replied.

"There's not much currach construction going on in Dublin," I said, speaking gently so as not to discourage him.

"I know," he said. "Don't you think I don't know? And I'm not sure there's much work for philosophers either."

I was home early and was sitting, sipping a small sherry when Dorothy returned. There was a casserole cooking in the oven. Her face was flushed and her eyes danced in her head.

"You got it. I know you've got it." I was pleased for her.

She kicked her winter boots in the air and flopped on to a bean bag.

"Yes, I did. It won't be official for another week yet, but yes I've got it." She snatched another breath.

"You are now speaking," she announced, "to the new Principal of St. Stephen's National School."

I kissed her on the cheek and she hugged me. I poured her a vodka and orange.

"Am I glad that's all over," she said. She stretched out her long legs towards the log fire. I like logs and the smell of burning wood.

"How was your day?" She asked this when she remembered me.

I told her about the woman on the radio that morning who claimed that all the song-birds were disappearing from the land. I told her I believed that had happened during the Famine because little birds like sparrows and larks were eaten. I told her I had looked up the etymology of the word 'steadfast" and

that it was a Greek word meaning 'strong" and
"persistent". I told her what County Kerry had to
endure.

"I mean how was the job-hunting?" she countered.

"We registered," I told her.

"What do you mean "we"?"

I hadn't realised I"d made a plural statement until
she queried it.

"Myself and Kevin," I replied. "There's this man,"
I added before she had time to ask, "there's this
beautiful man I met there - his name's Kevin – and he
and I registered at the same time."

She wanted to say something else, ask a supplementary, in fact, but I forestalled her. I'd remembered
something important. I went into the kitchen and
filled a tiny vase with cold water.

"He's upstairs," I told her, as I carried out this
delicate operation. "Having a wash. He's going to
have dinner with us."

"And what on earth's that?" Dorothy asked as she
watched me take my prize from a cup, pop it into the
vase and place the vase in the centre of our dining
table.

"Oh that." I tried to sound offhand. "You mean
that?"

"Yes, that." She dropped the word, like a useless
nothing, downwards towards the floor.

"Kevin picked it for me today," I told her. "It's a
leaf...it's simply a leaf."

LUCINDA ON THE SEVENTH DAY

The woman was nervous as she approached the big house. That long avenue trailing through prosperous suburbs intimidated her. So too did the prospect of working five mornings a week in such a place. She'd never done it quite like that before, like she was a real cleaning woman with a permanent job. But it was easy on the first day. The lady was nice. She was very nice. On the first day she sat the woman down in the kitchen and gave her tea.

"Tell me about yourself," she invited.

"There's not all that much to tell really," the woman responded, fidgeting, unused to being scrutinised like that.

"You are separated, you say?" the lady continued.

"More like abandoned," the woman replied with a vigour that surprised them both.

"Very good. Very good." The lady scooped some crumbs from the table and put them in the bin. Then she put the cups away. "Now I'll show you what I need doing," she said, "and you can get on with it, dear."

She popped her head into the kitchen a few times during the first morning, on one occasion to make sure the cups were facing the right way round in the dishwasher.

"When you're finished that," she said to the woman, "perhaps you would like to clean the scullery floor?"

She was very large and moved slowly, sinking into a low chair in the corner, watching carefully as the woman carried out her instructions.

"I could never get down on my hands and knees like that," she remarked to the woman who was on all fours in front of her.

The woman nodded. A gritty deposit of stink and fat was of long standing and yielded reluctantly to her efforts to remove it. The woman used strong, rhythmic movements of her right elbow and wrist, while balancing herself on her left hand. The watching lady noticed the shoulder muscles ripple under the pale green thinness of an acrylic jumper, but could not see how much the woman ached. Three hours later, by the time she was ready to leave for home, her muscles were twisted and sore.

The lady greeted the woman at two and a half minutes past ten the following morning. "Oh, you're here at last, dear. I've got a lot of vacuuming for you to do. You did say you enjoyed vacuuming, didn't you, dear?"

The machine fretted its way around the house for about fifteen minutes without making any major change in the condition of the floors. The woman decided to open it up. She found the bag sweating its contents down the hose pipe. No new dirt was getting through and the small amount she had lifted was piling up along the way.

"I think the bag needs to be changed," the woman suggested through the drawing room door. "Where do you keep the bags?"

"That can wait for a moment," the lady responded. "Come and have some coffee with me, dear."

She was sitting among several copies of 'SHE', 'WOMAN', "HOSTESS', 'VOGUE', 'HAIR', and 'HER', a pot of freshly brewed coffee resting on the table in front of her. There were cream cakes there too.

"Fetch yourself a cup and saucer from the kitchen," she suggested.

A few moments later she filled the woman's cup from the coffee pot and threw in a liberal dash of cream.

"I don't ever take cream," the woman said. Her tastes were simple, her metabolism long attuned to slender things.

"Nonsense, dear," the lady interrupted. "It's a little luxury you should allow yourself occasionally. I do. Now tell me," she continued, "what is it you said, you're divorced or something? Why is that?"

"He went away," the woman told her. "We didn't love each other. We didn't even like each other much in the end. He wanted to be married to the whole world. Felt tied down by me. And I ......" She hesitated, searching for a reason to continue with this explanation. The lady regarded her carefully from out of a deeply pan-sticked face. "I was too young to begin with. I was a wife before I was a woman, if you know what I mean?" She flung out the question as a novice fisherman might a first cast on a darkening beach. But there was no response. The lady was busy opening a cupboard under the drawing room window. From there she withdrew a box, and from the box she retrieved a bunch of letters which were tied with yellow and pink satin ribbons.

"Edward sent me all these," she said, pirouetting demurely around the room like a little girl angel in a Nativity Play.

"I'll do the windows now," the woman suggested. She already regretted the shorthand telling of her life story."

"Sit down, dear. I want to show you the first one."

The lady extracted a single item from the bunch, took the letter from the envelope and handed it across the table.

"What do you make of that?" she demanded, dropping into her seat again, breathless from the effort of her impromptu dance. It was a long letter from an address in Kent. It began "My Most Gorgeous Lucinda."

The woman began work early on the third day. She wanted to be home at the proper time. The previous day several of Lucinda's letters were presented for her comment, and as the woman read each one Lucinda purred. "We were blissfully happy, dear. Such a sweet man. I miss him awfully. Really I do." Later the woman had to rush through the cleaning, and in spite of the extra effort the work continued until three o'clock. The advertisement had specified a four-hour day, from ten in the morning to two o'clock, and that suited the woman fine. At three o'clock, however, she expected to be back in her own home with Sean and Lawrence, Mary-Ann and Kate.

"He was so much older than me, dear," the lady confided. They were both in the lounge examining photographs of Edward and Lucinda's wedding. It was midday on the fourth day. "But he was so generous," the lady continued. "I really was an old man's darling."
The woman nodded. There was no reason at all to doubt the truth of that assertion. And when she saw the lady's accumulated jewels fondled with such tenderness the woman felt sore and empty in all the parts of her that longed for a man's touch. It was then that she noticed how beautiful the lady must

have been once, and might yet be if she were not so fat. She also noticed the bad limp in the lady's right leg.

She hummed to herself as she walked to work on the fifth day. It was pay day. That meant one hundred and twenty euro extra in the kitty. She'd planned some slight improvements to their daily lives - and maybe even some surprises. The lady met her at the front door.

"We'll wash and starch and iron today, dear," she said.

A short time later the woman discovered that the old washing machine plumbed into an outhouse in the back yard did not work. Washing had to be done by hand and with carbolic soap. By two o'clock she had endured a morning of soap, suds, eulogies and tears. The tears puzzled her.

"Edward was such a darling," the lady repeated over and over. "I'll never get used to not having him around." And the grief was ushered in - with trembling lips, with a high-pitched wail, with the dabbing of the corner of the lady's eyes with a tiny pink handkerchief - but the woman saw no real tears. She had read once that as the body ages it produces less fluids, and if this large, heaving body in front of her refused to cry should she doubt the genuineness of its sorrow?

"I'll go now," she said finally, moving towards the hall door. The lady pulled herself together and made as if to usher the woman out. "See you Monday, dear," she said. "Bye now."

It was left to the woman to remind her that she had not yet been paid.

"Oh, I'm sorry. I absolutely forgot to allow for it

this week. I'll have a double payment for you next week. Won't that be nice to look forward to? It's better when it mounts up, isn't it, dear?"

The woman was miserable as she set out for work on Monday. The children had been disappointed. She had hinted that she'd bring then to the zoo on Sunday, and the treat had to be cancelled. Her first task on arrival at the lady's house was to clean out the budgie cage. He was a blue bird who occasionally uttered the word 'shit'. The lady had no idea where he'd picked up "that word," but it seemed to amuse her that he said it. At twenty past eleven someone rang the front doorbell. The lady called the woman aside and asked her to say that she was not in. As the woman headed down the hall she tiptoed to her bedroom. It was a television licence inspector.

"Hold on a minute and I'll ask the lady of the house if she has a licence." The woman did this deliberately, yelling up the stairs towards the bed-room until the lady had no option but to come down. Her pink face was full of fury. She had a licence, she insisted. It was just that she could not locate it right then. She persuaded the inspector to come back another day, and when he left she ordered the woman to clean all the silver and to wash and polish the downstairs windows. Later she pulled the woman away from the window and insisted that she dust everything in the drawing room. She was having her coffee and cream cake there.

"I don't know what's come over this country these days," she remarked as the woman dusted around her. "No idea of commitment, no loyalty, no integrity." She dangled the day's newspaper headlines before her. "TDs EXAMINE NEW PLANS FOR SPEEDING UP DIVORCE PROCEDURES" it reported. "In my day," she droned, "you got married and you stayed married. You worked at it, not like people today. You developed a sense of duty. You didn't make a run for it the first time the going got tough."

The woman continued to dust as the lady read and tut-tutted. The place became one heaving mass of words and sighs and agitated dust. It was the sixth day.

On Tuesday morning the woman was late. Baby Kate had a cold and became very clingy. She wasn't a baby, of course, but an eight-year-old, the youngest child, born five months after her daddy had gone away. The lady was preoccupied and didn't seem to notice the delay in getting started.

"There's some baking to be done," she droned. "My son and his wife will be visiting this evening. I always have home made brown bread and a straw-berry flan when they come. Can you bake, dear?"

"I think so," the woman sighed. "I don't do it often but I'm sure I can." She glanced at the letter in the lady's hand. The words 'ST. CORMAC'S HOME FOR THE ACTIVE ELDERLY' were printed in large lettering on the top. The woman immediately let go of her resentment, remembering the day her own mother entered the County Home, pushed up a ramp in an invalid chair, all her possessions in the black plastic sack which she held tightly to her chest. She'd never made a flan before but the woman said she'd try.

Someone rang the lady at half past eleven. The woman was working in the lady's bedroom at the time. With the door open it was difficult not to hear the hysterical, one-sided telephone conversation downstairs, the lady screaming hard into the receiver and stamping her foot. In the corner of the bedroom the woman discovered some paper things, press cuttings, birth certificates and suchlike lying untidily on the floor. She lifted one item. It was a short news piece with a large headline in an English paper dated May 4th. 1984 and the caption read "AGED MAN DIES IN PRISON." The screaming downstairs had turned to weeping, furious, gut-catching weeping which filled the house. The woman tried to shut out the sound as she read:-

"Edward Leroff, convicted of inflicting serious bodily injury on his wife, Lucinda in 1979, and sentenced to six years imprisonment, died in prison yesterday. He was seventy seven year old and had suffered from emphysema for some time. Mrs. Leroff, now aged fifty nine, suffered severe damage to her spine and right hip in the incident. At the trial she testified that it was one of several such incidents during their thirty two year marriage. Leroff is to be buried later today in Kent."

The woman folded the press cutting and filed it away inside a pile of papers. Then she finished tidying the room. When she finally went downstairs she found the lady, dry-eyed, in the kitchen.

"That was Derek, dear," she called out. "He's going to bring Christopher and Alan along tonight. They're my grandchildren, you know."

She was filling the flan cases with cream, carefully smoothing the lush mixture out towards the tattered edges. "I just love to have the boys come here," she continued. "But especially Alan. He's so like Edward, you know."

It was the seventh day.

BETWEEN THE HIGH CEILING AND THE CORNICE

This morning the world is purple. The small slice of sky which I see from my window is purple. So is the empty beech tree. The faces of people are purple, as are the cobwebs in that corner and the dust under my bed. I haven't seen it yet today, but, for all I know, the spider may have escaped. He may be beige.

Earlier Nurse Ashling Byrne was here. She fed me my breakfast and left. For some unknown reason she shut the door while I was still speaking. I speak only in my head, of course, but I thought she understood that. Now my words drift in empty spaces before returning to me. I try very hard to keep them up there where there is air and light, try to assemble them into sentences which have a certain sparkle. A few months ago someone hung a piece of crystal on my window so that it catches the sun, crowding the walls and ceiling of my room with dancing colour and light. I thought my words might, some day, dance like that. On my pillow, under my quilt they cannot shine. On more than one occasion I abandoned these grand plans and forced myself to think terrestrially - if they couldn't float I might at least take my words for walks. But spread on the floor before me, as near to the door as possible so that I could see them, they appeared sluggish and reluctant to move. The next person crossing the threshold would almost certainly kick them away.

It's quiet now, and in the silence which neighbours me, I suddenly hear a bell ring out. I'd like to be where this bell is, see the delicate mechanism in action, address its message straight away. In more deprived moments I can summon up the sound of the pealing bells of St. Patrick's Cathedral and have them sing for me. I try to keep faith by singing along with them. But it is a task which demands all my strength. Inevitably the effort drains me, and I end up cursing the singing bells until they become mute. There has to be complete honesty here. If I call them back too soon they will not come.

When the bell down the corridor quietens I hear water trickling slowly through the pipes embedded in the wall behind me. It is an ambivalent sound, as ambivalent as water itself. Once, having picked my way through a terrain of rabbit holes on the Blasket Islands, I arrived at a high point above the cliff, and sat there, picturing the wind-blown islanders ploughing the sea as others did the land. But a small boat tossing about in heavy waves reminded me that water is capricious, often snatching those men who were merely seeking a living out there on the ocean. The sea has no conscience - it takes what it wants in the end. Is this amorality a property of all water, I wonder, or specifically of the sea? I quickly remind myself of the reality of rivers and of lakes.

They come in later, full of their business, and make me up a fresh bed. It is a purple bed. When they've finished fussing about the place others come and lift me up and stretch my arms and pummel my legs. They smile and chat, but complain about the weather outside. In here I can be very tolerant of wind and rain. If the streets and fields around filled up with water until mud flowed over everything I would scarcely notice. And if the worst came to the worst I'd become a flying frog - spread out my feet like a parachute - and soar.

I like animals. Human beings can be quite dangerous, but I like animals. I see them quite often on the tele. At this stage I've been with the tele more than I've been with anyone in my whole life. There was a programme on recently about the Oil Birds of South America. They are sometimes called the Birds of Darkness. Strange, that nature did that, gave them wings and no sight. I tried to picture a miracle for them, their seeing the world for the first time, jungles and precipices and valleys and streams - and the tiny, tortured faces of their young. I will never have a child now, but I can see my baby's face - soft pinky, downy thing, bright lips, blue questions for eyes. He cries, and I try to run my fingers over his waiting body - waiting for my caress - but still he weeps. Is it he who cannot feel that touch right now, or is it I? They come back into the room and take him away from me. They are shush-shushing, thinking the tears are mine.

Though here a long time I am not at home here. I envy the hermit crab. In one deft movement he can climb from the old to the new shell. I'm always falling and climbing and falling back into the slim space between my own two fragile shells. The problem is, my new shell appears to be smaller. I realize that in time I may fit snugly into its awkward shape. On the other hand I may hesitate one day - another purple day perhaps - and remain forever trapped between two worlds.

A scurry of feet along the corridor and a scattering of

trays. I have lunch. Yesterday it tasted like butter-milk. Today it tastes like sour cream. The spider has come out. He is, as I suspected, not purple but beige. Once he came right down and strolled across my pil-low until he was so close to me that I was able to puff a light dusting of breath across his tiny body. He scurried away. I worried that he might have thought me unfriendly - but I was just testing. These days he meets me half way, dipping down from his web like a trapeze artist, staying just long enough for me to glimpse the beige flutter of his little life before hauling himself back up again. I never see it, but I suspect there is another spider up there too, who is less of a show off, whose home is near to his, in the crevice between the high ceiling and the cornice.

I often wonder if ... if there's a place where the dead continue to exist -and if the others forgive me my life. After the accident, when I finally knew how things were, it was far too late for me to mourn. I had not seen them go down into the earth. On the tele, on a programme I once saw about African elephants, I learned how the remains of their dead have a special significance for the living elephants, how they sniff out the bones and carry them carefully away to a place of burial. It seemed to matter that they had the opportunity to do that. It was almost a year afterwards before I found out that the others had died. If I'd asked I'd probably have been told earlier, but that was not possible. I know the people here say there is no medical reason for it, but words don't reach my tongue any more. It is of little consequence really. There is no security in language, in communication, and in realizing this fact there is a wonderful freedom. What gives us joy is, after all, indefinable. And we all know that it is life itself which makes us sad. It's not safe then, to assume that our own unique sadness and joy can be understood by others. We're all on our own really. And no one can help anyone else. We just go on.

There's that voice again. I think it is the man in the room two doors down from mine. I see him some-times when we all socialize together, but he never speaks to me. Sometimes he smiles, a thin pale smile which causes me to turn away. You see, I cannot afford to look too deeply into those eyes of his. The eyes lead to the heart. And to see inside that troubled place would be too risky by far. I'd never be the same again. As well as my own I'd know his pain. When he first did that - started screaming and shouting - it was about six months ago -they flooded the place with music through the public address system -the 'Overture to The Barber of Seville'. They don't do that any more. They just let it happen.

Someone once said that it is one of our best characteristics as a species that we cherish the maimed. But I disagree. That man two doors down who is howling out like a wild thing just wants to be free. As it is you can hear his agony all over the building, and his shouting. It is silence which would set him free. I realize that might sound ungrateful, but there it is - truth will out.

During the summer they used to dress me up and wheel me outside. I inevitably became drunk on air. There was a lavender crop nearby, and its colour and perfume soothed. Now, in wintertime, I look to the pale yellow noonday sun for consolation, rather than the fruits of the earth. But it is so far away. It can not offer the intimacy and benevolence of the earth. Under its frail gleam I cannot even imagine how it might be to dig the earth, to plant seeds, to have my fingernails covered inside and out with damp soil. What I can imagine is what might happen if someone planted seeds there, in a box on my windowsill. I'd hear the seed cover crackle and burst. I'd hear the radicle push furiously down into the earth, hear also the frail new shoot struggling upwards and the music of the first new leaves opening out. I've done all this before, you see - in a previous incarnation. But they've never seemed to pick up on these thoughts. I don't blame them at all. It is the nature of things.

At last the purple of this day is darkening. Evening comes in faster these days. There is laughter in the corridor - people visiting somewhere down the line. My visitors usually come midweek, when it is quieter. They bring me gifts, they read for me, they babble away. If they knew beforehand the colour of certain days they would probably not do all that talking - but they don't, of course, so they babble away. I can hear perfectly, but I can mind read too, and I know the things they omit to say. Tough shit! Great guts! Imagine a life like that! In their mid-week eyes I am always heroic. And perhaps they are right. Perhaps I am.

Now the purple is quietening down into black night. I drift. I allow myself to drift. I welcome sleep. When sleep comes I might dream of getting up tomorrow, of putting my arms and legs back on, of walking far away from here.

SOLITARY

Twice. Not once but twice within an hour the phone rang and when I answered it there was no one there. It rang again a third time and I ran down the stairs immediately so that I could grab it and insist that it speak to me. But the ringing stopped before I picked up the receiver. I'll sit beside it for a while, I thought. He's probably finding it hard to get through. Eventually he'll succeed and I'll be there.

I went on holiday once. The twins and Laura were eight and ten.

"Come on away for a break, Kate," my friend, Bronagh had urged. "Leave the kids with Raymond. You need a change of scene. You need to get right away."

We went to Belfast. Strange, some of my neighbours said, strange for a woman to leave her lovely home and her young family to go to that brutal place. Of course Raymond was due a break at Easter. He was a teacher, and he had Christmas, Easter and summer holidays. Taught twelve-year-olds. Said he needed every minute of his holidays. Said that the kids at school drained him, said they were excessively demanding, recalcitrant and reprobate, that's what he said. Before that I'd broached the subject of a holiday that included me.

"Just to Connemara or somewhere, Raymond."

"We'd have to take the kids and we can't afford that."

"We could if ...." I remembered just in time not to ask him to cut down the smokes to a reasonable ten or twelve a day.

"We could if I was very careful with the house-

74

keeping, used less expensive cuts of meat and all that," I said instead. "Then I could put something by."

"Ah no, Kate," he replied, smiling benevolently into his soup, "the children need their nourishment. They're shooting up these days - bone formation, muscle consolidation, hair, teeth and nails and so on - no, we'll have to wait. The good times will come later, dear," he added as an afterthought. I realised immediately that I'd proposed the wrong economy. I might have offered another one, but he walked away.

During the summer Raymond would go away of course. Teacher-plan cultural exchange. He travelled abroad each year, alone and unencumbered.

"I know you're a home bird, Kate," he announced once when every ounce of me wanted to escape with him. Designer blindness, I called it then. Elegant, like solicitude or thoughtfulness or reasonable care. He never dressed up his annual desertions after that. Just flew away. And I knew he had 'friendships' in foreign places. I discovered his capacity for friendship in the summer of '94 when Timmy broke his leg. I needed to ring him while he was in Quebec. Timmy cried all day for his daddy and wanted him to come home. The embassy helped me to locate Raymond. A French-Canadian female answered the phone.

"Ici Joselyn la Grande et aussi le petit Raymond", she purred, "quel 'qu'un desirez vous?" She was drunk. Raymond came home at once. He had been throwing a party for the 'native teachers', he said. Joselyn was one of the guests there. He spoke with such authority that there was no more room for enquiry. I accepted that.

Belfast was good fun while were there. In Bronagh's company I almost managed to keep anxiety at arm's length. We shopped - I'd removed four hundred pounds from the family emergency fund - and we went to the theatre and visited a museum. Towards the end of the week we took a coach trip into the Glens of Antrim. It was March. It snowed heavily, and as we travelled through them the glens were enveloped, before our eyes, in flawless white. Bronagh said how beautiful it was, how remote and peaceful, how ultimately reassuring. I experienced something altogether different as the fine white drape was pulled, by some invisible hand, over the countryside in front of us. I pictured myself in white, before a priest, and under filigree of lace, a smiling Raymond standing beside me.

I seldom see a priest nowadays except perhaps on the tele. Raymond tried to use one against me when I returned from Belfast. The thin, semi-detached little man called around the following Friday. He waffled on about 'holy vows' and 'testing times'. He beamed at each of us in turn.

"It's a tremendous honour," he intoned, "to be a mother." He nodded in the direction of my navel. "A unique blessing from Almighty God." He tried to imprison me - they both did - in that holy chat.

Raymond always made a big impression locally, a pillar of the community, a rock solid family man. Each week at the altar, each alternate week ready and available to take up the collection. But I eventually fell out with Raymond's God.

"Won't you come to Mass just for the sake of your children?" the priest pleaded.

"No. I can't."

"But they're getting big now," he continued, kneading his hands awkwardly together. "Beginning to examine the world for themselves. It would be good if they could see their mother practice her faith. It's by example they learn."

"It's not 'my faith'. I'd be a hypocrite if I let them think it was my faith," I told him. "I cannot do that."

He leaned away from me then, as if I were a pollutant fouling up his air. He and Raymond whispered together in the hall. And that night the family rosary routine began. Raymond would call Laura and little Timmy and Terence to the front room. He'd say how great a thing it was for a family to pray together before God and his blessed mother like that. I was exiled then. If the weather was reasonable I'd go out. I'd go to where it was busy, with many people.

Twenty minutes now and the phone has not rung. I think I'll make some more coffee. A few minutes in the kitchen won't alter anything. He will ring again after not speaking to me twice. It's his way. His amusing little game which he plays all the time. I've got to remember that and try not to attempt to secure anything. Try to float evenly in every situation. Try hard not to attempt to make things happen. Others will do that.

I see the pattern of my marriage clearly now. Of course I should have known earlier the way it was going to be. If I'd looked with the heart I would have seen all. Raymond left soon after Laura went to University in Wales. The twins were in Australia by then. Raymond cleared out overnight. I scrubbed the hairy arc of scum from the wash basin one Saturday night but on Sunday morning the bed was cold on his side and there was no one there. That was twelve years ago, and I've never had any communication from him since. It was easy, it seems, for him to disappear, and easy for him to stay safely away.

There! It's the phone. I need to put this mug down. I never go to the phone with a full mug in my hands. I need all my wits about me just in case.

"How long?" he'd first enquired.

"As long as forever and forever, Amen," I remember answering. It was a frivolous answer. But I was lonely. I wanted him to continue talking to me.

"Is that a fact now?" He laughed, a funny, tortured little laugh.

"I'd better be off," he'd sometimes say. "I know you're cheating on me. There's someone else. There's someone there."

"Oh no. Don't go. There's no one. Absolutely no one. We can talk about anything, anything you like. Don't go."

He'd giggle. "How often?" he'd ask. "And when? And where? Do it now with me."

The voice dropped to a low, teasing, rhythmic whisper. "Are you ready, love?" he'd ask. "Are you ready now?"

His voice hummed along the line. It was almost tender. I'd tell him I was - was ready - that I'd always been ready - always would be ready - always.

"Then come on, luv," he'd urge, and for a few demented seconds I'd forget, and it was beautiful, like he was my beloved beside me in the bed, like he was holding my breasts to him, like his mouth and fingers were here, there and everywhere.

It frightened me the way he screamed down the phone when he came. I was glad that he did not even know my name. He was a total stranger, a one-night stand I'd tell myself afterwards, feeling sick with self-loathing and regret. But it was a secret. No one knew he was there. In fact no one knew about me either. Here I have no neighbours to speak of and the twins and Laura are still away. But it doesn't happen like that each time the phone rings. Sometimes it's my sister-in-law, Barbara. She asks if I have heard from Raymond. I tell her no, it's been twelve years now and it's silly to expect to hear from him after all that time. She sighs and says she's sorry it's turned out like that. Other times it's my stranger playing a variation of his game. He uses a 'yes' and 'no' tactic until he's got me hooked.

"I have to go now, luv," he announces then, "there's someone on the other line."
The phone is replaced at his end.
I hear a low-pitched, electronic whine. It is all I hear.
I am alone again.

TIME TO BURY THE DOLL

I'll grow my fingernails, and when they are long enough I'll drag them through the skin of the world, scratching the planet 'till it bleeds and oozes and stinks. And if my lovely, manicured nails shatter and break, so what? I'll have had my satisfaction. I'll have had my revenge. You see, up to now I've been too quiet. It took Christmas Eve to put the appropriate noise back into my head. It was then that it finally embedded itself into my soul. But I'll soon release it. I'm getting ready. In a little while it will be my time for confrontation and I'll know how.

My mother took me in as soon as I was old enough to spot a tear that did not match a hurt arm or a grazed knee. I was about nine. You might consider that a little young, but believe me I've met others like myself, people who at a very tender age can detect the storms gathering inside the souls of others. I found her desolate one day, her long, slender neck bowed as she stood by a small window, looking out.

"Mummy," I said as I tugged at her skirt and allowed my eyes to wander upwards towards her face - for she was quite tall - "Mummy, are you very sad?"

I surprised myself when I said this, for I'd never used that word before. It must have crept from the back of my head, or leaked from my stomach or journeyed from somewhere even more hidden than that. And it triggered a response in her. It was then that she first wept in my presence, and I thought I saw the edge of the hurt that did not bleed.

"Catherine child," she said to me in that character-istic, slow drawl which eased every syllable into my brain, "I am sad, very sad indeed." She sat down at my level and threw me a long, sideways glance. The wide-openness of those desperately searching eyes dismayed me. I began to cry.

My father had long ago absconded with my brother and mother and I were alone. She'd told me my daddy was cruel. I remember sitting in the garden, under the strong heat of a July noonday sun, swinging on the swing that he had made for Alec and me, allowing the heat to filter through the leafy tissue of my skin, owning all that luxury - until she appeared.

"That swing is dangerous," she snapped.
"Don't you use that swing again."
There was no danger that I could calculate and I must have said so for she came back at me.

"He didn't do a good job on it. Didn't secure the ropes. His heart wasn't in it at the time. He didn't really care."
I knew 'he' was my daddy. I remained very quiet and still because every movement of that word alarmed her.

"Anyway, you're getting too big for a swing now," she said. "I'll have it taken away."

It wasn't such a huge loss really. The holidays were almost over and I was soon enfolded again in the security and activities of school.

Sister Agnes was a large nun who carried out a small business somewhere deep inside that cluster of dark and musty rooms that was the convent. We girls loved her for her industry and hated the way she clipped our tentative French sentences into two, sarcastically, with that twisted smile of hers. But she made sweets. And between eleven and ten past eleven each school morning she was permitted to sell us the fruits of her labours. Sister Agnes also took us for religion and surprised us all one bright, spring morning by arriving into class with half a dozen dolls under her arms.

"Divide yourselves into groups of six," she ordered, "and take a doll for each group."
We giggled for a minute or two until we had attached ourselves. Sister then strode up and down the room, her skirts swaying with the movement of her hips, her leather strap flapping by her side.

"How did sin come into the world?" she suddenly demanded, as though it were a new topic, fresh and exciting.
We told her that when we stole something from our friends, or said nasty things, or lied to our parents, sin came striding in.

"But why?" she insisted. "Why does that happen?"
We had no idea. We hadn't examined the matter closely at all.

"Girls," she then told us conspiratorially, "the reason evil is presently in your lives - and mine - is because of 'original sin'. She paused, allowing adequate time for the significance of all this to filter through. "Do you understand that?" she then demanded, and we nodded, willing to be convinced that we were naughty and spiteful because of that mysterious occurrence in the garden long ago.

"Babies," she continued, "are born in a state of original sin. They've got the stamp of that first sin on their souls when they come into this world."
My friend, Rosemarie shot me a puzzled glance, but I found that acceptable. I had the stamp of my father

on me. In his youth he'd had red hair. His father before him had red hair, and I also have red hair. The world is full of people marked with the past. This was no different, just a little bit subtler, that's all.

"It's your duty, girls," Sister Agnes continued solemnly, "if you ever come across a baby that is dying, to be sure to baptise it there and then so that it can go straight to heaven."

She filled six small bowls with water and handed one to each group. "If you find such a baby," she said as she handled one of the dolls, "cradle it in your left arm with its head tilted back like this, take a small drop of water and sprinkle it over the little head." She paused briefly and then continued. "While you do that you should say the words:- I baptise you in the name of the Father and of the Son and of the Holy Spirit, Amen."

She carried out these manoeuvres deftly, and we were very attentive, intimidated by the awesomeness of the duty life might one day impose on us.

"Such a baptism," Sister Agnes assured us when each of us had carried out the practice task, "is a true sacrament and will send the little one directly to Jesus."

I'd often seen my mother's 'acquaintances'. I needed to look up that word in the dictionary because it wasn't one I naturally owned, and when I asked her that's how my mother had described them. The day I spent practising on the dolls is indelibly etched on my mind for that was the day she first called me into the room where they 'visited' with her. I'd never gone into that spare room without her permission. It would have been too enormous a trespass, that much I knew from as early an age as I understood anything at all. When invited, I hesitated before carrying my doll with me into the room. She immediately removed it from my arms.

"You're a big girl now," she said sharply. "You should be well beyond the doll stage."

I tried to explain that I was baptising a dying baby - practising that is - but she quickly pushed my words away. Her visitor was in the bed and he was smiling. He had large eyebrows, which stood like thick forests, on the outer edges of his eyes. Otherwise he was long-necked, fair-haired and quiet. I thought he was a little like the daddy I longed to have, being an older man but not too old, regarding me kindly and speaking sweetly, saying Catherine, come here, Catherine my girl come here to me. My mother left the room and I heard a key turn in the lock.

"If you knew how difficult it was," she screamed at me a few weeks later, "if you had any idea what it's been like for me you'd change your tune."

"I'm sorry, Mummy," I said quietly, afraid, as always, of her fury. I knew my daddy had gone away and left her to cope alone with me, but I hadn't asked for all these new daddies she was bringing in. On the first occasion I cried all evening because he wasn't nice. I asked her not to send me into that room again and she shouted and screamed at me. After that I went in quiet often. Sometimes she seemed to be happy that I did exactly as I was told, but she was often cross and I was never sure.

Rosemarie was my closest friend. Her father was a surveyor or something like that. I really liked her and we hardly ever quarrelled, but after the day she laughed at me I seldom spoke to her. Anyway, I left that school soon afterwards and my mother and I went to live in a country cottage three counties away. Rosemarie laughed with the others because one girl - she was called Georgina and I hated her - said I was getting very fat. I'd noticed that myself - and how the other girls gathered in groups which whispered at me across rooms and down corridors. But I didn't expect Rosemarie to betray me like that. I wanted to be able to tell her how sick I had been and how I wished I could crawl into a hole and die.

I was on the phone now.

"Mother," I said, holding on tightly to the years of accumulated rage in my heart, "I've decided to come home for a while."

"Have you, Catherine?" she drawled back down the line at me. The question did not invite me home; neither did it veto my plans.

"I'll be flying in a week before Christmas," I continued. "I've arranged a car hire so I'll drive down. Will you be there?"

"I'll be here," she answered in that put-upon tone which had long imprisoned me.

I made no reply. I could no longer accept her martyrdom. Neither could I bring myself to openly reject it.

Two years ago, when I was twenty eight, I had a breakdown. It was then that I began to see how my spirit had shrivelled. I remember waking from those oppressive nightmares and pleading with God to send me one day, just one single day of unmitigated joy. My doctor concluded that it was essential for me to go back to the roots of those bad dreams, to the remote cottage, to the tiny room, to the nearby woods. Under her guidance I led out much of what was hidden in my psyche. Like recalcitrant children,

I led out my thoughts and my memories and half memories and the guessed-at things. To console myself in this newfound desolation I turned to love. I did not succeed. Later I evicted myself to cynicism. It could only be guessed that a heart still beat inside of me. Truth is however, I knew exactly how small and mean that heart had become.

"Mother," I told her on my third evening back home, "I keep having these dreams."
Her large eyes scanned my face as they had often done, but she said nothing. She was fifty-eight now, not old, not young, and still beautiful, with her long back and slender limbs and that black hair around a strong and sensuous face. She was, even now, more lovely than I would ever be.

"Mother, I've had some analysis," I told her.
"What?"
"I've had to be in hospital. Had to talk to psychiatrists."
I saw her shift to the edge of her chair like a wary animal preparing for attack.

"Mother," I began. "I want to know about those men."

"You were only eleven, twelve," she flashed. "It couldn't have harmed you. You were only a child. It should have been no more than a bit of attention for you."

"What's that you've said, Mother?"
She regarded me squarely but did not reply. For the first time in my life that gaze did not intimidate me.

"Mother," I began again, my voice rising as I continued, "you made a whore of me."

"Shut your mouth, you ungrateful bitch," she yelled.

"What is it I should be grateful for?" I demanded,

"answer me that."

"You were well looked after, Catherine. And I did it on my own. You always had a nice home, good clothes, toys, schools."

"What did you get out of it, Mother?" I demanded.

"Very little, it seems."

"Is that why he left?" I asked. "Did you drive my father away with your whoring around?"

That wasn't how I had intended to say it. Truth without grace can be a brutal thing and I had wanted it to be a little kind. But, though I longed for it, pity wouldn't come.

"I couldn't stop myself, Catherine," she sobbed, agitated now. "It was like a drug, like I had to take men like that or I'd cease to live. Like it was the only life that was left to me."

She paused. She seemed to be inspecting her very soul.

"And then when Brady asked for you," she continued, "I thought well, why not? And there was the extra money too."

"You are pathetic," I told her, wanting desperately to hit that revealing mouth of hers. "Do you have any idea what you did to me?"

Without waiting for her permission I told her about my life after I'd absconded to London, the squalidness of the early years, the guilt and self reproof later, the agonies of my late twenties when the jigsaw pieces began to fit. She looked away from me as I spoke and inhaled in a shallow way. Too much of the air I had breathed out would cause her to take in my hurt. Above all she wished to avoid that.

"Mother," I said, the storm inside of me eventually subsiding into a smouldering hiss, "if it has to happen we should be able to choose when and where our spirits are going to die. But you killed mine off long ago."

On Christmas Eve night, in my old bed in the little gable room, the past became so urgently involved with the present that I was a girl of fourteen again, writhing in agony in my bed, sweating, pleading with my mummy to take the pain away. She was there all right but nothing she did could remove the spasms of sheer agony which engulfed me. Then there was this huge, searing splitting in my guts so that I thought my body had been divided in two, and after that no more pain, but strangeness, numbness, and a small, far-off sound like a bird or a kitten or a tiny trapped creature of the wild. The sound did not last for long, and I must have slept weeks away. I awoke to the sound of my own weeping and my mother, in a blue nightgown, was standing at the door.

"It was for your sake," she pleaded, her words tumbling awkwardly across the frozen air.

I continued to weep.

"It was sickly," she said then. "It had come too soon."

In an instant the last, dogged jigsaw piece slotted into place.

"Mother," I demanded, shaking her, "did I have a baby and did you murder my baby as soon as it was born?"

She looked at me blankly.

"Did you baptise it?" I demanded, pushing her backward across the bed.

"No. There was no time. Things had to be done quickly if people were not to know."

"My baby didn't go to heaven," I yelled, trampling

over my mother with my fists. "You wouldn't even let my little baby go to God."

For several days she sat staring into the fire. The weather was not too cold, just misty and damp, more like late October than December. I cooked some fowl and a pudding, but we ate little. It was becoming clearer by the minute what I needed to do to be free. On New Year's Day I'd have mother march before me into the woods. I'd make her carry a spade. She'd lead me directly to the place where she had buried my child. I'm certain now it is the place I've frequently visited in my sleep, a small fresh mound of humus surrounded by mossy stones. Of course my dreams were tuned to the past and now it will probably be overgrown. It all happened sixteen years ago. But she will know how to find it. And I'll make her dig there until she uncovers my child. I'll take my baby's bones from the earth, away from that place. I'll pray some prayers to undo the past and bribe God into accepting my little one into heaven. He must know how much I would have desired that, how often I had practised salvation on my doll. And then I'll put the doll down. I'll take my doll from the top shelf of my old wardrobe and when the baby is lifted from the earth I'll inter the doll instead. I'll make my mother refill the grave and cover it over. Until she goes down into hell I'll not allow her to forget.
Yes, tomorrow I'll take my baby away. Then it will be time to bury the doll.

GOING HOME

"Are you afraid of death?" he asked.

Oh dear, devoted Franciscan holy man, I thought, I'm afraid of life. It is because of the life I see around me that I am here talking to you.

"It's common," he told me, "that fear."

"I don't think ....." I began, but he was there before me.

"It's not always a conscious fear, my daughter," he said. He spoke it softly so that I would not defend myself against the possibility. "It's not necessarily something that any of us think about at a rational level at all."

"I saw my grandmother die."

"Did that trouble you, daughter?" He smiled, a placatory, encouraging little smile.

"No," I said candidly. "And I don't think it bothered her either. She just eased herself away from life. Like a dry twig floating in a slow stream she just drifted out."

"I see. I see." His expression altered as he searched for a more reliable set of words with which to reach me. "Guilt is the problem," he announced then. "Guilt is what makes us unprepared." His voice dropped to a secret whisper as he enquired "how long, my child, have you been away from Mother Church?"

"Since I was twenty eight," I told him. "That's nine years now."

"You need to come back," he said, gently puffing his words across the glass-topped table between us. The room was warm and the perfume of burning incense filtered in through every ancient pore in the big oak door, The priest was about sixty five, old enough to be my father, and the way he called me 'daughter' and 'my child' melted me. I told him I would come back if that was possible, if it was not too late, if he could show me how. Before I had time to change my mind he donned a purple stole, asked if I was truly sorry for all my sins and when I mumbled 'yes' he hurried some prayers towards heaven and pronounced me free.

"You'll have communion now," he said, his words swinging delicately between the twin poles of invitation and command.

"But ….," I stammered, "there's no Mass on. I'll have to wait."

"No daughter," he said emphatically, "there'll be no waiting. I'll bring it here. You just sit there and prepare yourself. It'll take only a minute or two. I'll be back."

I heard him sing 'Jesus I am Coming' as he hurried down the corridor towards the tabernacle and the host which he intended to carry back to me. For a split second I was torn between the fear of disappointing this seemingly warm and tender man and the terror of being absorbed by all that - that suffocating religion - again. And I hadn't come for spiritual help at all. I had another, more pressing problem, one which this priest seemed unable or unwilling to deal with. I decided to go. I ran from the room as fast as gleaming polished wood would allow. When I got outside the February sky was full of snow. I went home alone.

"Shush," I heard one of them say. "She's back. She's in the kitchen."

"Ok. Ok," my husband replied, "the bitch'll not say nothing anyway."

"I'm not sure of that," the one called Kavanagh insisted.

"Ach no, Kavanagh." It was my husband again. "You don't understand. I've got a well educated wife." The emphasis on the words 'well' and 'educated' made me cringe.

"You know how well educated that girl is, Crowley," he continued, "weren't you there when she had her last lesson."

Crowley had stumbled in our most recent row after I had decided to ask what all those 'huddles' he and his pals got themselves into were about.

"My wife is kinda' curious," Stephen had told him then, "she keeps looking back. She's so curious she'll end up in as sorry a state as Lot's bloody wife."

Crowley shuffled inside his huge overcoat.

"Remember Lot's wife?" Stephen yelled as he hit me, "she got herself rightly stuck."

"Does she know anything?" I heard Crowley persist as the room spun about me and I hit the floor.

"Ah no, Crowley," Stephen replied, "Of course not. She forgets things easily, don't you dote?" He flipped an index finger briefly under my chin. "And when she doesn't forget," he elaborated, "she's got me to teach her how."

He was gone for five weeks before I began to panic. I hadn't a penny. I'd used all the money in my Post Office account. I suppose I should have continued to 'sign on' like they all do, but I wanted to be at home with the child and I decided it was not right to say I was available for work when that was patently untrue. When the child died in his cot when he was five months old I was too shocked to attend to things. I'll do something about that later, I told myself, when the ache eased - if it was possible that would ever happen. I was down to my last teabag and tin of sardines when I went to the Citizen's Advice Bureau. I'd no intention of hinting at anything strange with them - that would have been most unwise. I just told them that my husband had gone and that I had no money at all. A pleasant woman told me about the local welfare office and how I might apply there for some funds. "Relief", she called it, suggesting that I go there straight away.

The office was in a grey stone building situated in a laneway between two busy streets. The building housed a doctor, two nurses, a dentist and his assistant and the person I was sent to see. There was a large waiting room which, when I arrived, was crammed with people of all shapes and sizes. I sat down, but no sooner had I done that than a big, florid woman pounced on me.

"There's a queue here," she yelled - and then to the assembled roomful - "this wan thinks she can see yer man, Looney straight away. Must think she has something special to offer him!"
Several teenage girls sniggered as I retreated to another part of the bench. An old man sighed and moved up a little to make a space for me. No soon- er had I sat down again than a howling toddler rammed his toy tractor into my shins. When he saw me wince he stopped his howling and smiled. My baby's unexplored blue eyes swam in my head. I began to cry. When I finally entered the welfare man's office my face was flushed and red with tears.

"What's the problem?" he demanded. He was very young, far too young, I thought, to peer into other people's lives like that.

"I've no money," I told him. "My husband's gone."

"Gone?"

"Yes. He hasn't been home now for five weeks."

"Don't you know where he is?" he asked.

"No." I hoped he had not noticed how my tongue hesitated over that tiny word.

"No?" he repeated. "No? You've no idea? None at all?"

I said I hadn't while a mental picture of what I'd discovered formed in my head - a plastic bag - in the tool shed - under the old, abandoned rabbit hutch which had been in the back garden when we moved in - and inside the bag several maps, routes across the border, Donegal and Monaghan, farmhouses marked with red X's, main routes indicated by parallel blue lines and secondary roads in green biro. There was also a list of names, just first names, and something else which I found hard to contemplate at all.

"Are you going to attempt to trace him?" the welfare man demanded.

"I'm not sure," I stammered. "I don't know how."

"Are you working?" he enquired. I'd hardly be sitting before him if I was but I suppose he had to ask.

"Not since I got married," I told him.

"Children?"

"There was one but he died - it was a cot death."

"Oh." He softened visibly. "Oh, I'm sorry."

He shuffled through a mound of paper and produced a pen.

"You'll have to do two things," he told me. "You'll have to attempt to track down that husband of yours, and you'll need to start signing on for work."

"I see," I told him, conscious of the hunger growling inside of me. I was frightened. I'd never encountered this need at such a basic level before.

"In the meantime," the man continued, "I'll visit you in your home this afternoon. When I've done that I'll be in a position to offer you assistance until your dole comes through. And hopefully, it won't be long before you get some work."

I never discovered precisely what my husband had hoped for. But I know how that hope shaped his life and how that shape defeated me. Even before the child died Stephen had drawn away - all those sessions at various locations - night and day - and the ones he presided over in our front room - and the weekends which might have been filled with hill walking - or something else.

"Don't interrogate me," he yelled when I took my first tentative step towards finding out. I wanted our life together to be different, I told him. I wanted to share. And I wanted him to do the same. He just laughed and walked away. The crucial row came on the night I cried during the Nine o'clock News. Bombs had exploded in the main street of a market town - victims's blood congealing on my television screen - shreds of human flesh scattered in the
yellow privet hedge of a garden just like mine - a shocked woman moaning so hard I could feel her agony in my heart. It was all only yards away. And the tears came, like a swollen Niagara, like I could replenish each of the Great Lakes.

"Cut out that sniffling," Stephen fumed. His supper was in front of him, toasted sandwiches and beer which he took in an easy chair by the fire.

"I can't," I told him.
He kicked the coal bucket to one side and stood up.

"Doesn't it affect you at all?" I asked. It was a

foolish question.

"Cry for those bastards? What do you take me for?"

"They were murdered in their beds," I yelled back without weighing the possible consequences of what I'd said.

"Murder?" he roared. "Is that what you call it? Murder? You bloody shoneen bitch." He strode across to the television and turned the sound of the news commentary even louder so that it might fill the room. "Shoneens like you, my dear wife," he spat at me, "are the lowest form of animal life. Positively the lowest form of animal life."

I remained silent. There was far too much fury in him and no through route to the heart. Upstairs the child had begun to cry.

I got some money from the welfare officer. It wouldn't keep you alive in the head and in the heart but it held back the threat of acute hunger. Funny. In those days of coming to terms with Stephen's absence I began to see why my baby had died. There wasn't enough love for him where he was and he'd decided to go. We were both preoccupied, his father and I, Stephen all secretative and aloof and I, wandering on the perimeter of his say-nothing world, both longing and dreading to know.

There was a name etched in black on my brain so that I would never forget. It was on the largest, most used looking map. I wondered as I read it what type of place it might be. A small town set in a valley among stony hills? Orchards perhaps? Or sheep country? Something like that. It was a barely angelised name, and it rolled off the tongue with double vowelled eloquence. But it was ugly when I heard it again. A bomb in a culvert - near that place - no warning - ten injured - badly mutilated - three dead. The priest squeezed his right hand into his left hand as I tried to tell him about the name on the map.

"I'm sorry you left so quickly the last time you were here," he'd said.

"Me too," I lied, "but I felt ill. I had to go."
I noticed that he was wearing shoes, not sandals, but it was very cold and perhaps that was the reason. There is always an explanation, a reason for everything which happens on the face of the earth. There is always a sensible reason, like the one that Franciscan might offer for his choice of footwear. He don't hold rigidly to the old rule anymore, he'd explain. It doesn't make sense in this age, in this climate to stick to wearing sandals. We've let go of the past. On cold days we wear shoes.

"My husband was always reading Pearse," I told the priest in a rush.
He stared at me.

"Padraic Pearse," I elaborated.

"What do you mean 'was'?" he demanded.

"It's weeks since I saw him," I told him, "months actually. Two and a half months now."
He said nothing.

"You know that 'blood sacrifice' idea?" I continued. "Jesus, atonement, redemption through blood? My husband read all those things in Pearse and wrote about them too."

"Oh."

"One day I heard him reciting some of it aloud. I think he was practising for a speech. 'Bloodshed is a cleansing and a sanctifying thing and the nation that regards it as the final horror has lost its manhood' I quoted.

"Is that all?" the priest droned. "Is that what has you so upset?"

"Father, I saw bits underlined. We make mistakes in the beginning and shoot the wrong people - that's what it said - that's what goes along with this glorification of bloodshed in that book."

"It's just rhetoric. Every nation needs the stimulus of a bit of rhetoric. It's not at all important," he soothed.

"It can't be right," I pleaded with him. "It can't be right to talk about the gibbet being the noblest symbol in the world, linking themselves with Jesus dying on the cross and all that."

"Did he do that?" the priest asked, a puzzled expression on his face, "Pearse, I mean."
I ignored his question. "And he wrote about taking Christ's sword," I continued. "In Christ's name, Father, tell me what is Christ's sword?"

"Where's your husband now?" the priest demanded.

"I'm not sure but I think ...."

"Is he up there with the others?" he pressed.

"Father", I spluttered, "did you see that bomb the night before last? In the culvert? That's the place they had mapped. That's the place they were planning to visit. I know that now."

"Child," he said, "you're overwrought. You're imagining things. You're reading too much into everything. And I think you're missing that little baby of yours."

"But I saw the dead people and the maimed people in my front room," I yelled.
He frowned. "There were no dead people in your

front room."

"Names," I hammered out. "Names. A complete list of names. Guns. Maps. Explosives. They were all in a bunker dug out under our rabbit hutch."
He must have pulled the service bell because the housekeeper suddenly arrived with a tea tray.

"This young woman is going through a tough time grieving for her little baby," he told her. "She could do with a bit of help, I think. Would you ring Dr. O'Hara?"
She nodded.

"Don't be troubled, daughter," he said after she had left the room, "we'll soon have you sorted out."
On no. I should be going now, I thought. I had made a bad mistake in coming back here. It had finally become clear to me that there was no way of persuading this man to help me deal with what it was I had discovered. Absolutely no way. I was bone weary of trying to draw him out of whatever blind world it was he occupied and I just wanted to leave. Maybe I'd have to ask for Jesus in order to get the opportunity to sneak away. That's it. I'd ask for Communion. And I'd be humble. Plead if necessary. Plead with the priest to go and fetch Jesus for me. But I'd need to be quick. I'd need to do it immediately if I expected to get away before the doctor came.

LOUIS AND LOUISE

Now, I ain't got nobody, babe
And there's nobody cares for me

Louise Robinson drives along the South Circular
Road and on the car stereo Louis Armstrong is
alternately singing and blowing his horn. Louise
holds the steering wheel lightly with her left hand
and strums the dashboard with her right. There is
colour as well as music in this movement, her
brightly painted fingernails flickering like humming-
birds in flight. By the time the song is finished she has
pulled into a service station and has served herself
fifteen pounds' worth of juice. Afterwards she heads
for the car wash. Switching off the engine, she
engages the handbrake, inserts a token in the
machine and the magic begins. The spread of water
over her little world is at first very slow. It comes in
a light drizzle, but by the time the green rollers have
enveloped her car she is in an African jungle and the
monsoon is beating down. She settles to listen to the
heavy thud of water on her tiny tin roof. For a
while—only seconds, perhaps—she hears nothing
but the hot rain as it meets the inevitable opposition
of the earth. But shussh! Listen! There are footsteps
outside. Her heart begins to pound, and the new
sound is as loud as the first. Water cascades down
her window but, even so, she can detect a shape
outside. She peers hard into the wetness and finds
that the shape is smiling in at her. He is very big, very
naked, and very black. Louise has been warned not
to open her door in such circumstances but the man's
smile is benign, and she'd like to discover if the soles
of his feet are pale, and he is out there in the rain and

it's dry inside. He eases himself into the seat beside her and immediately flicks his pink tongue around the perimeter of her left earlobe.

"Are you saved, sister?" he whispers, as he carries out manoeuvre. "Are you saved?"

She shakes her head.

"What a pity," he replies, his broad forehead shaping into an attractive frown. "But never mind, salvation is at last on hand."

Taking her face in his huge hands, he kisses her full on the lips. Later, much later in fact, when the flood has subsided and the sun is shining through once again, she notices the tiny bubbles of oxygen in the water cascading down her windscreen. And she is pleased to see that a spider's web, carefully constructed on the side mirror, is intact. It shimmers with luminosity in the after-rain. She smiles to herself as she drives away.

Brown and white chairs are spread across the hotel terrace. Interspersed with these are black stools. Music comes from inside, from a small hexagonal extension to the hotel. In the centre of the hexagonal roof is a round window, and through it the sun relentlessly beats down on the musicians. The neck of a steel guitar sends out prisms of colour and light in all directions. Though the place throbs with couple-speak and with noisy family groups Louise sits alone. She wears a short pink dress, frilled at the hem, and in her slender left hand she languidly handles a cigarette. She knows she is fifty today, but no one else does. Her hair is auburn—with assistance—and her eyes are brown.

"Here's to you, Mrs. Robinson," she whispers under her breath as she sips her gin. It is the second today.

The first came at breakfast time, after the flowers—
a stunning bouquet of roses Interflora'd from Burma
with an accompanying note. "Sorry I'm away for this
special day," it said, "but we'll whoop it up when I
return." Louise shredded the note into the refuse bin
and arranged the flowers in the crystal rose bowl
Malcolm had given her last Christmas. He'd filled it
himself that day with the remaining pink Elizabeths
from their garden. But he'd escaped since then, away
from their agreed enclosure and into the open
savannas of the world, prowling, she knew, and
howling with sex; she was no longer sufficient, and
she'd accepted that. It was he who kept up the
pretence of an imminent reunion. And now the
breakfast gin was simply to celebrate the fact of a
half-century's survival, even though she was alone.
One piddling little gin.

In the hotel grounds small boys kick a football
around the sunken lawn. Little girls splash at the
edge of a pond. Larger girls—the young and
beautiful variety—toss their gleaming tresses in the
sun and laugh together at the young men. Louise
stretches her legs out and away from her, watching a
girl called Tara and a man called Clive. The girl is
sitting in a chair, her sparse red garment held over
her breasts by insignificant straps, its skirt ending an
inch or two below the pubes. She has a straight back
and long brown legs, and wears flat canvas shoes.
She is probably twenty-two. The man is older, maybe
thirty, and is very small. He wears a white sweatshirt
over dark green trousers, and his blond hair lies in
a quiff on his forehead and is short at the back.
He places his hands on the girl's shoulders and

moves the knuckles slowly, deftly burrowing into the soft flesh. She squirms with delight. Again he approaches, kneading the pressure points along the spine, moving lower and lower with each movement. The girl sighs, yawns and smirks at her watching friends. Louise fidgets, her legs become anxious, her body hot.

When the barman comes to her table she orders an iced lager. But when he attempts to collect for the drink, she discovers that there is no money in her purse. The young barman is confused. He has been warned about customers like this. When she offers to go to the car park and fetch some money, he reluctantly agrees. Louise walks away arguing with herself. There was money in the inside compartment of her purse, she is sure of that. She'd put it there that morning. But had she? Maybe she was thinking of her other purse. A tenner? And two twenties, perhaps? How much had she put where? And when? Her high cream-coloured stilettos beat out a hurried staccato down the fifteen steps to the car. In the glove compartment Louise finds the other purse and there is a twenty there, and three one-pound coins. The coins are for the toll bridge, which she uses when visiting her Uncle Harry, who is an Alzheimer sufferer. Too much aluminum in the brain, they say, leading to forgetting things, to confusion. Might be an hereditary element. Louise begins to cry. Hot tears urgently coast down the cool translucence of her cheeks. But she checks her tears as she makes her way back up the steps to the brimming terrace. The young barman is relieved. How elegant she is, he thinks, as she hands him his money.

The musicians range over wide emotional territory.

> No one to talk with
> All by myself
> No one to walk with
> I'm happy on the shelf
> Ain't misbehaving
> Just savin' my love for you

Another Louis Armstrong number!

Clive is in the middle of a group of older men and Tara is nowhere to be seen. At the table nearest to Louise there are three girls and two young men. The earnest brown-haired girl is singing the song and stroking the longhaired young man's arm. Ignoring her attentions, he is staring at Louise. She blushes and looks away. When she thinks he is unaware, she appraises him. Sturdy. Reddish hair pulled back in a ponytail, a high forehead and green intelligent eyes. He glances in her direction again, this time at her feet. She pretends to be engrossed in the sound and movements of the trumpet. It is five o'clock and the sun's rays are oblique, casting shadows on people and place alike. Above all, there is the shadow of the musicians on the tiled terrace, a misty swirling movement which tells its own story.

> I'm confessin' that I love you
> I'm confessin' that I care
> I'm confessin' that I need you
> Honest I do.

The group members are tired, for it's been a long afternoon, and this is their swan song.

> I'm afraid some day you'll leave me
> If you do you know you'll grieve me

Time, Louise decides, is definitely running out. When he looks again, she is determined to hold his glance. By now his companions are invisible, and he alone strides among the shadows, solid, sensuous and with articulate eyes. She is not surprised when he comes forward with two drinks and sits beside her. His is a shandy, which he quickly drinks, but she leaves traces of her gin behind in the glass as she hurries with him towards her car.

He fidgets with the tin opener on her kitchen counter. "I can't open this damned thing."

"Give it here." Deftly Louise opens the tinned beans.

"Have you any bread? I'm starving." His accent is slightly rural, but quite fine. Obviously he has breeding.

"Toast? Shall I make you some toast?" Her hand shakes a little as she extracts two slices of thin white bread from a wrapper. When they are nicely browned she butters them, tips the heated beans on top and offers the lot.

"Aren't you hungry?" he enquires.

"No. No. You go ahead," she stammers. 'Eat any-thing you fancy. Take your time." She throws open the fridge and some cupboards, indicating cheeses, fruit, and a variety of tins. Then she moves quickly out of the kitchen.

"I'm going upstairs to tidy things," she says. She dislikes the coy way the words have assembled them-selves on her tongue but it's too late now, so she con-tinues. "And then I'll have a bath."

Packed away in the back of a wardrobe are black satin sheets. Quickly, for her heart is a steeplechaser on a grand run, Louise strips her bed and makes it up again in black. The pillowcases have a primrose filigree design. She distributes a light sprinkling of patchouli oil on each pillow, at the same time pounding them well so that they settle into comfortable dreaming readiness. She opens the window wide but draws the curtains so that only a small glimmer of daylight enters the room. Downstairs she hears sudden music, and knows that he has discovered the record player and her pile of records. She is glad that there is music, that there is no great urgency on his part, for she is sure that he will come to her when he is ready.

In the apple-green bathroom Louise undresses and sinks slowly into water perfumed with chamomile. A purple bathrobe hangs on the door. She lifts her legs and allows them to float free, wallowing in the sensation of weightlessness. Louis Armstrong is singing downstairs, expounding his unique gravelly interpretation of the world. Louise is pleased that the young man likes Armstrong. It is another point of contact, and she can listen with him as old Louis sings. There is a cabinet by the bathroom door, and she helps herself to a drink. Malcolm, she remembers, disapproved thoroughly of the practice, insisting that there should only be one type of liquid available when having a bath. Louise instantly banishes Malcolm back to Burma and, when she is drying off, pours herself another drink. It is only the third—no maybe the fourth—she argues, as she slips between layers of black satin. She begins to fondle herself as she waits for him.

A rattling sound awakens Louise. She shivers. It is very cool and the curtains have parted at the open window and wind is whistling in. A digital clock in the corner records the hour of five a.m. She stumbles towards the door and turns on the light. She is alone in the room. She moves outside to the landing and descends the stairs. As she reaches the hall she hears the sound of the record player in the lounge—now baby you know, now baby you know, now baby you know, now baby you know—repeated over and over, the record obviously stuck in a groove. Louise frantically searches the kitchen, the breakfast room, the bedrooms and finally the lounge, for her young man. In the lounge she finds that the small drawer in which she kept all her cash and jewellery has been forced open, and every slight, unwanted thing has been strewn around the floor. A great deal is missing. And there is no sign of him.

Mechanically Louise moves towards the record player. Carefully she adjusts the needle so that the music can continue.

> I'll always love you
> Now baby you know
> You can depend on me
> Oh, though someone you met
> May have made you forget
> You know you can count on me

She sits in a rocking chair in the bay window. Soon its rhythmical movements begin to soothe.

THE BONES OF THE DAY

Eileen O'Brien knew well the geography of the body. She understood especially its bones, the monorail of the spine, the curve of the clavicle, the great dark bowl of the skull. She knew the shaft of the femur too and how its round top fitted cosily into the pelvic socket. Even the minutiae of fingers and toes were familiar to her, those tiny pieces of magic that made music, dance, homes, meals. She understood that the knee bent gently to the rhythm of her body, that muscles extended and flexed so that she would always be carried safely forward. She was aware of all this, how she walked, how she talked, how she breathed, how she ached, but not how she might love.

On her way to the supermarket Eileen paused at the canal bridge. The trees along the banks were getting ready for summer. While they stretched upwards they also spread out in the opposite direction. From an early age Eileen had taken exception to covert things, like roots feeling their way about underneath the earth. She wanted to see and to understand everything, exactly - how it is that mankind and the stars are made of the same stuff, why is it that the world does not spin off into outer space - what it is that is going on in her own head. She knew that Theresa needed her. She knew that she needed to be needed. These facts were spelled out clearly above ground. What lay buried was the detail of how she'd argued with these facts. Could she care for Theresa if she were free not to care? What had happened to the many mutinies she'd suppressed? Could she do anything about them now?

Though it was late spring a cold wind lingered, lifting little waves along the canal. Eileen watched as a wave carried some debris. It looked like a child's plastic ball. She noticed how the wave took possession of the ball and how it could not escape the wave but only go wherever it went. Movement without independence seemed to be the inevitable fate of anything possessed by powerful forces without being itself empowered. She moved on. A few minutes later, at the lock gates, she attempted to catch her image in the water. A forty-five-year-old woman, dark haired, grey-eyed, without any dreams? But the water clamoured frantically around the wooden gates, and the image fragmented, its meaning multiplied into many meanings.

As she passed the local church Eileen saw some people gather for a wedding. Several guests stood chatting together, and a large woman in a print floral dress and cappuccino hat struggled hard to keep the first few drops of rain away. It was over ten years since Eileen had been inside that place. She'd confessed her frustration then, and her unease, to an aged priest.

"The wrath of God is swifter against women." the man had told her," "because He has elevated the female sex so high in the overall scheme of things." Eileen struggled hard to explain that she only wanted occasional 'time out' from her sister's infirmity, but the reverend father was having none of that.

"The essence of Christian love," he hissed at her through the grill, "is to forget yourself and to help someone else in life." He went on to spell out exactly how God had dealt with poor Job. "And

Jacob," he concluded with relish. "Jacob dared to wrestle with God, and he came away wounded."

Eileen began to cry.

The memory of her mother's death was lost in time. When she tried to retrieve it, all Eileen managed to conjure up was the smell of lavender in a large bedroom and dark blue curtains pulled tight across a summer window. Seven years old at the time, she was oblivious to the difficulties her father faced in carrying on as sole parent to her and her fourteen year old sister. Some of his problems seemed to have been solved when Theresa, at seventeen, decided to become a nun.

"That girl won't be a worry for me now," Eileen heard him confide to someone at the other end of a phone line. "But of course there's still Eileen. She's bright, but she's a headstrong one."

Eileen took great pleasure in reading. Her father, however, did not approve of his youngest daughter "having her nose stuck in a book all the time" and made many rules in order to discourage her. In those days he seemed to be afraid of day dreams too, on one occasion snatching Eileen away from a shop window which showed a series of images of ballet dancers in action.

"I was just looking at the photographs, Daddy," the child protested as he jerked her arm and dragged her away.

"Trivia. That's all it is. Trivia. Not worthy of your attention, child."

Eileen hesitated. "What's 'trivia'?" she finally asked. "And why does it make you so angry?"

"Look, it's just rubbish. Fills people's heads with

notions. Notions they can well do without. Now come along."

The pictures might, Eileen realised years afterwards, have given her the wrong idea about life! Later, when she received news that she might qualify for a place at medical college, he put his foot down.

"That kind of thing is for people who have a lot more money than we have," he told her.

"But it's subsidised, Dad. I'd have a chance of a scholarship."

"What would your poor mother think?"

"If she thought I'd have a chance I'm sure she'd be pleased."

"She'd think that you have notions above your station, girl, that's what she'd think. She'd say that you'd better cop yourself on. Scholarship indeed."

Soon afterwards Eileen took a job in the office of a local solicitor and earned the money her father insisted the family needed. But in October she accepted a nursing place in a training hospital in Liverpool and left without discussing the matter with her father. She wrote a few weeks later, explaining her work, letting him know where she was. He never replied.

His phone call to the hospital administration office two years later took her by surprise. She squeezed in behind the Staff Nurse's desk in order to take it.

"Daddy, it's me," she whispered, "what's wrong?" His familiar voice floated back to her, washed clean by anxiety.

"Eileen, I'd like you to come home. I need you to come home."

"Why? What's happened?"

"It's Theresa," he told her. "She's back from the

convent.   She's ill."

"But......."

"It's bad.   And she won't get any better.   She'll not be returning."

"I ......"

"You're practically a nurse now, Eileen. You can help me. We can manage Theresa together."

Eileen hesitated. "I'll come home and take a look at what needs to be done," she heard herself say. 'But that's all I can promise right now."

"Good girl. I knew you wouldn't let us down."

She requested a month's compassionate leave. That should be plenty of time, she thought. When Theresa had settled back into her old home again she'd make a strategic retreat.

The plane took off from Speke Airport as evening folded over the suburbs of Liverpool. The city looked beautiful down there in the smoky dusk, and almost innocent, as though newly emerged from the primordial dust. Eileen watched its lights flicker and flush until they were mere will-o-the wisps on the horizon. A couple opposite her then attracted her attention. The young woman wore a shocking pink tracksuit, and cradled the young man's head on her breast. But it was the young woman's face which was bloated from crying. Were tears a part of everything we do, Eileen wondered, as she drifted off into a fitful sleep? She awoke to the sound of a public announcement advising that they were about to land in Dublin.

Her father hurried her through the crowded airport to his car.

"Is Theresa really as bad as you said?" she asked.

"What do you mean "is she really as bad"? You don't think I invented....."

"It's just that she's only twenty seven. It's hard to accept that it will all be downhill from now on."
He shrugged. "She's been seen by the top specialists. A rare bone disease. Incurable. They all agree."

"And the nuns? What about her vocation?"

"It seems it's vaporised into thin air," he snapped.

"They threw her out then?"

"No. Not really. They just 'suggested' that she might be 'more comfortable' in her own home. And she agreed."

"I don't understand. I thought ...."

"You though?" he interrupted, "well so did I. But in the convent it seems it's not virtue that survives but strength."

Eileen never returned to Liverpool. It was supposed to happen after a month, or in six months time, or at least within a year. She could resume her studies after a year without too much trouble. But fate intervened when her father died and the responsibility of looking after Theresa became hers alone.

Last night she'd lain awake, examining the years that lay scattered around her, the past and the future, naming, as she sometimes did, the things that were absent - like fun, like the companionship of equals, like leisure, like love. Of course it was assumed that her life was full of love. Perhaps it was. Perhaps the priest she'd spoken to all those years ago was right. Maybe love was sitting still in the evening watching a woman struggle with a piece of knitting. Maybe love was hearing her moan in the night or having to listen to her incessant, high-pitched prayers. Maybe it was being there to monitor every movement of that disabled body and spirit. Above all, maybe it was having to lie awake at night wondering what it would be like to have the arms of a man around you and to enjoy lovemaking with that man.

Eileen passed through the rows of supermarket shelves as though sleepwalking. It was second nature to her now, negotiating the aisles, grabbing the food needed to keep herself and Theresa going for another week, making sure she had included magazines and chocolate for her sister and the lotto for herself. They'd had an argument last night. Theresa wanted to visit the relics of Saint Therese for the fifth or sixth time.

"You couldn't wait for them to come to Dublin so I took you to Wicklow when they were there," Eileen yelled. "But that wasn't enough. No, Wicklow wasn't enough. You wanted to go to Blessington and to Naas. You wanted to go to Cootehill and to Athboy. You wanted to go to Drogheda. You wanted to follow the poor bitch halfway round the country, didn't you? And for what, I ask you? For what?"

She stopped when she saw her sister's face crumple into quick confusion. "I'm sorry," she mumbled. "I didn't mean it. I didn't think."

"But you did," Theresa said quietly. "You did."

Eileen swallowed hard. "What is it you want of me?" she pleaded. "I'm not sure that there's anything more I can do. You've got to tell me what it is you want."

Theresa sighed. "It's not you who will help me now, Eileen. It's her. I can smell her roses all around me. I know she's going to touch me. I'm as sure of that as I am of heaven. It's just that I don't know when or where or how."

"I'm not taking you to the church again tomorrow", Eileen blazed. "I've had enough."

"You'll burn in hell," Theresa screamed after her as she left the room.

"Then so be it. So bloody-well be it."

Maybe it was the stormy night and the shining morning and the design of her own heart which softened Eileen's resolve. Or perhaps it was the canal and the lock and the fluency of water weeping continuously over that wooden weir. But she knew she couldn't heap blame on Theresa. Her sister had every right to dream. And those dreams needed to be acknowledged. And her hopes ought to be nourished. Eileen walked quickly now towards the small house with the suffocating room in which Theresa was probably still sulking. She'd not changed her mind about her sister's request. Instead she had formulated her own plans. She'd say nothing. Just get on with the day's chores. The action would come later.

Confetti lay scattered about on the ground, but in the evening there was also the new colour and splash of the bunting that hung from every conceivable place around the church. People made their way there, alone or in groups, some excited and garrulous, others quiet and withdrawn. Everyone's happiness is different, of course, but for one mad moment Eileen wished she could believe in the rationale of the occasion and rejoice in it. It would be comforting, she thought, to fit in - just for once to belong - to be warmed by the acceptance of others -

to be normal - to conform. But if there was a God out there somewhere there had to be an obligation on Him to love humankind simply because of its vulnerability. Didn't she react immediately to lost little children crying in the supermarket? And while she was attempting to reunite a distressed child with its mother didn't she love that child with a ferocity that was beyond imagination? Why should God be any different? And why have a 'magic tricks' department? Oh no. There she was again, slipping back into her old ways. But she wasn't hoping for the impossible, was she? Just Theresa's liberty and her own. Wasn't God omnipotent? Couldn't He do anything? If He existed at all then surely He could manage that?

Inside the church the air was hot and stifling. Eileen squeezed into a seat near the front and listened to the music as it filtered down from the organ loft, soft, plaintive, relaxed. She just had to sit it out. The priest intoned all fifteen decades of the rosary as the people filed past the glass cabinet within which lay a wooden box containing some of the mortal remains of St. Therese. They shuffled by in an orderly fashion, waiting patiently to see and to touch. Then, as the last few stragglers returned to their seats, silence settled over everything, like a quiet death in a familiar house. The only sound heard was the inhalation and exhalation of stale, trembling, expectant air. Eileen glanced around to the colourful map of stooped shoulders and bent heads and kneeling hearts behind her. Then suddenly, as though at a prearranged signal, people began to cough, in several different tones and pitches, like an orchestra tuning up before a concert began. Inside that awkward music something happened to Eileen. Her memory was strangely stirred, bringing her rapidly to a safe place beside her mother. She struggled to hold back the tears as the detail emerged. It was Christmas and she wore a new coat and hat of scarlet red. Her mother looked warm and soft in a fake fun fur. Yes, there was no doubt it was Eileen and her mother, in their Sunday best, seated side by side in that very church. Strange. She'd never been able to reclaim that part of her childhood before.

As the final dry whisper of priestly prayer faded away, and as the congregation swelled towards the doors at the side of the church, Eileen made her move. Checking that no one was watching her she slipped into the central compartment of the nearest confessional. As the last voices echoed far away into the night she sat quietly there. She heard footsteps then, tracking down the long aisle of the empty church. One door was slammed and the keys turned in the lock, and then the other, after which there was a welcome stillness. It had a soothing effect - but Eileen could not afford to relax. There was work to be done. She needed to take her torch now, and her tools, and to make her way to the casket where the relics lay. She'd unscrew the lock, lay it carefully aside and open the wooden box in which the bones of St. Therese lay. She'd remove only a small fragment, from ulna or tibia, or femur or skull – it didn't really matter which - and she'd put that fragment safely away in the old snuff box she'd brought along. Afterwards she'd fix everything back in its proper place so that in the morning, when people came in for early Mass, it would not be noticed that the casket had been plundered. She'd slip out of the confessional then, and mingle with the Mass goers as they moved about. Later she'd carry the box home to her sister. The dead bones of the little French nun, lying close to her sister's withered, living ones, would produce the required cure. Yes, that's what Eileen would do. It would be easy. And it would work. It was all a matter of psychology really. Eileen sighed. She was happy now - and fearless - because her mother was there.

GIN - AND A LITTLE BIT OF TONIC

Rose-Ann Hannigan is having her very first gin and tonic - at the age of forty-eight. She bought it herself in an off-licence. A tin. A double measure, it said, and ready to drink. The liquid sparkled as she poured it, and bubbled in the glass. She had to let it settle slightly before taking the first sip. It was sharp, and she held it on her tongue for a long time. After a few minutes she filled her mouth with the stuff, but drew back immediately from that impromptu extravagance, spitting it out as she had done sometimes with the cod liver oil her mother fed her as a child. She sipped again. When the drink was completely finished she laid the glass aside and allowed the taste to linger, watching from her apartment window as dawn pawed gently at the city of Dublin.

Rose-Ann had been up all night. And the gin was a 'night-cap', she told herself, and not an early morning 'tipple'. She always worried that she might drink too much - three sherries instead of two, or a second shandy at lunch. And now she'd sampled this other alcohol of which her mother heartily disapproved. Gin. Rose-Ann shuddered, automatically reaching for a cardigan and pulling it tight about her shoulders. Her mother used to do that too, muttering away about the vagaries of the Irish weather.

Rose-Ann fancied she'd like to have been born in the South of Spain in high summer and not on a Dublin January night when, as her mother had informed her, a blizzard blew in from the north east and the midwife did not reach the labouring woman until an hour after the birth. She felt each unnecessarily searing pain as the story was retold. And she knew the pain was intended for her, as was the guilt. More than once she'd been tempted to check out the whole thing. She'd even reached the point of calling up the newspapers for the time in the National Library, but she fled before they were brought to her desk. If the weather charts confirmed her mother's version of events she'd immediately feel guilty for doubting her. If they did not, she'd have nothing to do with her anger, since her mother had consistently disallowed any aggression but her own.

That was why Liam went away. He was twenty-three. Rose-Ann, six years younger, overheard the final, fatal clash. Initially, he tried to deflect his mother's anger with humour.

"If I'm going to be charged with all those sins," he joked, "then I might as well start committing some of them."

"Go on then," his mother screamed, "laugh at me."

Rose-Ann heard Liam try to rein her mother in.

"Look Mother," he said, his voice blurring to a whisper, "would you sit down and, for once just listen to me."

But it was not to be. Rose-Ann couldn't remember how long the ensuing savagery lasted, but words like DUTY, FAIR, COMFORT and AUTONOMY gave way to other, biting ones. At the time the seeming subtleties of the dispute were beyond her, and it was years before she realized that there was nothing subtle there at all, that what she had witnessed was an old-fashioned power struggle, and that her mother had lost. But then, she still had her Rose-Ann.

Her father went away when she was fifteen. Rose-Ann fell in love with jazz soon afterwards, and listened to it often, and cried her heart out for her missing father. Her mother, on the other hand, became afraid.

"I can't go down there," she'd say to Rose-Ann. "You'll have to go."

The local shopping centre thus became her mother's first 'no-go' zone. Later she refused to travel on the buses, finally limiting her outdoor activities to her back garden. Rose-Ann even had to put out the bin.

"It's too heavy," her mother used to say if her daughter protested, "and I'm getting old."

"You have to go out sometime," Rose-Ann pleaded. "It's years now. Nearly three years. You'll have to go out."

The woman smiled. "I don't have to do anything, do I, Rose-Ann? Haven't I got you?"

"But you won't always," Rose-Ann said. "I might get married. Or go away. Do something extra-ordinary with my life."

The woman grinned. "You might," she said, "you just might."

Bright sunlight shot through the narrow slits between the bedroom curtains as Rose-Ann awoke. She could hear her neighbour's radio, and the mid-day Angelus bell was ringing out. It was Saturday. No work. She wrapped the gin tin with the other rubbish and sent it sliding down the disposal chute. She would buy a full bottle later. She'd have coffee now - just coffee - and not "a proper breakfast," as her mother might have insisted. She'd have lunch in town. And she would not visit the cemetery in Glasnevin - she'd go there in a few weeks time - or whenever she was ready.

The Centre City shopping arcades beckoned. Rose-Ann decided she'd have a proper look around and start rigging herself out for the summer. Her holidays were due in July. Maybe she'd make plans to "go foreign" after all, prove to herself that her mother's dire warnings about the stranger and the strange land were already fading in her mind. She thought - as she'd often though - of Spain. Sun. Sea. Sangria. And? And perhaps sex? The word tumbled about in her mind like a blind creature in an unfamiliar place. She fought the terror of that initial struggle for a few seconds until things settled. He would be handsome, of course, but not excessively so. He would not be a Spaniard - probably an Irishman on holiday at her resort, or an Englishman. Yes. An Englishman! And he'd call her his "wild Irish Rose." He'd loosen her up. Stir her. She'd love him for that. Even if they said 'goodbye' at the end of the holiday, she'd love him for that.

Her skirt might have been a mini except that Rose-Ann was small - barely five feet three. It was her first really short skirt, bought exactly a month after her mother's death - a sort of Month's Mind! The jacket fitted neatly over it, making a pleasing whole. It was yellow, a sunny colour, to match her new mood. In one of the big department stores she flitted to and fro between the various cosmetic counters, eventually opting for a 'free makeup' from a fussily blond lady, who afterwards sold her over two hundred euro worth of gear. Rose-Ann enjoyed relaxing on the reclining chair, having her face examined like that.

"You've got great eyes," the woman told her. "And a good bone structure. You don't need a heavy hand."

The saleswoman's 'light' hand did wonders for Rose-Ann, and the new face she carried out into the street was quite pretty.

"You'll never be beautiful," her mother had told her. "You're like your Aunt Sally. Homely. Bits fitted together awkwardly. No symmetry there at all."

Rose-Ann hid her lack of facial symmetry under a grand splash of frizzy hair. But she had it cut on the day she bought the yellow suit, and the hairdresser also suggested a light sprinkling of blond streaks. Rose-Ann succumbed. It felt strange to have sleek, short hair bouncing about her head. She ran her fingers through it, and it settled back into place almost immediately, the anarchy of her previously unruly mop banished in one fell swoop.

At the corner of Henry Street a man played the banjo and begged. He had a crumpled face, all the youth sucked out of it, eyes now fixed and staring at some invisible thing. Rose-Ann put a few pounds into the little cardboard box he had placed on the ground in front of him. Doing this, she felt both good and bad at the same time. She wished she were not afraid of these feelings, of finding out that nothing in life is ever as simple and easy as she would like. The last time she'd tried to help someone in distress her efforts had gone seriously astray. She was at the local shopping centre at about ten thirty the previous Saturday morning when a woman drove up, parked near the video shop and strode towards it, dressed only in a flimsy nightie. When Rose-Ann tried to lead her back to her car she got a slap across the face for her troubles. Rose-Ann had never - absolutely never - indulged in "lingerie frivolities." But today was going to taste and smell and be entirely different. She wandered among rows of tantalising nightwear, slowly fingering the silk and satin of them in the same way she'd finger the first buds of spring or the petals of early crocus or narcissi. She bought four nightdresses, and two new, perfectly fitting bras. An unnecessary extravagance, she realised, smiling to herself.

As soon as she stepped inside the door of the travel agents Rose-Ann felt as though she were in a foreign place. A young couple was in the process of negotiating a deal with one of the assistants, and a few other individuals flicked through brochures. Rose-Ann decided she'd not do that. She gathered as much information on Spain as she could find and left quickly, brushing aside an offer of assistance from a tanned young woman who intercepted her as she made for the door. She'd go and have a meal, find somewhere to relax, and browse through her treasure throve at her leisure. By the time she set off for home she'd know her exact holiday destination.

Four courses. Such waste. But she had them anyway, finally flushing down her morsel-sized profiteroles with a Gaelic coffee. In the lounge she chose a corner seat and spread out the brochures before her. The 'Costas'. Bravo. Dorado. Blanco. Del Sol. Everything blue and green and gleaming gold. No winds. Just balmy breezes. Jungles of colourful plants, their tendrils trailing over the white walls of cool villas and apartments. And the interior.

Andalusia. Granada. Sevilla. Madrid. Toledo. Salamaca. A man sitting alone in the far corner of the room must have noticed her excitement. He smiled. And she smiled back, glad that someone knew how happy she was. She thought of ordering gin, but decided she'd enjoy that later in the comfort of her own home. As the lights began to flicker in the city below, she'd stand at her window and toast her recently departed mother - and her new life. Right now she'd content herself with another Gaelic coffee before setting off home. Her head spun slightly as she stood up, and she did not notice the smiling man follow her out.

WILLIE AND CHARLES, ALLELUIA, PRAISE THE LORD

Once I heard someone say that mankind had developed language in order to tell lies. And another sage claimed that the mirror was the most capricious invention of all times. However, in spite of owning these titbits of wisdom I used to sit each day at my dressing table, close my eyes, and slowly exhale close to the surface of its rectangular mirror. Only when I was sure that I could inspect my face through this newly introduced fog, did I look. The outlines were blurred, but surely I was still pretty? The hair was a dark froth framing a perfect oval. The lips were full and well formed, the eyes luminous in a flawless face. This was my regular lie, the fogged mirror my language to myself, no one sharing this morning ritual, since Charles left early for his office far away.

His mother used to pray for us. Novena followed novena once it became apparent there might not be any heir apparent. I recall the night the telly first came to our house. When the face of a man filled the screen she pulled her skirt way down over her knees so that this intruder would not plunder her. Charles had inherited her tendency to 'modesty', but soon abandoned it. He might have enjoyed his new freedom were he not so anxious to prove himself to her - and to the world – and to me. But after a few months my wishes were trivial considerations and his obsession uppermost. Yet the baby did not come. Once I actually dreamt a baby into my arms, but Charles' mother, that toothless old crone, tugged it away from me. When I appealed to Charles for help in repossessing it, he merely grinned and walked away. Waking clipped the dream but left the root firmly embedded in my head.

On our fifth anniversary she brought rosary beads home to me. She'd acquired them at a meeting dedicated to Our Lady of Ephrata, USA. It seems that a devout woman of that place received regular visits from God's own mother, who told her what she disliked most about the world. 'The lady' was upset when recipients offered their hands and not their tongues when receiving the host. And when women carried out the tasks which had hitherto been reserved for male priests. And because jeans and shorts were becoming fashionable attire at Sunday mass. Perhaps I am naïve, but I would have expected the Queen of Heaven to be a trifle more concerned about wars and famines and religiously inspired pogroms and those sorts of events. But no. As far as I could determine these did not concern her. A couple at the local meeting had seen Jesus materialize on their bedroom room door and when the man handled rosary beads they became pure gold. I took the 'golden' beads Mother gave me and hid them in the bottom of my bottom drawer. If there were magic to be made let the 'lady make it there.

We were nine years wed, and still childless, when Mother died. She'd parted from us six months earlier to take up residence in the Veronica Home. Charles agonised for months before she went, and only signed the papers when he was convinced that the nursing home would be a safer environment. She'd taken to walking about at all hours of the day and night, you see, and when a skinhead lad delivered her back to us one evening we were forced to consider the alternatives. It seems the young fellow had very nearly fished her out of the sea. Well, not exactly fished her out of course, but she was sitting on the rocks at Sandycove, sunning herself, with the legs of her cotton pyjamas turned up to the knees, when he'd thrown out a line from his beach-caster and accidentally hooked her up. Veronica Home guaranteed her safety. I admit it was a kind of prison, but isn't life itself a prison for us all? Even at the 'home' there were a few minor incidents in which she'd attempted to 'escape'. In the end she abandoned the small-time stuff and made the grand and final gesture. Charles mourned her fiercely, blaming himself for her death, throwing himself into his work with an enthusiasm and dedication I'd never before experienced.

I thought the past was tucked safely away forever when he began to be obsessed with the notion that her passing must surely have heralded the immanent arrival of another little member of the clan. An exit preceded an entrance – that sort of thing. He counted the days on the calendar and made sure he did the business frequently on the most 'auspicious' days. But this wearied him, irritated me and produced no tangible result. When he began to stay out late several nights a week, I convinced myself that he had found another woman. I allowed myself to be pleased about this. But on April 1st he rang from work and told me he was bringing home some 'brothers', and would I make sure to have a 'simple' supper prepared for them. Now, I'm not one for jokes, and neither is Charles really, but it was April 1st and why else would he, an only child, ask me to prepare for a visit from his brothers?

It was the precursor of many visits. On the first night the 'brothers' gathered around me in a circle and prayed. Since Charles was there beside me, holding me firmly in place, it was not easy to resist. I was required to bow my head and close my eyes, but I stole the occasional upwards glance and saw the shadows of the 'brothers' praying hands dancing on the ceiling overhead, their fevered magic throwing black shapes which mirrored the 'darkness' they wished to defeat.

Something was 'blocking' God's grace, they claimed. I needed to be cleansed, they insisted.

Wouldn't I like to receive Jesus as my Saviour? they demanded.

Get myself saved and get a baby in the process, they suggested.

Charles would like that.

It would make him a happy man.

He would at last be the contented husband of a fulfilled woman.

Baby in the cradle and all's right in Charles's world. I had nothing to do except to submit to these ministrations which would bring Jesus knocking at the door of my heart.

And then eureka!

Door wide open.

Invite Him in without delay.

Submit to God. To God's order. To them. To Charles. Forget that I have forgotten – long forgotten – comfortably forgotten to demand explanations for the world and my part in it.

Believe that I am important because God has died to 'take my sins away'. And that belief would operate to clear away the cynical debris from my cramped womb and open it up to receive my husband's seed.

Without lies we'd be stuck with truth. But my regular morning 'lie' led to quite reckless behaviour on my part. It began when one of the praying men called in on his own one day and announced that he'd opted out of the brethren's scheme of things. I quite liked him once he'd divested himself of his pseudo-religious garb. Soon afterwards he shed his other clothing too and we got on marvellously well. He became my regular lover. For a while my weeks were crammed with activity. Sessions with the brethren. Prayer meetings in which I played the part of Charles's placid wife, and passionate afternoons with Willie in my own bedroom, or in the woods above the city, or in a secluded cove on a stretch of County Wicklow beach.

Hope is a desperate animal for an eager husband to have stalking around in his head. I hardly knew what to say to Charles once I knew I was pregnant. Obviously Willie's child. I'd gone for tests many times (at Charles's request), and had always been assured that there was nothing wrong with me. And now Willie and I had proved that fact. We had made a baby between us, a new life growing in my much prayed-for womb. I kept the news to myself. Time, I persuaded myself, was still on my side. In a few weeks things would become clearer, and we'd discuss it calmly and decide what needed to be done. I kept the news from Willie too, since the shock might have dulled his passion and the last thing I wanted was to lose my enjoyable new life almost as soon as it had begun.

Maybe the whole of life is a steady process of educating our nerves. Mine were taut as a trapeze wire during the weeks that followed. It did not help that Charles was at home for his annual leave a great deal of the time. On three consecutive mornings he caught me running to the toilet to be sick. I said it was something I'd eaten, and he seemed to believe me. But he watched me closely, was strangely solicitous, and even brought me breakfast in bed on the morning before the big meeting on Sunday night. Charles insisted that I go, but I was quite self-conscious and began to believe that I showed, even though the tiny cluster of cells growing inside of me was only a little fingernail in size. Willie was there too. He still consorted with the brethren (for career reasons, he assured me), and seemed to be able to enter into the hymn-singing, hand-clapping frenzy with no effort whatsoever. Charles was awkward about these things, yet I could see that he longed to fit in and to do and feel everything the others and did and felt. During a particularly significant hush in the proceedings, when those present had been called upon by the main preacher to open up their hearts and to share God's blessing of their lives with the congregation, Charles cleared his throat, stood up, took the proffered microphone and spoke.

"I want to praise the Lord," he said. "I want to give thanks for His presence in my life. I want to praise His wonderful name. I want to give thanks that He has reached into the life of my wife and brought her abundant blessings. He has blessed her, I know." (Charles looked at me briefly and alternately winked and smiled.) "She hasn't actually told me yet, but I know," he beamed. "We've been waiting a long time, but now that Jesus has touched her she's with child. I know the signs! Praise the Lord! Praised be the Lord!"

The biblical description of my pregnancy seemed strange and incongruous among this well-heeled late twentieth-century gathering. I caught Willie's alarmed glance through the corner of my eye. I was about to excuse myself from the few people with whom I was sitting when the whole room chorused an excited 'Alleluia' and then the song began, a girl with a frenetic guitar strumming out her chords as the crowd sang 'Freely, freely, you have received, freely, freely give.' The women around me placed their hands on my head, mumbling their prayer 'in tongues', while the men hand-clapped and 'alleluia'd the next ten minutes away. I barely recall leaving my seat and walking across the large hall to climb the stairs to the stage. But I arrived there, and found Willie there beside me, pleading that I leave Charles and set up home with him. He declared to the entire, enthralled, congregation that he knew this was his child, and that he wanted to love me and it together under the same roof. I briefly caught sight of Charles' astonished expression before Willie and I were physically ejected from the room. In his car outside Willie kissed the steaming tears from my face, and his tongue found mine, and we were together, locked in that ill-fitting embrace, when Charles drove our Volvo straight at Willie's car.

The baby died. I was discharged soon after the miscarriage. Willie is still on traction, and likely to be in that position for a few months. Charles suffered a fractured jaw as the impact of his car on Willie's forced his face down on to his steering wheel. He's out on bail now, having been charged with attempted murder. One of the brethren risked the disapproval of the others to put up the £10,000 required. I found that very strange. But maybe he is one of a few such people who understand passion outside the framework of constant prayer. Maybe. Perhaps. If that's possible. I don't know.

IT'S A FREE COUNTRY IN THIS KITCHEN

Here I am in the kitchen ironing a 'non-iron' shirt. It's a blue/green one, the colour of the Mediterranean on a cloudless day. Mark wore it the other night when we met up with my youngest brother, Daniel and his new girlfriend, Aoife. Strange, he said, how her eyes were the same colour as his favourite shirt. I don't know why he told me that, except perhaps to indicate that he didn't care any more if I noticed that his attention strayed from time to time. He had a laugh with Daniel too. Boys together, kind of stuff. Just because I'm on a diet doesn't mean I can't look at the menu, kind of stuff. Ha. Ha. Ha. Men together being ultra male. I'd have to accept that if we were to continue to live together on this island we call our home.

It is an island. An isolated territory. Hard to reach. Difficult to leave. Winds, tides, the twists and turns of a maverick moon and an indifferent sun making it an ambiguous place. A prison whose bars are bent and broken but which still contains. I cannot help it when I look out from here and crave freedom. It is human, isn't it, to want to be free? Nor can I help the panic I feel when I am out there and the urge I have to be safely back behind familiar bars. Sometimes I believe I am at odds with my 'real' nature. My real nature wants to be part of a space probe that is searching beyond this universe into outer space. My real nature wants to time-walk down the many corridors of the past and to meet with the people who have contributed to my life. Never mind the human genome! How can a string of microscopic data compete with the romance of history and the prospect of my ancestors lining up to meet me? This would be a different universe, as elaborate as the first, but I would hold it in the palm of my hand, move my fingers softly over it, savour its warmth.

Headstones do not hurt me anymore. I can walk through acres of limestone and marble and not sigh. But there was a time when I matched every mile my father peddled, every brick he laid, every load he carried, to the place where he now rests - and failed to balance the equation. There was a time too when all those white sheets blowing in the wind, my mother's hands pegging and unpegging them, made little sense when set against her silence as she lay, forever hushed and still, under black earth. It was the wasted effort, you see. I couldn't accept that work disintegrated almost as soon as it had been done, that in the end nothing added up. I used to examine specific days - like the day my mother came home after hours of hard fruit picking for a local jam factory - and had a miscarriage and lost her youngest child.

"Maybe it's just as well," she said to me matter-of-factly as I brought her home from the Rotunda Hospital on the bus, "there isn't enough for everyone as it is. Your father and I wouldn't be able to feed any more babies." I was fifteen.

Days like that do not stand up to any logical scrutiny when matched to the mystery of eternity, so I do not examine them any more. I am content to accept them as mere will-o-the-wisps, pieces of cosmic debris to which we have become far too attached.

My child once asked me if there were any wild men like there are wild animals. The question bothered me. Maybe we should all be wilder than we are - in our spirits, I mean. Can you imagine? Wild-spirited men and women among civilised things in a wild world? Everything is so sanitised now - supermarkets, shopping centres, suburbs - we might shrivel up with the artificiality of it all. When I first came to this 'nice' house in this 'nice' estate twenty-five years ago I thought I'd be jumping over the moon. But I haven't jumped over the moon. Far from it. I hear now that the Society for the Prevention of Cruelty to Animals is taking in domesticated foxes and helping them, giving them back their wildness, and I wonder who will rehabilitate us.

It isn't Mark's fault, of course, that I am confused. My husband is a good man. When I said I'd have to accept that 'boys having a ball together' bit I was speaking tongue in cheek. And when I talk of islands it is because of me and not of him. There's is a certain disunity of course, but he's as much a victim as I am. We are like two branches of the same tree growing in opposite directions. And I think he has a job that's too small for his spirit, and it pains him. He is in the bank. Counting money. Adding and subtracting money. Advising on money matters. Coveting other people's money. Once, when he was very drunk, he told me he'd like to have been a rally driver and to have won the Grand Prix.

That child of mine - the questioning one - asked me another awkward question. He wanted to know if flowers know when they are dying. I wasn't able to offer an adequate answer to that one but my son's mind soon skipped to other things. Mine stayed with the issue of 'dying'. In many people, I decided, the soul dies long before the body. It shouldn't happen like that, of course, but it does. It's as if, most of the time, we want to get as far away from ourselves as possible - or perhaps its just carelessness - our losing something which we have never truly found. Of course the question of 'soul' is highly problematical. In 'High Babies', for instance, our class was told that the soul was matched to the body before birth. It was like a white sheet which wrapped itself closely around our inmost core, and stayed beautifully there until we sullied it. We were told that we were likely to be poor guardians of this special entity and that we were sure to damage our very own wonderful white souls over and over again. Little wonder then that the whole idea sat uneasily with us and that some of us never discovered what soul is and that others tried to escape its claims by denying them. I think I escaped from my soul into domesticity and suburban trivia. The 'matching china teacup to china saucer' syndrome. The 'your conservatory will never be as appealing as mine' syndrome. Me and my women neighbours pouring over Habitat catalogues together. The menfolk heroically shelling out. There was nothing wrong in that, of course, but I had come at these things from a bad angle. I thought there was security in such a life, and that was my sin. It's as if I tied everything up which ought to have been rather fluid and sloppy. And it wasn't even as if I imagined myself one of those esoteric creatures who never have to deal with the ordinary things of life, the kind of woman who, in a previous existence, would have had an army of servants above and below stairs and a wet nurse to look after her babies. I was happy to get my hands dirty. I carried in the coal and cleaned out the fire. I didn't mind wearing wellies and getting stuck into the potato plot at the far end of our garden. When my children were infants I used cloth nappies and washed them all by hand. I even learned to change a wheel on my ten-year-old car.

Recently I've been carrying out a radical reappraisal of my life. If the house where I live has functioned for years as a safe, dark place in which I could hide, that is no longer the case. If the details of my role as a wife and mother seemed set in stone - as they may have been - that stone has crumbled. I could run away, of course - not even Mark really needs me any more - and travel in Africa or Asia and come home and write a book, perhaps. I could 'discover myself' that way and bore people for evermore with the minutiae of what I'd discovered and have them salivate over my foreign adventures as they munched Rich Tea biscuits around my kitchen table. I could take a boat and follow a pod of dolphins in some far-flung corner of the ocean, and swim with them and see where that pelagic extravagance might lead me. Why not?, I ask myself, and there is an instant answer hammering about in my head. It would be a false trail. It would avoid the issue. I could set out in search of exotic epiphanies and avoid the realities I have decided I need to confront. Oh no, not the 'being and nothingness' question. Not even desire. Or value. Not frustrated possibility, not freedom, not anguish - but one thing only - ignorance. Our living and dying without knowing who and what we are. Our not even knowing the points on the spectrum of life where we might find ourselves. Our not even knowing - or trusting - what it is to be human.

Maybe our dreams accuse us of forgetting who we are. I've often wondered about that. I mean we run amazing risks each time we put our heads to our pillows, considering the frenzied worlds our sleeping minds conjure up. It's there, surely, that the absolute anarchy of our lives is evident, in that mish-mash of untamed stories and images that sometimes delight and often frighten us. Mark sometimes tells me his dreams and I laugh, or comment, but do not tell him mine. I think I need to begin to do that.

And it's a free country in this kitchen. Here I am now, within its four walls, committing a most unforgivable sin - ironing a non-iron shirt. But I've claimed this kitchen as another sacred territory - like the dreaming bed at night - where I can shelve many of the orthodoxies of my existence. I can take my arguments for walks around this room and not be afraid if I do not know my destination. I can accept that sometimes it's a little better to travel than to arrive. I can learn that painful but exciting truth inside these four walls and take it with me when I go out. I can learn to sniff the air and watch the skies and get to know the weather patterns around this place. Then I can row away from my island. I can risk the seas, setting out from here on uncharted waters to see if I can find out what 'soul' is. I can do all this because it's a free country in this kitchen. I have at last established that.

THE HOUSE THAT MICHAEL BOUGHT.

If I said to him "why do you hate all women?"
he would reply that there was one he loved - his
mother. I'd need to pull back a curtain in his head to
show him that she is the one he most hates. But I
doubt I'd succeed.

We met at the theatre one windy and cold December
night. He trampled on my toes as he found his seat
in row D. He apologised, of course, smiling my
frown away. And in spite of the seven seats which
separated us we were together a lot that night. Our
'conversation' consisted of occasional silent glances
directed at each other. But his mother was there. I
saw her nudge him once or twice, offering a large
bag of sweets. He took several, but I don't think he
ate them. She chewed loudly, cracking down on her
boiled fruit balls with all the determination of a
lumberjack felling wood. Without remembering
everything I remember her on that occasion, the
beanstalk neck, the baleful eyes, the sharp crunch
echoing in the silences between the actor's lines.
When she spoke I saw him half attend to her,
offering his obviously say-nothing replies.

On our third date he paraded her foibles before me.
Look at this, he said - this is how she feels, thinks,
acts - this is my very own mother. I greedily
consumed these revelations, flattered that this
virtual stranger should confide in me. He etched out
words in my head - like 'respectable', 'sensible',
'prude', 'proud', 'practical'. No single word shone.
Each was ushered in unsung, but a brittle laugh
accompanied all of them.

The play explored a bleak world populated by ghosts, devils and demons - the darkness of alleged possession.

"Why did you choose that play?" I asked later. It was our fourth date and he'd insisted he did not believe in ghosts. We were straining the last few yards to the mountaintop retreat known as the Hellfire Club.

"She wanted it," he said tersely.

"Your mother?"

"Yes, my mother."

"Does she go to the theatre often? Does she like drama?"

"She seems to," he replied offhandedly. "She's been lonely since my father died. But she goes out a lot more than she used to - mostly with me," he continued, screwing his face into a kind of benevolence, eager for me to know he cared. His mother was a frequent topic of conversation over the following months, as Michael and I dated and began to get to know each other.

"Why are you telling me this now?" I asked his second cousin recently. He was walking the laneway with me, having hand-delivered a message for Michael. They were junior partners in the same firm.

"Because you are well married and scalded at this stage," he answered. "It will do no harm."

"Michael never mentioned it," I said, bewildered at his revelation.

"That's not surprising," Terence answered. "His mother puts him into the nearest monastery at the age of seventeen and tells him to get on with it, to turn himself into a priest. He marches in there to the sound of the town's number one band, and slinks silently out five years later without as much as a single 'Orate Fratres' under his belt. Not a story to tell the world, now is it, Elaine?"

I stared at him without speaking.

"You don't believe me, do you?" he demanded.

I nodded and shook my head all at once. How could I have a husband of several years standing and not know this, this most crucial of facts about his previous life?

"I tell you, Elaine, it's true," Terence added. He assumed a grave and alternative tone. "This secret has been buried in the family closet for a long time now, and I happen to believe its high time it came out."

I was twenty years and one month old when we married. His mother cried at our wedding. I believed hers were the traditional tears of joy - son now taking a manly role in life, blushing bride at his side. I considered myself secure and strong in his love and her approval, and the only secret I knew was that Michael and I had already 'done it' without the sanction of church or state.

Our wedding took place in April. It was an exceptionally warm spring day. Thereafter it was cold. I waited for seven years for my world to turn towards the sun. Spinning in its own peculiar orbit, it avoided that. Immediately Michael begun to go the long way round to and from work so that he could visit his mother. Mornings were never soft and leisurely and tender. "Stay just a little longer with me," I urged more than once - but he'd go ahead out. After a while I no longer pleaded, knowing he would be haughty and stern in his reply, as though addressing a wayward child. I booked the tickets for my birthday celebration myself. It was he who suggested I do that.

"Elaine," he said wearily a few days beforehand, "be a good girl and get the tickets for the concert yourself. I've got a lot on at the moment."
This was to be my twenty first birthday treat. He must have seen my disappointment and ignored it. But I was determined to be positive. I persuaded myself that he would be glad of an evening out alone with me, of some good music, and afterwards some wining and dining and perhaps a degree of real passion once again. I went ahead and booked two of the best seats in the house. They cost £65.00 each. Michael thought them far too expensive, and he complained that I had not bought three.

Four or five weeks after my birthday Michael came home with a suggestion which shocked me.

"I think it's about time we moved out of here," he said.
We were living in a luxury, two-bedroomed apartment in a good part of town. I knew there was some connection between the property and his mother. but I was not aware that it was hers, that she had provided it to him rent-free until the day he married me. I thought it was his own place, that he had more or less inherited it, or that he was buying it from her through some arrangement of their own.

"But why do we need to move, Michael?" I asked, "I like it here."

"My mother wants to sell it."

"She does?"

"Yes."
I immediately understood how it was – had always

been - her ownership of our home and her inability to accommodate me in her scheme of things.

"I've looked at a place near mothers," Michael explained. "It's down at the end of Mill lane and second left."

He became absorbed, showing me the detail of the place. With his fingernail he sketched it on the leather seat of our suite. He made two or three deep indentations to indicate the roadway and the lane up to our secluded house. I tried hard to see all the trees and shrubbery surrounding it. They were there somewhere between the lines remaining after the initial leather tracks had faded. I tried to see what Michael was seeing, to get inside his head.

The apartment was sold almost immediately and the money lodged in a 'special' account, which my husband might later have as his own. The house that Michael bought was beautiful, of course, and decorated according to his tastes, but we seldom had visitors, and he had little time for socialising out and about with me. When I mentioned that I would like a baby Michael laughed. He said I'd have to grow up first. I tried to persuade him to let me give up using the pill, but he said he'd divorce me if I became pregnant. When I began to scour the daily newspapers in the hope of getting a job he took to bringing home copies of 'Home and Garden' and leaving them lying around for me. But he was seldom at home, being only five strategic minutes away from his mother's place.

Eventually I thought I'd learned to stop wanting. I began to see the truth of what they said - I'd made my bed. I dug the garden. I preserved fruit. I went for long walks with my dog, Toby. My favourite route was along the shore for about three miles, and turning inwards through a small copse of trees, to our house. I knew each stone on the beach as though it were a part of me. I talked to Toby. If it were a bright and breezy morning I'd explain to him how ships in former times had linen sails which carried them around the perilous oceans of the world. If it was dusk, and the sky was smeared blood red, I'd recall the battles listed in my old history books, and I'd tell him about the heroes I had studied, their lives, their loves, and how they finally fell. Toby listened to it all without comment. I hated being indoors. I especially hated my bedroom. When I looked in my mirror I saw a woman already wise and sighing. My childish ideal of emotional plenitude had vanished.

Toby died on February 29th. - Leap Year Day. He was fine that morning, bounding across the yard to greet me, following me into the kitchen, routing me out of the library, lying asleep at my feet in the lounge. Night came, and he stumbled in from the laneway whining and foaming at the mouth. Within an hour he was dead. The vet called back next morning with the results of some tests. Toby, he said, had been poisoned.

"I'll take him out and bury him," Michael said as soon as the vet had left.

"No you won't," I countered.

"Elaine, what ever do you mean?"

"I said I don't want you to do that."

"Don't be stupid, Elaine. The animal has got to be buried." A vivid flush of anger and frustration rose on Michael's face.

"I don't want YOU to do it. I don't want YOU to

TOUCH him," I yelled.

Michael moved to the scullery door. "I'm going to the tool shed now," he said, enunciating each word clearly, as though he was an infant teacher attempting to reach a rather dim child. "I'm going to fetch a pick and shovel from the shed. I intend to dig a great big hole, and as soon as I've done that I'll be back for that dog."

Automatically I placed myself in front of Toby's body but Michael brushed quickly past me.

"Say your goodbyes now, Madam," he barked, "I won't be long."

Even though she was unable to walk unaided Michael's mother began to go to daily Mass. Initially she made her way to the church alone, progressing slowly with the help of a walking stick, but she summoned Michael's assistance on one auspicious occasion, and from that day on he left our house after seven each morning, and accompanied her. She seldom came to visit us, but my life and hers continued to entwine and overlap about the edges. Six months after Toby was poisoned she died. It was sudden. I held my husband's hand firmly as he walked behind her mahogany coffin in the church in which she had spent many of her final days. But when they lowered her into the ground, the size and shape of the wound in the damp, yellow earth carefully measured, all I could see was the ugly jagged scar in the darker soil in which Michael had buried Toby. But I did not cry. My task was the future. He had been released to me. My day had finally arrived.

"I'm pregnant," I announced in a matter of fact

voice, having considered many ways in which to deliver my news. Three months had passed since his mother's death.

He stared at me.

"We're alone in the world now," I told him, "and I'm twenty seven and I thought it was about time."

I had anticipated an initial negative reaction but his utter fury startled me.

"You bitch," he yelled. "You devious little bitch."

"Michael," I pleaded, "I'm your wife. We've been married for over seven years. I'm expecting your child."

"Didn't I say NO CHILDREN?" he fumed. "Didn't I give you clear instructions to that effect?"

"I know what you said, Michael," I replied, struggling to be calm. "And I paid attention to it. I've not said a word on the subject for seven years. I've done what you said. And I've kept silent all this time but now ...."

"Silent? Silent? Since when did women know how to be silent?" he roared.

"Michael."

"Women whisper and men cringe, Elaine. That's the way it's always been." He grabbed my arm. "Women whisper themselves daintily into men's lives and once in they sit there shouting - shouting out loud - shouting out so that the entire world can hear - occupied territory - totally mine."

"I'm not like that," I pleaded, knowing that the aberration he so vividly described was, for him, the absolute and only state of things. For him all women were like that. He simply shut out the stories that didn't fit. He moved towards me so quickly that I had little time to plan a strategy to protect the little baby from its daddy. His thin fingers and the smooth

147

palms of his lovely hands were suddenly strong and sharp against my face, and very soon he was battering me about the head. Blood trickling from my nose was the last thing I remember before I passed out.

There was a nurse at my side when I awoke. She was holding my hand. A bottle of liquid, propped at an angle above my bed delivered its red juices along a transparent tube. A needle in my arm was held in place by a large wedge of skin-coloured sticking plaster.

"Elaine," the nurse whispered, "I'm afraid you've lost your baby."

It seemed that I was fine, but the child I had dreamed of would not now exist.

Michael came to visit me. The nurse who ushered him in did so only after she had established that I would received his visit. And she was wary. She asked me to use the pull bell on the wall if I needed any help. Michael sat down as soon as she left the room, but it was left to me to break the antiseptic silence.

"I don't want to stay here," I told him. "I want to go home."

"I'm sorry," he said, ignoring my plea, "I'm so sorry." He laid a dozen slim white roses on the bed before me. It was a formal gesture.

"Will you forgive me, Elaine?" he asked, the thinly squeezed-out words trailing painfully away from him.

"What made you go away to be a priest, Michael?" I asked, mentioning the subject for the first time. I'll never know what brought it into my head at that precise moment.

"It seemed like a good idea then," he answered confidently, but it was obvious he was truly startled that I should ask.

"Why did you leave?" I asked him then.
He stood up and nervously pulled back the pretty hospital curtains, revealing a weak sun blinking between the tops of tall birches.

"Because I could no longer allow her to decide for me."

"But she was right, wasn't she, Michael? She was right."

"No."

"Of course she was right, Michael. She was your mother. She understood you. She was always right."

"It was just that she was the only one that ..."

"Cared, Michael. Is that it? Really cared?" It was a furious question.

"Yes," he spluttered. "No. She meant well but she was wrong."

"You allowed her bully you, Michael."

"She merely suggested that ...."

"You allowed her bully away five years of your life."

"I did no such thing. That's ridiculous, Elaine."

"She would have stuffed you squarely into a round hole for the rest of your life and sat basking in the glory of it all."

"You're wrong. Very wrong."

"What did she do when you came home without your precious Holy Orders? What did the lady do, Michael? What did the lady say?" I must have raised my voice considerably because the nurse rushed in and shooed him away. After he was gone all the false energy I had shown left. I was exhausted. They gave me some medication and I slept.

Throughout the next day, when I was not dozing, I watched the trees outside my window bend in the breeze, and in my several dreams that night I saw them ravished by a storm, their long, slender trunks overturned, the leafy brilliance of the upper branches buried in the mud. Even the truth of the morning, that nothing like that had happened at all, did little to dissipate my sadness. On the sixth day I began my preparations. Michael was to come that afternoon with my clothes. I could go home, they said, but I would have to return to the Out Patient's Department in a few weeks time. They took his word when he spoke about the incident that had brought me there, accepting that it was unexpressed sorrow for his mother's death that had caused his anger. They were sure it would not happen again. And I believed them. But there was something I desperately needed to know. And in a few weeks, or months perhaps, when we were settled again into the house that Michael bought, I'd ask him if he had married me in order to spite her, to disenfranchise his mother in his head and in his heart. I'd need to be certain that was not the case before I could love him again, before I could begin to teach him how to love me.

SEASCAPES

It was late September as I walked along a beach which faced towards the east. Overhead the sky was clear, but in the north heavy, grey clouds plodded, like hard-working drays, across the sky. A high wind blew from the west. Occasionally the waves were met in mid-stream by the force of the wind and sea-spray rose, like a delicate kiss, into the air. I held that picture in my head and savoured the kiss on my lips for as long as I could. Soon it was evening and time to go home.

He told me he had belonged in many places.
"Your behaviour is very Irish," he said accusingly.
"I am Irish," I replied.
"There's no need to accentuate the fact."
"I'm not," I replied, "not at all."
"Why do you always argue so much?" he demanded.
"There is very little that you say that I can endorse," I tell him, "very little indeed."
"You are opinionated," he said.
"Yes," I agreed. "And so are you."

When I had walked as far as I needed to I turned back. The tide raced towards the shore and I had to clamour over a rocky promontory in order to make my way to the place where I was to meet him again. If I'd had binoculars with me I might have spied him in the distance, the creases on his face, the hard, blue eyes, the curved upper lip, the elegant legs. As it was I observed a small dot a long way away from me.

He never wrote home. Never. He left Dublin for

London when he was eighteen years old and never wrote home. After his departure his mother filled the silence with little things, bingo, rosaries, retreats. His father frowned at the future and cursed the only son who had gone away. I cried, slept and married another man.

"Hello," he called out in that south east of England accent of his. The wind swept his long, fair hair about his face.

"Kiss me here in the spray," I demanded.
He did. Sweet and sour sea kiss is what we had then, taste of other long-gone days.

"Is the sea cold?" he asked. He'd noticed that I carried my shoes over my shoulder. And he saw my bare feet.

"The sea is always cold," I told him. "Even in spring, even on the warmest summer day the sea is always cold."

"You're shivering." He put his coat around my shoulders and we hurried away.

I'd walked the beach for many hours before he arrived. I studied the stones. Truth is, I did more, I loved them into life. A scientist once said that nothing is ever still, that even in the deepest recesses of the most inert objects molecules moved. I imagined the busyness of stones, their trade, their industry, how in the time before man, they first came into being. I imagined the manufacture of fossils, the scraps of trees and flowers and fruit, the tiny crawling creatures, how time wrapped up this life and delivered it up to the present. Mica dazzled me. The smoothness of limestone comforted me. Sandstone, quartz, shale, chunks of marble and slivers of slate were enigmas. They intrigued.

"It was the suddenness of your going away," I told him, "and the secrecy that disturbed me."
Silence.

"And you never wrote," I continued. "Not once did you write home."
He shrugged.

"What happened?" I asked, longing to put a degree of sound and movement inside that long silence.

"In twenty five years?" he queried. "You want to know the whole story of twenty five years?"

"Begin at the beginning," I invited, "or anywhere at all. I just want to know something more."

We'd lived next door to each other since we were five. We'd made sandcastles together in the local playground. On my seventeenth birthday we went down to the sea. We each etched out an initial in the wet sand. The outline of my A inside his O resembled the anarchist symbol.

"Aileen," he asked solemnly, "will you marry me?"

"Maybe," I replied, shrugging my shoulders. Inside I was churning up with excitement. "Maybe when I am older I might just do that."
With a large stick he made a circle in the sand and enclosed our O/A, and in another linked circle he placed two entwined hearts.

"What did you first do in London?" I asked, so as to mark a direction for his disclosures.
He dragged the toe of his left shoe through heavy wet sand, saying that I'd probably rather not know.

"Did you get work?" I demanded.

"Yes, eventually," he answered brusquely.

"Please tell me," I invited.

"In my first digs I couldn't afford the rent after the third week," he explained.

"Yes. Go on."

"Well .... there was this woman .....my landlady .... Mrs. Foster ....she was about forty five ...."

"Yes?"

"She was married but her husband was hardly ever at home."

I nodded.

"Well .... she let me stay rent free .... I sort of began to work for her..." he muttered.

"You worked for her? What did you do?"

"Nothing. I just ..... well, eventually I went and lived with her."

"Lived with her?" I echoed blindly, unable to appreciate the full significance of his story.

He paused briefly and then rushed headlong at the final elaboration.

"Can't you see, Aileen, I became a gigolo."

I mourned for a long time after Oliver left. I longed for him day and night and wished he would come home - but he never did. I became obsessed with making some large gesture to mark the fact. It was foolish, I know, but I returned all the little things he had given me, bracelet, Claddagh ring, a pair of jasper earrings - to his mother. She was full of venom when I produced the earrings, maintaining that Oliver had stolen them from her. Clearly she resented me.

"Why did you settle for that?" I demanded, when he had explained his first 'job' to me.

"It was comfortable."

"How could it have been?"

"It just was."

"But .....", and I hesitated, words briefly failing me, "but you were eighteen years old and you allowed yourself to become the paid lover of a woman of forty five."

"Yes", he agreed, "that's what I said. I warned you that it would be something you'd really rather not know."

"Did you not look for work?"

"No. She was well off. I had a good life."

"A good life?"

"Yes, a dammed good life."

"You disgust me, Oliver."

"I suppose I do."

I called frequently to his house after he went to London. If he had written home I wanted to know. Of course there was his mother's animosity to contend with, and obviously she might not readily disclose his whereabouts to me, but I suspected she would be glad to discover that I had not received a letter from him and that her satisfaction would show. If I detected such satisfaction I would attempt to prise the address from his father or his sister or someone else. But he never wrote home.

I'm sexually employed by wealthy, forty-five-year-old, half-married Mrs. Foster - I suppose that was hardly something you could brag about in letters home.

"How did all that end?" I asked him.

"She died."

"Oh."

"She went skiing twice a year. I went with her. During our third winter in Italy she had an accident.... it was damm serious .... and a few weeks later she was dead. I returned to England, alone and penniless."

"Poor Oliver O'Hanlon," I snapped. It wounded me deeply to know that he had gone from my eight-een-year-old freshness straight to her commercial, middle-aged bed.

"I got work eventually," he said, ignoring the ice in my voice, "in sales."

"What did you sell?"

"Encyclopaedias."

"Oh no."

"I made money, Aileen, so there's no need to scoff."

"Sorry."

"I became an area rep and later an area manager."

"Where?"

"In Surrey. Initially I realised that I couldn't go any further unless I changed certain aspects of my presentation - my personal presentation, that is - so I set out systematically to achieve that."

"What did you change?"

"I changed two things, Aileen, my name and my accent."

"You changed your name?"

"Yes, by deed poll. To Oliver Handy."

"And your accent. Surely you didn't set out to deliberately change your accent?"

"Yes I did. I took lessons in pronunciation and diction - Standard English, they call it - and I worked at it until my Irishness was invisible."

"But were you not lost, Oliver, totally lost?"

Out on the horizon a tanker slowly made its way southwards. Closer to the shore a small ship lurched about in substantial waves. On the beach Oliver and I discovered pieces of debris which may or may not have been the one-time parts of a ship. I imagined the initial trauma, the sundering of the matched and welded parts and how the timbers might have drifted about, captive of the waves, until they were finally beached on my own home shores.

"Tell me about you?" he invited. "All we've done since we met up again is dissect my life. Now it's your turn."

"You know I was devastated after you left," I offered, still loving him a little. "In the beginning I kept in touch with your mother but she did everything to discourage me."

"I'm not surprised," he said. "It was she who sent me away from you."

"She sent you away from me?" I echoed.

"She packed me off to London because she thought I was getting too serious about you. I resented the deal so much I cut all ties."

"What had she got against me, do you know?" I asked.

"Your poverty. Your lack of social status," he said. "She wanted me to marry a doctor's daughter, or a judges' or something like that."

"About a year after you left," I told him then, "I met Peter. He was older. Fifteen years older, in fact. He was anxious to get married so I married him."

"Just like that?" Oliver asked, "without passion, without love?"

"I felt safe with him," I responded.

"Safety. Yes, I see."

"As time went by I didn't need his 'protection'," I elaborated. "It was like a prison. It stifled me. And the more I struggled to be free of it the more he filled up with the terror of losing his protégé - of losing little me."

He nodded.

"Do you know what a terrified bully is like, Oliver? Do you have any idea at all?"

"Yes, I believe I have."

"It took quite some time. I had to go a long way away to be me."

"Are you sure you are 'you', Aileen?" he asked, smiling at me. I found that smile unnerving. It probed.

"At this stage yes," I blustered, "I'm totally sure."

We climbed Killiney Hill together. It was a cool, blue day with a light easterly wind dancing about us. We sat on the stony, whin-covered sloping places above the railway and overlooking the sea.

"It's so beautiful," he announced. "I don't understand why anyone leaves."

"Beauty does not feed and clothe, Oliver. You should know that."

"Remember the lilies of the field, Aileen."

"No Oliver, I'd rather not."

"Why are you so cynical?", he accused.

"I'm not. Just realistic. And haven't you changed your tune a bit?"

"Aileen, I'm going to buy a bit of Ireland," he countered. "I'm planing to have my own place. I'm finished with cities."

"Really. Where are you buying?"

"Galway probably, or Kerry."

"What do you hope to achieve with all this? Is it really what you want?

"What I need most now," he said earnestly, "is to be real. To be really me."

"You can't borrow identity that easily, Oliver. Standard English has made you a partial Englishman. Now you think that by buying a field you'll become Irish."

"I am Irish," he asserted, "I was born here."

"No. You're not Irish," I said, "not any more."

"You believe I'm more English than Irish?" he queried, "just became I worked there for twenty five years?"

"You wanted to be English. You almost made it but not quite. Now you want to remedy the situation. But I don't think ...... ," I said, breaking off when I became aware of the acute pain in his eyes.

"Go on Aileen, finish what you were about to say."

"I'm sorry, Oliver. As I said, you're not English. Neither are you Irish. You don't even tolerate the Irish very well any more. It's like I said on your first day back here - you belong in neither place."

"Aileen," he pleaded, "help me. Please help me."

"How can I help?" I asked cautiously.

"Come with me to Galway - or to Kerry - love me again - live with me."

"Oliver," I said steadily, "I care. I really do. But your mind is full of heaviness. And if I love again I want to love with lightness there."

When I was leaving my house the postman handed me a letter. I glanced at it for a long enough to see that it had been posted in London. I thought that it might be from Oliver. I had not seen or heard from him in three weeks, since that day on Killiney Hill when I had refused to enter his make believe world. Dry, dead leaves whirled about as I made my way through Miller's Lane, to the beach. Autumn was harsh and threatened a severe winter. The wind howled in the trees, and when I reached the shore a large amount of seaweed had been beached by the severity of the night's gales. The air was permeated by the smell of the sea. I sat on the edge of a high and savage tide and opened the letter -

Sorry I intruded on your life, it read. I'm now back in London. It was foolish of me to think I could belong again, could capture your heart again. Ireland was hard on you and toughened you - but it also strengthened you. You know who you are, are certain of where you belong. I don't think I'll ever return to Ireland again. I almost wrote 'return home'! I'll have to watch that. I'm leaving for Spain soon. I might teach English there for a year or two. Don't worry. I won't ever upset you again. There has been enough damage done.
                            Yours,
                            Oliver.

Oh poor lost love, I roared at the sea. And I cried for him, all the weeping I had done when I was eighteen threatening to overwhelm once more. In my mind I saw his mother knitting her black rosary through thin fingers and lying, telling me that Oliver had voluntarily gone away. I saw him in Mrs. Foster's money-laden arms, and me and Peter on the altar promising to love each other until the day death decided that was no longer necessary. Oh poor, lost love, I roared at the sea, I haven't let him know it, but I'm more that a little lost too. His mother - this country - their ways have exiled us all somehow.

LOOKING FOR ME

Only some of us will be remembered. I know this even as my husband and his congregation attempt to ignore it. Of course religious sentiment sanctions many real evils and I should not complain if it is now peddling a popular deception in order to console. The highest degree of reality in this situation is its raw grief. I hear the widow whisper to her daughter and her daughter cry. I see the son strain an arm around his sister and the mother manage a faint smile. There is space here for only one idea, that of the importance of the man who has died and of the desire and ability of many other individuals to remember him. Eternal life has been taken for granted. But in order to be believed, temporal remembrance needs to be stated over and over and over again.

Occasions such as this one bring back memories. I played the organ at the first funeral service Harold conducted after we were married. The hymn 'What a friend we have in Jesus' seemed entirely appropriate at that time, coming as it did out of a double bereavement of the writer, a certain Mr. Scriven. That unfortunate man lost his fiancee in an accident and, years later, the young bride he had just married. I can appreciate how soothing his words were then and how Harold used them to assure the family that their loved one would not be forgotten. Later that day he seemed depressed.

"I make no difference at all," he said when I questioned him.

"I think you do," I replied. His self-doubt really troubled me.

"But not nearly enough," he responded. "These people want more than a funeral service, you see. They want to believe that the dead will be remembered – really, importantly remembered in times to come. They want a guarantee."

"You can't give them that," I protested. "In most cases it will be a lie."

Harold and I met at a garden party held to mark the retirement of Archdeacon Tennant who was, as he put it himself, "about to live at last in the real world." He'd been a close friend of my fathers and I'd always regarded him as being well grounded in the realities of life. His wry statement startled me. But on that afternoon I'd other, more pressing matters on my mind. I'd just met a stranger who'd offered me some home-made lemonade, and I was immediately smitten by his enigmatic half-smile, his blue eyes and his elegant hands. He constantly pushed back a lock of fair hair from a boyish face, and I liked that too, the understated, equivocal promise of the boy/man. I soon learned that he was to be joining the parish as a junior minister, and we were married six months later without discussing any theology at all. The clergyman who conducted the marriage had a lisp, and whenever my grandmother, sitting proudly in the second pew, found it difficult to understand him, she simultaneously cocked her ear and opened her mouth.

"Gillian dear," she called out to me later that day, "what about a bridal kiss for your old grandmama?" I moved quickly to her side and kissed her lightly on the cheek. "Congratulations," she said as she held me in a warm hug. "I know you'll be very happy –

Harold is such a lovely man – but remember dear, you've married his parish as well."

When Sophie was born I knew for the first time how intrusive parishioners could be, coming into our home all smiley-sweet with their 'advice' while Harold stood helplessly by, unable to defend me. Of course they came bearing gifts, and the biblical resonances had to be respected, but I longed for the space in which to learn how to be a mother for the first time. It took weeks for that to happen and months for me to fully repossess my home and family again. And it took longer – much longer – for the truth of my grandmother's remark to sink in, to see that they had indeed measured up my life. By 'they' I mean the church officials and the parish patriarchs who seemed to know instinctively how and what a rector's wife should be. Even the ordinary parishioners had their specific expectations. As Harold's wife, I should be available as a sympathetic ear, a discreet secret keeper, a bible study strategist, an after Sunday Service tea and coffee lady – and much, much more. In defining me according to their expectations – gentle Gillian – Rector Harold's perfect wife – they also confined me. But like many of the captives of history, my slavery was so much a natural part of my life that, for a long time, I failed to notice it at all. In fact I was alienated from the Christian story long before I was alienated from the role Harold's commitment to it imposed on me. I listened to it all, the hymns, the silences, the preaching, but there was no connection of any kind for me. Yet Harold's parishioners seemed to enjoy being together so much that I envied them. I was forced to the conclusion that knowing what to believe had its advantages – that if I could lie to myself successfully and appropriate all those awesome 'truths' wholeheartedly, everything would be better all round. I couldn't. Harold never noticed, even when I opted out of playing the organ, offering "a touch of rheumatism in my fingers" as an excuse. A new parishioner named Pamela was more than willing to take over, and as it was Harold's desire to include "as many people as possible" in the running of the church, there was no blame or fuss.

I had noticed Harold change over the years. In many ways he was still the same husband I'd married, loving me awfully in that relaxed and affable manner of his, but he had altered in one highly significant and fundamental way. Little bits of other people's experiences had somehow stuck to him, you see. Now I know that's how we all grow, seeing and understanding how the world handles humankind, but in Harold's case it was as though he was being made out of his parishioners' difficulties and sorrows without ever really groaning under any of them. I hesitate to say he was a phoney – he was much too honest for that. What happened was far more haphazard. And I'm not saying that he lacked compassion. It was obvious that he had that in abundance. But he failed to be wounded by what he had seen and heard as spiritual guide to his few hundred parishioners. And with all that new, pirated knowledge clinging to him he was not mine in the way he used to be. At night we'd lie close together, so close indeed that even a rush of air could not filter between us. By day we occupied different planets.

Sophie went away when she was eighteen. I'd like to say that she'd been a happy girl but that's not true. On the surface things seemed fine, but I think we let her down by not having another child to keep her company. She was often very lonely. For a while she became totally engrossed in the church and we thought she'd offer for the ministry, but at seventeen she decided on a career in architecture and went to college in Edinburgh. After she qualified she got work there and now has her own apartment in the centre of the city.

I had a dream around that time. There was a lot of activity. Many people familiar to me were involved. I saw the activity take the shape of a circle and the inside of the circle was quite empty. Reason has no place in dreams, of course, except in a most peripheral way. But emotion has, I'm sure, and my dream was speaking to me. I told Harold about it and he laughed, dismissing my desire to discuss its significance as an example of "New Age codology". I laughed too, but the dream returned on several occasions and I began to dread night-time and encroaching sleep. What had started out as a subtle message became a blunt instrument, relentlessly hammering away at me. I decided to take advice.

My therapist had wide eyes in a placid face. His voice was fluffy and soft, and for a while I allowed my spirit to sink into it and rest. He told me that in dreams, separate and contradictory truths can be mingled. I might love Harold and despise him. I might refuse to see what was in that dreaming centre while longing to see. I might be as the woman who watched trains go by, mortally afraid and yet longing to journey.

Sophie rang just as we were leaving for the funeral. While Harold took the car from the garage I answered the phone. She told me about a baby, my grandchild, who was soon to be born. She asked if I minded, and if her father would be angry that she was pregnant without the benefit of marriage. She told me that she couldn't let his life control hers – she was sorry about that. But we owned ourselves for such a short while, she said, and it seemed reckless to hand over to the dictates of others. In a hundred years time we'd all be dead - even the baby in her womb - and who'd remember, who'd care? She sighed and said "goodbye" so longingly that I knew I'd soon fly out to see her, to assuage her longing for family at this most vulnerable time. And I too might be helped by her. She might teach me to be less anxious about life. Indeed, she might even show me how to look beyond the rector's wife for me.

HOME AND AWAY

Drifting. She is fitfully drifting into a soft sleep. The open curtains of the hotel bedroom allow her to see the plump moon sitting on the rim of the bay. She half watches as it rises slowly into the air, as it grows smaller until it is only a pale, yellow balloon at the end of a long string. Somewhere down there among the narrow streets of the old town is the little boy who controls it. He might tug it to him at any moment, make it sit right back into the water again. Winnie closes her eyes and banishes the moon away.

Next morning. Half past nine. She and Isabel are in the dining room. Outside a thin wind fingers the flags of many nations. The women exchange smiles when they see the tricolour among those honoured at their hotel. A buffet offers many foods but no boiled eggs. They call a waiter to their table and explain their desire for hard-boiled eggs.

"Six min-uhte," he says, flashing those dark Arabic eyes of his.

"Make it seven," Isabel replies, winking at Winnie. "We're not in any hurry, you know."

He comes back smiling, four boiled eggs in silver cups on a silver platter. Isabel slips him five hundred escudos and he melts away into the busy room. An old couple enter as Isabel and Winnie leave. He is in a wheelchair and has obviously suffered a broken leg. His fuzzy-haired wife struggles hard to keep his chair on a straight path.

"Got that windsurfing, I imagine", Isabel says with a giggle.

Winnie frowns and pulls away from her. They walk

separately into the crowded foyer and when Winnie enters the lift Isabel is nowhere to be seen. She goes directly to her room on the eight floor. The hotel staff has serviced it and the balcony door is open. The window which last night offered that intriguing floating moon now displays the waking town, the harbour and the sea. A heat haze hangs over the blue Atlantic waters and through it Winnie discerns the shape of an old galleon in the far distance. Nearer to the shore are several small pleasure boats. Quite suddenly Winnie wishes for the intoxication of a trip on such a vessel, but this remains a peaceful wish and she is free to set her mind to other things.

The pool is her ocean. She sits by it for a while. Others are there too, large bare-breasted women and the men who mind them - and their children. There is a loud splash and a dark, moustachioed man is moving on the surface of the water like a walrus or a seal. A child dog-paddles towards him. He takes her on his back and she is carried into the deep by her daddy. She waves and shouts towards the shore, her face shining with the audacity of her adventure. Winnie cannot understand why the small face is so familiar. Without taking her eyes off the little girl she drops into the pool and swims underwater in the direction of the man and child. When she surfaces she finds that the small girl, brown skinned, sloe eyed, an Asian is singing. Winnie struggles hard, but the image of a familiar child does not return. She flips over and the water laps about her as she drifts on her back, the sky above a clear uncompromising blue and not the grey, cloud-streaked canopy which she feels ought to be there at that moment. And a few yards away, where the waves disperse into innocent trickles of water there ought to be a stony beach - with one stone - just one single stone the colour of a ripe raspberry. Winnie swims for the shore. It is midday and a fierce sun is blazing high in the sky, its worshippers retreating to cooler corners of the world. Shielding herself against it's arbitrary attentions, she withdraws to her room. She dials room service and orders lager and a toasted sandwich. Sleep comes immediately afterwards, the first siesta of her holiday.

Winnie is awakened a few hours later by the loudspeaking voice of a young hotel hostess organising a game of 'vater polos'. Winnie takes out the binoculars Isabel brought along "to see the mountains", and focuses on the game. She is surprised to find envy in her heart as she watches the lithe and vigorous participants prance about in the small pool under her window. When she was their age, she thinks..... but checks the descent into self-pity as she flings the binoculars aside. She dons a pair of tailored shorts and a tee shirt with a Pierre Cardin sticker ironed to the pocket. It is a blue and white ensemble, matching, Winnie tells herself, her blue eyes and her white skin. Leaving a note for Isabel in case she should return while she is away, Winnie leaves the room.

The old town simmers in the heat. A profusion of smells waft on a gentle breeze, escaped from market stalls, kitchens, from the fishing trawlers down by the harbour, from the open sea. Winnie wanders among the stalls, her head reeling from the impact of so many new sounds. She attempts to sift through them for some familiar word, but the conversation around her is too rapid to extract even the key phrases she learned before she arrived. A black-hatted woman tries to persuade Winnie to buy some knitwear, but she smiles a refusal and moves to where the leather is. Here handbags hang side by side with sandals and shoes. Winnie sniffs, closes her eyes and sees a band of Portuguese cowboys riding through the valley of the Ribeira Guadiano, and later racing down the mountains from Monchique. Conjuring images out of nowhere is second nature to her. Her father used to call her "a fanciful child", full of fairy stories and tall tales.

"No one will ever believe you when you tell the truth," he'd warned, explaining about the boy who 'cried wolf'. After that she'd tried not to see the pictures, or at least to keep them to herself when they came, unbidden, into her head.

A teenage boy is beside Winnie. "Five thousand escudos," he chants, nodding in the direction of the bag she is admiring. "For you, lady, only five thousand escudos."
Winnie laughs and moves away.
"Four thousand then," the boy calls after her. "Is good value for four thousand."
Winnie turns and saunters back towards the leather stall.
"I'll give you three thousand," she says. She writes it down in case the boy's English is not equal to her Irish accent. He is happy as he wraps the bag she has chosen. The deal is done.

There is music in the far distance. Winnie moves towards the source, negotiating several narrow streets before coming to the Town Square. The music is South American Indian, guitar, drums, pan pipes. It is Jacaranda blossom time and a flimsy mauve tapestry trails against an azure sky. Oleander scent saturates the air. The little square is crammed with appreciative listeners. Winnie searches and soon finds a bench, but has to share it with a young German mother and her child. Several cafes, which open out onto the square, are serving cold drinks, barbecued fish and chicken piri-piri. Winnie is glad that she has come, grateful to Isabel for helping her break through the four stifling walls of her home to this delicious freedom. She trembles as the sweet, breathless pipes echo from ever corner of the square. The final note is held, dips down, flutters awkwardly, and swells out again before the instrument is still. Silence is in the air, in the people, in the sweltering stones. But soon there is movement again, a quick, spicy tune, and the German toddler is dancing in the middle of the square. Winnie is watching him and fails to calm her own feet.

"Don't dance like that," she once screamed at Cathy. The child was about seven.
What way did the little girl dance? Winnie can not remember now. A vague hint had come earlier with the image of a grey sky and a stony beach on which lay one raspberried stone.

The musicians eventually pack away their instruments and Winnie leaves. She blows the little boy a kiss and he waves her 'goodbye'. The walk back to the hotel proves far more difficult than the journey there. It is an uphill struggle, and the heat is still intense. Winnie steps into a restaurant for some respite, and stays for over an hour, opting to dine there rather than return to the hotel. As she begins her meal she is the only diner there, and the waiters fuss about until she wishes they would stay away. But other tourists soon arrive, quickly filling the room. The women are all dolled up, though it is very early evening. Winnie has met women like that at home - dripping with jewellery - covered in sequins - totally unable to dress down. She is as uncomfortable watching them here as she is at home. The men are less formal, short sleeved, denim trousered, a little more relaxed. And the children are at ease with foreign menus. They obviously know well how to handle choice. A father throws an arm around his small daughter, whispering to her, appearing to encourage her to eat. The mother smiles but the little girl pushes her daddy away. Winnie's coffee grows cold as she watches these three. Her pulse races. She despises herself for this obsession but she is powerless to dismiss it. Suddenly the dining room is disappeared. There are three faces only in the dark place where Winnie is - those of a woman, a man and a small child. Winnie alone can see what is happening. She alone can banish the evil that lives inside this little group, and offer salvation. There is an alarmed scream as she pushes the woman aside. She seizes the child, but the father is on his feet, blocking her way. Winnie holds the tiny sobbing body for a brief moment before the little girl slides from her arms and away. As the father restores the child to her mother Winnie makes her escape. She runs through the door, darting among the strolling crowds, and heads towards an almond grove. Eventually she glances back, and is relieved to see than nobody has succeeded in keeping up with her. She sits for a while on hot, red earth, her back propped against a tree. She struggles to regain her breath. When she is sure she has successfully evaded the people at the restaurant she returns to her hotel.

Tonight there is no moon floating like a balloon in the hot sky. Instead, the darkness is divided by a shaft of burning light and the skies mutter to themselves as they pour scorn upon the earth. Winnie knows now how her daddy swam with her, how he urged bravery on her, how often they sat together on a stony beach. She also knows why, up to now, she has not succeeded in teaching her daughter wisdom. She'll bring that new knowledge home with her tomorrow. They might scour the resort, looking for her, but she'll be away, soaring the high skies and wonderfully free.

A heavy footstep echoes along the corridor outside her bedroom and the sound of drunken singing announces the arrival of Isabel. She flicks on all the lights and immediately Winnie turns off those by her bed.

"Did you have a great time without me?" she asks, her speech awkward and slurred.

"I did," Winnie says quietly.

Isabel sits beside Winnie and takes her hand.

"I'm glad you did, Winnie," she says, "very very glad you did because I bloody well didn't have any fun at all."

Winnie pulls her hand away. "I'm going home tomorrow," she tells Isabel, "on the first flight out of Faro."

Isabel begins to weep. "You won't do that, will you?" she howls. "You can't leave me alone in this place." She stumbles across the floor and falls headlong onto her bed. "That Sebastian fellow was a right bastard," she shouts into her pillow. "Do you hear me, Winnie? A right B A S T A R D."

Winnie remains quiet and still. She has no desire to know the 'whos' and 'whys' of Isabel's most recent 'adventure'. She knows all she needs to know right now. She has enough knowledge to last her the rest of her life.

HUMPTY DUMPTY IN THE GREEN WOOD

When I was a child I pitied him. At least that's the word I now give to the overwhelming sensation that gripped me in his presence and which left me unable to look at him, emotionally swamped and on the edge of weeping.

The first time I met him should have been fun. It was after a wedding, when all the family gathered in his kitchen to eat, drink, talk and dance. But I broke the vase. It was a white one, which grew from a round base upwards into a square, and again, higher still, resumed a circular shape before fanning out into a scalloped edge. Its architecture intrigued me. But I also admired its colours. It had a flower and butter-fly motif, with many delicate petals around the base and one single, blue butterfly higher up on the stem, moving, and almost free. I have a vivid recollection of myself with the vase in my hands, trying to edge the butterfly into flight. But it slipped and shattered on the stone floor. Immediately they heard the noise the women ceased their dancing and fussed about, attempting to recover the bits. I heard Aunt Sal say that it might be possible to put the pieces together again. When I heard this I became excited.

"Will it be like Humpty Dumpty?" I asked.

"Silly child, no!" Aunt Sal seemed to be cross. She was down on all fours and, with her head under a large table and her rear end in the air, she groped around for the smallest, most elusive pieces. I could-n't see why it was not like Humpty Dumpty. They had tried - all the King's Horses and all the King's Men - they had tried very hard to put Humpty Dumpty together again. Of course they had not succeeded but the general idea was to make one Humpty Dumpty out of all the little pieces. And I though Aunt Sal was suggesting that one vase could be reassembled out of all the little broken bits. Today I know there's no easy way to cleanse the world of hurt. They happen - accidents - disasters - brutalities - and afterwards the pieces never fit snugly side by side. But I digress. Aunt Sal rose from the floor and let fly at me. She took a left-handed side swipe which caught me totally unawares and I lost my footing and fell, hitting my head on the corner of the hearth. I don't remember any pain, but the gush of warm blood which spread rapidly down my face terrified me. I feel its sticky presence there even as I now write.

"Get out of my way." It was Uncle Dick ordering Aunt Sal to move aside. I knew the music had stopped. I knew the room was still. I saw my uncle bend over me. Then he must have lifted me from his kitchen floor and I probably passed out, for when I woke later I found myself in a big, brass bed and he was holding a cold compress to my temple and sending 'poor child' messages to me with his eyes. I loved him very much then. He had saved me from the full onslaught of her fury. He was strong

"I'll talk to everybody." It was more a subdued scream than a statement.

"Sarah, what's wrong?" They were both outside the bedroom door and I was terrified they might come in. It was my third night in their house. No great damage had been done, the doctor said. There was no concussion, just three little stitches needed, and wasn't it terrible that little Annette had tripped over the dancers' feet and hurt herself? I should have a rest for a few days before I went home, he suggested.

"Nothing's wrong." She shot the words out at high speed. "Just stop your fussing over that wretched child."

"But we have a duty to ..."

She interrupted him almost immediately. "She's a sly one. I'm sure she broke the vase on purpose because she ..."

"Sarah!"

"Go on then. Make your fuss. Weep over her. But I'm not going to hang around being her maid. You're a fool anyway, Dick. Do you hear me?" The question soared into a full-throated, terrified soprano. "Do you hear me, Dick? You're a bloody awful fool. And you're mad. I'll tell them all what I have to put up with. I'll tell them what you say - what you do. They'll all know you're totally mad."

"I like yellow," he said to me a few hours before I was due to leave for home. I wouldn't have come to that knowledge unassisted. My first impression of him was of a grey/brown, undifferentiated shape with a twisted smile. The smile veered radically to the left. Years later I understood what they meant when they talked about his 'stroke'.

"So do I," I replied. It was true, but I don't think it was as true for me as it was for him. I said it merely to be friendly.

"Do your see this plot here?" We were in the far corner of the kitchen garden. "I've got sunflowers in here. Sarah says they are a waste of space but I know different. They're beautiful. And you can eat the seeds. I can grow great, big sunflowers, about eight feet high. They say you can't have decent sunflowers in this country but I do. I talk to them. That's the secret, you see." He used a conspiratorial tone. "I

encourage them. I flatter them and they respond."
I was staring at the words vaulting sideways from out of his misplaced mouth. My intense attention must have unnerved him. Suddenly he sank into silence and merely touched, ever so gently touched the centre of each small and growing bloom. After that he went away by himself. I used the garden swing. Then I lay on the grass and fell asleep.

When I was younger I dreaded old age, seeing the very old stooped and already tilting towards the earth. But I've listened a lot since then. I've looked. I've put out all my antennae. I know now there are worse deformities, that there are twisted souls in very healthy bodies, spiritually cramped and without flexible movement or grace. And there are dead souls in the eager living who stride confidently about. At some stage I realised that Uncle Dick's victory over Aunt Sal that day was a fluke. It was a once-off. He was not at all invincible. She crushed him. I feel angry when I think of her. She must have gone ahead and done what she had threatened. She must have told them. On my nineteenth birthday I saw a group taunt him. He didn't see me there behind the ruined schoolhouse wall, and neither were they aware of my presence.

"I hear you sing a mean song, Dick."

"Ah lads, go on. I'm not that great." He was glowing. He thought they meant to praise him.

"Heard it said you go up there where the big stones are." Their spokesman was fair, a beautiful young man except that he had a big mouth."

"Yes." It was a shy answer.

"What do you sing when you're there, Dick? Tell us now. We'd like to know. What songs do you sing?"

"Just songs." He stepped back from the fair-haired man. I think he was beginning to be afraid.

"You think we believe that, Dick?" They had all moved in closer to him now.

"We hear stories. Do you hear, old man? We hear str-nge sto-er-ies." The last words were split into separate syllables and delivered with menace.

"Do you dance with the dead, Dick?"

I didn't want to intervene. No, that's not strictly true. I did. But I was terrified and instead watched my uncle's twisted face cloud over with confusion. They had gathered around him. They began slowly, almost imperceptibly, to move. They linked hands. Eight ugly pairs of hands entwined and they side-stepped in a singing dance, around Dick.

> Sings to the stars.
> Dances with the dead.
> Got madness in his head.
> He's a visitor from Mars.
> He sings to the stars.
> He dances with the dead,
> with the dead,
> with the de de de dead,
>
> de de de dead,
> de de de,
> de de de,
> de de de dead.

They had matched their taunt to an abrasive air, and they spun it slowly round and round, down to the final drumbeat - de de de dead.

I should have known my silence would do no good.

But I sensed intervention would be equally unproductive. Dick stood hopelessly in the centre of their obscene fun, a terrified little boy. They pulled some nettles then, and feathered his hands and his face with them. This seemed to satisfy them. They grew tired and bored. They left. I never told Uncle Dick I had witnessed his humiliation. That evening he bathed the poisoned parts of his body in cold water, saying he had stumbled and fallen. Aunt Sal was getting old then. Its ugly, very ugly, ancient, well-fed hatred, bloated, contorted and evil. I saw that she was glad he suffered.

"You're a stupid old man, Dick," she said flatly. "Why don't you stay away from those lads?"

Just once I saw him at the standing stones. It was soon after the nettle event. A month perhaps. I must admit I was intrigued. I had known for a long time that, in the evening hours, my uncle whispered to birds and trees and flowers. This was not his special secret. He had told me, years earlier, that he loved yellow and spoke to his sunflowers in order to encourage them to grow.

"Dickety, Dickety Dock, with a face to stop a clock," I heard the children call after him. They'd run up to him and throw bunches of dandelions at his feet.

"These are for you," they would say. "They are lonely. They want mad Dick to talk to them."

I almost became used to these scenes as the years went by. During each of the summers I stayed there something like that happened. I noticed that he always tried to pull back from the jibes, as though his soul was wounded. And I never discovered how I might have helped him.

When I knew he had the urge again to go eastwards towards the mountain I went too. I didn't love him any more, not in the fierce and juvenile way I had first loved him after he had saved me from Aunt Sal. As I said earlier, I pitied him. But there was more. He was my uncle. People said he was mad. I was curious. I needed to know. For my own self I desperately needed to know.

Once, before Patrick came to Ireland, before Jesus in far-away Israel wept and walked his Via Dolorosa and finally died, this country had other stories to tell. In the oak woods people found ways of stretching out to the unknown. Along seashores are echoes of ancient pleadings and songs. Among the standing stones are the remains of incantations, barely audible after-notes held for millennia in the air. I followed my uncle to where a small plantation had been set among the stones. It was almost mature, and the trees were tall and swayed softly in the breeze. I crouched down in a hollow between two trees. A cloud dipped over the hillside and a mist hung precariously in the air. All things were in waiting. A mile and a half away, in the village, church bells tolled.

Dick walked into the clearing with an eagerness I had never before witnessed. He had authority. That's what it was. He moved around as though the earth belonged to him. For a short time he paced from stone to stone, laying a hand on each one. When this ritual was completed he sat in the centre, on a grassy patch. His songs soon became airborne. I know now they were entirely his own, both the words and the music. They were a mixture of slow, melancholy airs and crisp tones. The language was exquisite, all of it a celebration, of the words themselves, of the notes, of the trees, of the sun, of the clouds, of the air. Between each song he sat still, head uplifted, eyes closed, and I saw the mist lift and the sun touch his damaged left cheek. I remember that, when I stayed in his house as a child, he frequently came in very early in the morning, all wet, little beads of rain or mist or dew dancing in his brown hair. Now I saw excitement surge through him as he sang. And then the soothing came, infiltrating every pore of his skin. I watched this strange liturgy for about half an hour. A thrush sat in a branch beside me. It sang and then it was silent. Then it sang again. I think it answered him.

After I left Ireland I received many letters from Uncle Dick. He wrote that he missed me. From that day onwards, after I had seen him at the standing stones, I began to love him again. And he opened up his mind and soul to me. I never told him I had seen his celebration. It wasn't necessary to do so. He knew. And I did not consider him odd or mad. He was a pagan. And I loved him.

I'm sitting at his desk now. I'm trying to write. Sarah is downstairs. She is troubled. She constantly weeps. She wanders about the village and does not easily find her way home. I have to send minders out with her. Everyone knows how her brother died. He hung himself from a branch in the green wood. She doesn't understand that he did that. She just says that Dick did not "take to the lads." I have his journal beside me. It's all there. How they daily accosted him. How it became their favourite sport.

How they bullied him. How they shamed him. It explains too how those who did not perpetrate those deeds but witnessed them were silent. I should say it mentions their silence. It does not explain it. Dick was obviously puzzled. He had hurt no one. And he could discover no reason for such aggression.

Now I hear Sarah calling out to me.
  "Annette, come here, Annette."
I go down to her immediately. I find her on the floor. She says she is looking for the pieces of the vase I have broken.
  "Annette, child, go out and get your Uncle Dick. Tell him to come in here right away. He'll be able to glue these pieces together again."
There is nothing in her hands. She sees me hesitate.
  "Go on now. Hurry up. This vase is much too pretty to leave lying around like this."
She scoops up another little nothing.
  "Go on now, child," she says. "Go up the hill and call your Uncle Dick."

BACKTRACKING THE PAST

Even though I've been living in this area for over six years this winter landscape of bare trees and flat fields still enchants me. There's something timeless about it. It could belong to any century. If I pulled into the side of the road about a mile from here, switched off the engine and watched the point before me where two roads meet I might see the Lady Jennet Dowdall ride up to the 17th. century wayside cross that commemorates her husband. Or I might witness a 19th. century crossroads dance, bare feet bewitched by fiddler's music, the covert glances of a boy and girl who have been forbidden to meet. It's all there in the landscape, the hope and desperation, the grief and the joy of the past. It has seeped into the earth itself.

Kevin has come to this part of the country to live. His house is a mere twenty-two miles from mine. I read that in the local freebie which was stuffed through my letterbox a few weeks ago. He's the new Parish Priest. Kevin Taylor. P.P. — a former missionary, a busy curate —now a Parish Priest. We argued a lot when we first met. I told him that his job satisfaction was made out of little bits of other people's agony. But he already knew that. Hadn't I come to him because of the slow, confusing torment of my marriage to Brendan? Finding myself unable to share all that with friends, I found it easy to share with him. No one takes an immediate interest in the pain of others, of course, but in this country clerics are supposed to be the one noble exception. It is their duty to listen — at least Kevin believed so — though a natural curiosity ensured that it was always more than a dogged duty for him.

That was nineteen years ago. He was one of two curates working in a busy seaside parish in north Dublin. I rang beforehand, asking if I might come round and talk to someone. The other curate was away on holiday, but Kevin Taylor was available. If I preferred I could wait for the other guy, it seemed, but as I had no way of estimating the value of either man I chose to see Kevin Taylor straight away. On a summer's day, the air hissing with heat, I walked the ten-minute walk from my home to his. He met me at the front door. He was wearing a yellow, short-sleeved shirt and black jeans. Small blue eyes, set under a thin fringe, danced in a boyish face. I had never seen him close up like that before, but only on the altar, where he was a remote figure going through the motions of the Mass, piety insinuating itself into the very folds of his robes. Now, in this stifling heat, I had encountered a different person.

"Would you like to sit out in the back garden?" he asked, smiling.

"Yes, fine," I stammered. But I was already beginning to question my decision. After all, what could this priest understand of a marriage that was probably already doomed? He seemed so unworn - and so unconditionally happy and in tune with the world.

"It would be a shame to miss out on the sun by sitting inside," he added when he noticed my hesitation. "If it were Sierra Leone I'd be diving for cover from the sun and recommending that you do the same. But it's not. It's the Emerald Isle. Not much blessed in the sun department, is it?"

There were no sunny solutions. He and I soon discovered that. But we continued to meet long after the presenting problem was no more. Brendan had left home, but Kevin and I found things to discuss - the merits of various books, the well-heeled immaturity we saw all about us, the media, the nature of friendship, the wrath of God.

"Only equals make friends," I offered one day. Not long before that I had observed how things panned out in the local Golf Club.

"You think?"

"Yeah, I think."

"What about us then?" he asked. "What are we? Are we friends?"

"I - yes - no," I stuttered, "not friends exactly, no, not friends."

"Soul mates then?" he probed. "Would you settle for that?' A smile flickered around the corners of his mouth but his eyes remained steady. Soul mates. Would I settle for that?

In a world crammed with everyday mistakes I made an understandable one. I paid attention to the 'soul mate' thing. I examined it. Was this what was happening when, desolate at the final realisation that my marriage could not be salvaged, I ran into his arms for comfort, only to hear his heart, like a trapped bird flapping in a cage, beating close to mine? Soul mates? Was it a soul-matey thing when, one winter's night, he took me on a spin through the Curragh of Kildare and we returned together across that whispering blackness having counted stars? Soul mates? He was, of course, as lonely as I was. When I first realised that I was surprised. He liked Tolkein. I did not. I was bewitched by the scowling blackness of James Baldwin. He was afraid of him. But we agreed on one thing.

"We read to know we are not alone," he said quietly after I'd wondered out loud why people like us spend so much time shuffling through books.

"But all those parishioners you work with ....." I began. "Surely..."
I shut up just in time. Why should I assume that he would not be lonely? And perhaps being alone with people is even more painful than being alone alone. I tried to explore this idea with him but he wouldn't listen.

"It's a little more complicated than that," he insisted. "Every day, before I make it to the altar, I have to fight this gigantic feeling of senselessness. I have a battle on my hands every single day. Do you understand that?"

"Then why don't you let them know? Why don't you say how things are?" I demanded. "Why keep up this front of being the perfect believer in a doubt-free world?"
He sighed. I leaned across and rested my hand lightly on his. He grabbed and squeezed it so tightly that my wedding ring was embedded in my finger.

Since I found out that he is living in this area I've begun to imagine him, like a ghost upon the road, feeding that two-tone Wolsley of his across the miles, and holding on to nothing at all. I can still see the walnut richness of the car's dashboard, feel its worn upholstery, smell the leather as if I had sank back into its familiar comfort only yesterday. But the Wolsley is probably gone now. He'd most likely favour a Ford or a Rover 14 today. And the emerald earring I once lost in the old car has been crushed, no doubt, as it lay hidden behind the front passenger seat. There's something desolate, isn't there, about those scrap yard places where old cars are crushed? All those lives and hopes and journeys and songs seeping out, like melted ice, from between wafer-thin pieces of metal. But I'm convinced that not everything ebbs away. Microscopic bits of energy remain - maverick thoughts, sighs, sobs, kisses. I'm sure of that.

Kevin was transferred about two years after we met. He was sent to a curacy in Clare. A few parish workers organized a party for him. He was hoping I'd attend, but I couldn't bring myself to mark his going in that way, with coffee and cakes and hymns and little nicenesses. I said my own 'goodbye' to him earlier. And after he left I imagined him driving the narrow, coiling roads of his new place, living there where the only abundance was one of sea and stone. That might suit him. I decided, but knew instinctively that he would miss our times together as much as I would. He hadn't said so, of course. He would never do that. He protected himself. I didn't feel the need for protection because I had nothing to lose - but I protected him.

The roads around here are old ones, routes gouged out by long-ago horse riders, expanding later to encompass the luxury of carriage wheels. After my daughter left home to work in London I came here to live. I needed to escape the claustrophobia of suburbia. I needed a new perspective. And I wanted to become a different me. I began a new job. I took up cycling. I explored the ancient, trembling past of this place as fully as I could. Battle sites. Monastic ruins. Souterrains. Raths. Bronze Age cysts. Mesolithic middens. Neolithic burial mounds. The past is constant, tightly wrapped, dependable, I told myself. I liked that. I looked also to the small corners of life, to hedgerows smiling with tiny flowers, to the sibilance of streams flushing through woodlands, to the shimmering grasses of summer, to the abundance of autumn and the quiet closing of the year. This was my life. I was certain I was at peace.

But Kevin Taylor has come to this part of the country to live. And already I can see him slipping past me on the motorway, or pulling alongside at a petrol station, or striding down my road. It's always these outdoor scenarios that present themselves. There are no indoor views. Maybe he wouldn't recognise me, of course, if he drove near me or walked close by on the street. But I would know those familiar stooping shoulders and those dancing eyes. I wondered if he would slip across to me, or walk quickly away if I called out to him on the street. Funny, how I question myself like this. Had I kissed and told like the bishop's woman this would not be happening. There would have been one enormous explosion, followed by bitterness and recrimination and an unhappy-ever-after ending. I'd have lost my hope a long time ago. But I remained silent, and it was in that silence that hope grew. Like a tiny seed buried in black earth it became a larger thing.

What must I do now to be free? I could trot off to Mass next week and watch as he prayed for himself and his congregation and perhaps even for me. But there's a scream in me wanting to get out, and it might frighten some unsuspecting person if it emerged at Kevin Taylor's Sunday altar. I require quiet closure really, a clean, truthful, unsentimental leave-taking that will allow me to forget. And I'll need his help. That's why I'm planning to call on him soon to ask him to backtrack on the past with me. It's possible he'll be easy enough about this activity, but I doubt it. Nevertheless I'll persevere. I'll not rest until I have persuaded him to co-operate, and to explain to me what 'soul-mate' means. Only when he and I are clear - and agreed – about that - will I be satisfied. Only then will I be free to move forward – to embrace a healthy hope again – to start living the rest of my life.

AT THE AUCTION

I lose myself in this place. When Ulick Osborne indicates each piece of furniture, machinery, bric-a-brac, jewellery I immediately become involved with it. There he is now, smiling down from that lofty perch of his while his assistant, Libby, holds up a Victorian oil lamp for all to see. There is a definite interest here. Four bidders.

"Start me off at four thousand," he suggests, smiling.

There is silence. Inside that silence I see an old woman in a black shawl, her hair wrapped into a bun, and she is lighting the lamp. Afterwards she sits in it's shadow, waiting for her fisherman son to come home from the sea. The light flickers, wanes, dies. He does not return. My heart thumps as hard as hers must have done when she learned that his body had been found on the foreshore.

Ulick Osborne is working hard. "This is a sweet piece," he says, "will someone please start me off at four thousand." A hand is raised. "Four thousand I am bid." An elbow flaps like a flipper beside him.

"Four thousand one hundred. Four thousand two hundred. Four thousand three hundred." He continues his chant until he reaches five thousand. He pauses. Nothing stirs. "All done then at five thousand euro," he concludes. "All done now."

It was Gary who suggested that I sell the furniture I had inherited from my Aunt Sheila. He wants me to sell the house too, so that we can pool our resources and buy a few acres somewhere in the country and build our own bungalow. We've already been to see a parcel of land. There are several fields. All the fields have names. Poppy Field. Chestnut Field. Fieldfare Field. Clem Collin's Field. High Field. The Fairy Field. Gary thinks the Fieldfare Field would be the best place to site the bungalow, but the old man who is selling the land says that the birds come there each autumn and stay for several days and that it would be a pity to disturb them. He suggested that we settle for Clem Collins' field. The drainage was good there, he added. We walked the land with that old man, and he made us tea in his cottage kitchen later. He was too old, he said, to look after the place. His rheumy eyes probed a distant place we could not see and it seemed to us that he was almost ready to return to the earth itself.

Gary is over there beside a pair of wooden wheels and his six-foot frame is diminished by their immense size. He grins across at me as Ulick Osborne introduces them. They were used for removing timber from forests, he tells us. A team of horses pulled the load. Later perhaps they'd used a steam engine. I'd examined them earlier. Iron shod. Impressive. There's far too little left in this world that's ordinary yet remarkable and I'm glad someone is interested in them now. The main bidder is a middle-aged man. He pays three hundred euro. "All done now at three hundred euro," Ulick intones, beaming at the gathered crowd and nodding to his assistant. They are cheap at the price, I consider, but at least they have not been burned. Gary might have made a fire of them. It's only the future which interests him, he claims. I've argued that the future is a mere set of probabilities. These days we argue a lot about such things, about past and future, about certainty and contingency, about black and white.

A young couple in the corner are disappointed. Their three-piece suite fetches only a quarter of what they had expected. But it wasn't old. Just too big for their house. They will soon forget their loss. The violin Libby holds up is interesting, but incomplete. The E string is missing. I tuned it and tried it earlier. I played some of the Ballet Music from Rosmunde. The instrument has a pleasant tone. Gary tried it too but his big hand moved awkwardly across the strings. It is a child's violin, made long ago to charm some little one into the world of music. The Duke of Wellington played the violin as a child. Perhaps he even carried one into battle with him, something pure and sweet to soften the cruelty of that savage world.

Everything speeds up. Ulick Osborne is a conductor, urging the various sections of his orchestra on. Within minutes he sells a hand painted Chinese fire screen, a holly and rosewood chess board and a gilt over mantle. The room thickens with the odour of many people. The air grows tired. Attention dwindles. We have reached the halfway point and a break of fifteen minutes is announced. People begin to filter out.

I rejoin Gary in the yard.

"How do you think he's doing?" he asks.

"I'm not sure," I tell him. "He certainly can sell but I'm not sure."

"He's a wizard with words," Gary offers. "He'd sell ice to the Eskimos, no bother."

We accept some of the polystyrene coffee that is handed out. It tastes strong and sugary. Gary sips his slowly, but mine is gone in one gulp.

"The Crown Devon vases, I think I'm going to

withdraw them," I venture. "I've decided I'd like to keep them."

He shrugs. "If you want," he says then, "but I thought we'd agreed to a brand new start in a brand new place. I hadn't counted on your Aunt Sheila's vases being part of that plan."

"But they were her mothers' - my grandmothers' - I knew my grandmother better than I knew my mother, you know."

"Yeah. I know that, darling. What I mean is they're old."

A bell summons us back inside. The crowd has thinned out to about sixty people, all gathered now in the largest room, the one which contains, among other items, the contents of my aunt's house. It had been sparsely but elegantly furnished, with all the essentials of my grandmother's era and none of the clutter we have today. That's where the crucial difference between the past and the present lies, I think - in the rate of accumulation. I tried to discuss this with Gary but he laughed at me.

"What about those fussy drapes - and those vases?" he said. "They weren't needed. They were wanted. Your Victorian ancestors were as avaricious as any twenty-first century man or woman, but in a different way."

Perhaps he was right. I remembered Van Gogh's 'Sunflowers'. "This painting is worth at least four hundred francs," he told his brother, Theo. In 1997 it sold for forty million dollars. Maybe the distinction between quality and value, between need and greed is not as clear as I would wish.

I try to stay far away from the items Ulick Osborne

is about to auction now. I sit down on a green tubular steel chair and Gary sits beside me. There are two other chairs and a kitchen table. I think they were sold hours ago but I don't know how. They are an appalling pukey sort of green. Gary sees that I am nervous. He squeezes my hand.

"Lot number 365," Ulick calls out. "The oak sideboard over there. It's a fine piece. Comes from a house clearance not far from here. Will some one start me off at five hundred euro?"

It is raining hard as he speaks, discordant drumbeats reverberating on the building's tin roof. Nothing moves.

"Four hundred then, just to get me started," he pleads, raising his voice above the noise. "Four hundred euro."

I see a woman's hand flutter to her face.

"We have a bid here. Four hundred euro." He gestures towards the woman with his gavel while his eye scopes the room for signs of further interest. There are. Two other bidders enter the fray. Gary is watching the man with the bald forehead and the ponytail. He nudges me.

"He's the one," he whispers.

When the bidding has reached seven hundred and fifty euro there is a lull in the proceedings, followed by a frenzied escalation, tenner by tenner along the line, up to eight hundred euro. Ulick suddenly points to a man in the corner.

"New blood here. Nine hundred euro. New blood. Any advance on nine hundred euro?" He lifts his gavel and brings it down, once, twice .... but the ponytail guy is right up there beside him.

"A thousand euro," he shouts out, holding his auction ticket aloft for all to see. It is number forty four.

A few months after we met Gary and I set up home together in a flat. It was easy enough for me. There was only my Aunt Sheila to reckon with and she had indulged me throughout her life. I think it was because my mother - her sister - had died when I was five. Things were different for Gary. His family were religious zealots who put markers up for every step he took. His childhood had been tainted by frenzied discipline and by a total absence of joy.

"You can do many harsh things in the name of a loving God," he often reminded me.

That first flat we shared came into my mind now because of the auction ticket number - 44. It was a top flat at 44, Seacourt Ave. And it was near the sea. If we squeezed ourselves sideways as we looked out the window we could even see a lighthouse winking at us in the darkness. We often walked along the shore in the evenings and sat on the rocks singing to each other. In those days we were both a bit daft, I think.

Gary sees me smile.

"You happy with that price?" he asks. A wide grin demonstrates that he is. I care about him. But marriage - this country idyll he wants us to share for the rest of our lives - I'm not at all sure about that. I'm not convinced about the 'simplicity' - that's what he called it - of country life. And I'm not sure about promising to love someone forever. Could I possibly love myself forever, let alone another person? I'm not at all confident about that. I like the wisdom of horizons - shimmering goals in the far distance to which I can aspire but which I may never reach. I know that there is pain and longing in that, but there is also be the joy of human effort. Effort, not completion, that's what I was beginning to aspire to now.

Within the next fifteen minutes two storm lanterns, a gramophone horn, a hall stand, some kitchen utensils and several sets of china float out of my life. Next Sheila's Underwood typewriter, her chest of drawers, her patchwork quilt, her carved wooden planter are also sold. Everyone seems to be satisfied. Gary, Ulick Osborne, the buyers are all satisfied. Shouldn't I too be happy with this opportunity to set up a new life with a man who loves me? Someone once said to me that to be happy in an unfriendly world is to be insane. But for me it's not really a matter of friendly or unfriendly, sane or insane. It's more complex and more basic than that. It's about journey and arrival. Gary sees marriage as life's destination whereas I see it - and life itself - as a journey. I doubt there can be any genuine compromise around these disparate points of view.

We have reached the last item in Aunt Sheila's lot, a sailor figurine. Her father - my grandfather - had been a seaman all his life. He traded around the north of Scotland and into the Baltic. He traded southwards to Portugal and Spain. Once he even zigzagged westwards across the Tropic of Cancer to Port of Spain. He bought the figurine out there and brought it home to his wife as a souvenir of that exotic place which she had never seen. But she separated it completely from that location and made it into a reminder of her man, something to cling to when she was lonely and alone. There it is again. Journey. Arrival. Going away. Coming home. A fussy little blond woman is the only bidder for the sailor.

197

She pays twenty euro for it. She is a dealer and will sell it on at her market stall for twice the price.

"I'm not going to put the house on the market," I tell Gary later over drinks in a nearby hotel. I had finally made up my mind.

"No?" His tone changed from excitement to surprise.

"No. I'm going to rent it out - for the moment at least."

He leaves me sitting quietly with my news.

"You see, if I sold it," I try to explain, "if I went along with your idea of ......"

"I thought it was our idea."

"So did I. But it's not. I got caught up in your plans for a while, that's all. But they were your plans"

"Then you think we can go on as we were - as we are, I mean?" he asks. "You think we can just turn around and do that?"

I see his confusion.

"I'm sorry. Really sorry. But no. I'm going away. I'm going to take a few years out from work to travel. I've always wanted to do that."

Ulick Osborne is in the bar. He comes smilingly over to us and shakes my hand. Gary thanks him for his work.

"It's hard work," he admits. "But I like it. You never know what's going to happen. Every auction is an adventure."

He has been working hard on my behalf and now he looks to me for a response.

"I suppose it is," I agree. "But then isn't everything an adventure of one sort or another? Isn't life itself an adventure? And don't we have to meet it head on?"

He and Gary exchange puzzled glances before Gary
lays his glass aside and walks away from me.

RASPBERRIES IN THE PALM OF HER HAND

Madeline had become increasingly uncertain and
sour. In the Post Office a neighbouring farmer
attempted to exchange pleasantries with her and she
had sneered. "Isn't it a grand, growthy day?" he
asked, smiling, and she'd gone and laughed and
spluttered in his face. For a while afterwards she felt
bad about it, and resolved to check her tongue in
future. Earlier she'd allowed herself to be persuaded
to buy a royal blue two piece in the town's boutique,
only to discover how vulgar it looked, mirrored in
the supermarket window next day. And at the Town
Hall Charity Concert on Sunday night she'd met two
nervy, middle aged women and knew immediately
that if her mother were still alive she would regulate
her daughter's activities as relentlessly as these two
were managed by the eighty-eight year old despot
who was wedged between them.

Her mother had never approved of Hal and said so
frequently throughout her long life. When twenty-
year-old Madeline first brought her boyfriend home
her mother was rude and ungracious, and although
Madeline tried hard she could not fathom why. She'd
met him a few months previously in a chipper beside
Derrymore Green, and watched in absolute fascination the three-stage conveyor belt system by which he
ate. In the first stage the teeth grasped a single chip.
Afterwards the tongue sucked the middle portion
along, and finally the tail was snatched down in one
deft movement which anticipated the next helping. It
was the neatest trick Madeline had ever seen. Six

months later they were married in the tin church which had temporarily replaced the one burnt down at Easter. Madeline's mother said it was a bad start, her daughter being married "in that miserable old shed," and declared that the girl could not expect that much anyway, settling down in life with such an "obnoxious little fart." Her listeners nodded agreement, and whispered together whenever they saw the newly married couple about the town, but Madeline was blissfully unaware of their disapproval, and totally happy with her new man.

Four children and twenty-seven years later strange things began to happen. It started when Madeline returned from a walk along the beach and told Hal about the Christmas tree she'd seen there. Her husband laughed.

"It's just a bit of wood," he scoffed, "what's the fuss?" He turned up the sound on the television so that her reply was lost in the vacant spaces between them. She'd been thinking of writing a poem about the tide taking away a December tree and returning it to the beach in August. There must be a parable there, she thought as she hurried back to the house, a message, a crucial connection with a much larger reality. But Hal wasn't at all impressed with her find, and anyway there were other things to be done. She made spaghetti bolognese, and watched it disappear in less than ten minutes when Hal and his pal, Kevin took supper in the kitchen that evening. That was the really sad thing about a woman's work, Madeline concluded, how impermanent it was and how quickly it could be undone, how no tombstone ever told the fullness of a woman's life. Immediately the idea of a poem came stealing back and would not be banished. At three in the morning, while Hal snored softly into his pillow, Madeline crept from their bed and, with the sitting-room window full open so that she could hear the tide scurry along the stony beach, she penned her first lines.

Ever since their eldest child was born Hal had called Madeline "Mammy."

"Mammy, come here and see what little Garry has done." "Mammy, is the dinner ready yet?" "Are you ever going to come to bed, Mammy?"
She thought she'd die of embarrassment when he first said it in public, but nobody seemed to notice, and she survived. It was just a habit some people slipped into when their children were small, she knew. But their youngest had fled the nest two years previously and Madeline longed to hear Hal say her name. In the months before their wedding he had uttered it like a prayer, his tongue easing delicately over its three distinct syllables as though it were a medieval love song or a Shakespearean sonnet. That sound would be music now, she thought, but instantly dismissed the idea as absurd. His voice had become gravely with tobacco and age, and anyway wasn't she a middle-aged woman and doing her own thing? Why on earth should she stand about, open mouthed and open eared, waiting for Hal to pronounce his magic once again?

Trouble was, Madeline was not doing "her own thing." Indeed, she wasn't sure what "her own thing" might be. There was a time, babies at the breast, a hungry husband coming home from work, a hungrier husband in her bed, when she knew her exact place in the universe and how to negotiate its topography with relative ease. Voices from distant lands telling of the virtual slavery of women hardly impinged on her consciousness, so natural and comfortable was her life with Hal. Any slight blip from that other world was immediately dismissed as irrelevant. She'd agreed with him when he offered the opinion that "those media feminists" must have suffered some deep frustration of their basic instincts at significant points in their lives to make them turn out like that - but they deserved pity more than censure, she thought. That skinny one from down under was a hoot at times, and Madeline liked to listen to her when she was a guest on television. But if Hal was around when Germaine Greer appeared he usually switched to another channel. As far as Madeline was concerned this was no big deal. Television did not interest her greatly, and when all was said and done she had little in common with the fiery feminist from Australia. Things were slightly different however on her own patch. Clara, her neighbour, had once suggested that they get "a women's consciousness raising group" going and Madeline was mildly interested. But the idea was firmly knocked on the head by another neighbour, Fionnuala, and did not survive. Madeline found herself slightly intimidated by Fionnuala. Once, after admiring the impeccable bowl of fruit which occupied a prominent position on Fionnuala's gleaming mahogany table, Madeline attempted to produce the same effect in her own sitting-room, but realised things had gone drastically wrong when she returned a few hours later to an empty bowl and a table littered with apple butts and banana skins. In her dreams that night she heard the soft, apple-tart-

and-cream voices of Fionnuala and her friends discussing her 'failure'. The dream was telling her something, Madeline decided. Perhaps it was saying that domesticity was no longer "her thing."

Hal looked at her with horror the morning after her first poem. "You didn't," he remonstrated, "tell me you didn't spend two hours out of our bed in the middle of the night scribbling some daft poem?"

"It was three hours," Madeline said quietly. "Actually, three and a bit."

"You need your head examined," he told her.
She shrugged. "Maybe I do."

"Are you going to make a habit out of this kind of carry on?" he asked, "because if you are we need to alter our sleeping arrangements a little. I can't have you nipping in and out of my bed all night."
Madeline stiffened. "It was something I had to do," she told him. "I thought you'd understand."

It took a long time for Madeline to realise the futility of her longing for understanding. When a letter came one morning advising that her 'Beach' poem had won a prize in a nation-wide competition she was ecstatic. In the evening she met him on the doorstep with her news.

"No need to act like a teenager," he told her. "It's just a bloody poetry competition."

"But I've won second prize," she said. "And the first prize went to this woman who's been writing since she was twelve. I've only started. Maybe I'll be a First Prize winner one day."
Hal looked at her as though she was a stranger who'd just trotted into his life. "What kind of ambition is that for a three times over Granny," he

exploded, "to win a bloody poetry competition? What could that possibly do for you?"

"It would be like winning the Lottery," Madeline said.

"The Lottery would give you hard cash," he countered, "opportunities for a new life. How could a bloody poetry prize do that?"

"You don't understand," she said, "but poetry IS a new life."

The following Friday Hal came home early. He ate quickly and retreated to the bathroom where he spent half an hour soaking and sprucing himself up. Madeline was in the kitchen when the commotion began.

"Mammy," he yelled down the stairs at her, "where are my clean shirts?"

"In the linen basket," she beamed up at him.

"I mean the ironed ones," he yelled again. "Where the hell are the freshly ironed shirts?"

"I didn't iron any shirts this week," she told him. "I forgot."

"You forgot? You've hardly anything to do these days and you forgot?"

"I had something to do," she said softly. "I was writing."

Hal descended the stairs two at a time. "You were writing?" he roared. "You're telling me you were busy writing?"

"I was busy, yes," she said.

"I'm going out tonight, Mammy," he said then, attempting a placatory tone. "And I'm running late as it is. Could you please iron this shirt for me?"

Madeline turned away. "Iron it yourself," she told him quietly. "My hands are all red. See! I've just been crushing some raspberries

"Since when did you become interested in fruit picking – in jam making?" he demanded.

Madeline smiled. "I didn't pick the fruit," she told him. "Fionnuala gave it to me. And even though she gave it to me for jam making I have absolutely no intention of making any. I've been crushing the raspberries in the palm of my hand just for the smell," she explained, "and for the colour - and the sensation – see?"

"You're mad," he said, flinging the shirt on the floor in front of her'. "Stark raving mad."

She picked it up and smoothed out its multiple creases with her berried palms and fingers, working first on the collar and cuffs, then on the sleeves and finally on the body of the garment until she was satisfied it was all done. She watched him as he watched her, in shocked silence, unable to move.

"Well now," she said when she had finished, "it looks fine, doesn't it? That should do perfectly for the rest of the evening."

She handed him the shirt, its pinkish, once white elegance dangling, for one bizarre moment, between them.

"And by the way, Hal," she said slowly, "I'm not your 'Mammy'. Never was. Never will be. Do you think you could possibly remember that?"

BIN DAY

Have you ever sat where a river enters the sea. Well, I have – and when I did I closed my eyes and listened. The river made minute slurping sounds, like a baby at a full breast. The sea was altogether different. It fisted the sand and roared in my ear. It demanded that I see and hear it. I had to make a special effort to reserve space in my mind for the little river. Otherwise it might have been drowned out. This disturbed me. They had to co-exist, these two, little river edging gently into the big sea. They had to live a common life there on the foreshore, but the one made such a big noise it almost obliterated the other.

It was Friday, so I put the bins out early. I was due to visit Lydia in the home that afternoon. 'Lydia at home in the hills' she used to say. I disliked her chirpy slogan. And I hated that name which seemed to loom out at me from the distant past. I enquired about it once.

"Is that an English name?" I asked. She wasn't at all pleased at my ignorance.

"There was a Lydia in the early Christian community," she explained. "My mother was interested in her story and she called me after her."

"You'll come next Friday, won't you dear," Lydia said as I took my leave last week. She always said that and invariably I assured her that I'd be there. But I'd decided I'd soon have to make my 'Farewells.' She was beginning to drag me down. And I don't think I could deal with that very often. That mess. That unholy show. Last week I'd found her almost naked, with her catheter out and the contents of her bag on the floor. She had a look of absolute delight upon her face but it vanished when she saw me walk towards the nurse-call bell.

"Don't call anyone, Janet," she pleaded. "It's just a little puddle. You can handle it yourself. Here." She pulled one of her old interlock knickers from a drawer. "Take this and mop it up. Please."

"I'll have to get the nurse, Lydia," I said, but she knew by my voice that I'd softened. I saw her notice it as plainly as I detected my cat's ears twitch at something I could not hear.

"Don't, child. It's not necessary."

"But the tube?" I protested.

"That thing." She kicked the catheter aside with her absurd pink-stockinged foot.

"You've got to have it, Lydia, for the present anyway." I wished I was not the one to insist that she was not free.

"I've made up my mind," she said, her voice rising, "not to have anything to do with that contraption any more."

"You can't do that," I argued. "You have to have it, you know that." Lydia fumbled around in her mind for something safe to say. Strange. I was the one who usually had to do that.

"Did you have your walk by the sea this week, dear?" she finally asked.

"Yes, I told her, "this morning I went to a spot where a little river enters the sea. You know, it's a strange feeling sitting there on the sand and hearing both the river and the sea at the same time."
She nodded, and I confided that I thought the sea almost drowned out the little river.

"Eventually it sucks it right in," I explained. "It takes it to itself in huge devouring gulps." I was finding this thing with the sea really troubling, but she gave me her full attention, and that comforted me.

"You know, this morning, Lydia," I continued, strengthened, " I hated the damn sea."
She talked a great deal. Didn't say anything more about the river and the sea. Held up a huge chunk of her past for me to inspect. Asked me into her soul. If I could see her soul I would see things her way, she reckoned. Already she had burrowed right under my skin. But it was time to disengage. I'd not allow any more of her agony to filter into my heart, I had already decided. But I said "yes" again when she suggested "next week, Janet, next week." Later I approached Bob.

"What are you trying to say?" he coaxed.

"I can't take any more of Lydia," I told him. "I wanted to put an end to it today but I didn't."
I gathered crumbs into a little cluster in the middle of our pine table. As soon as I'd made a neat pile I began again to disassemble them. Bob watched in silence.

"She made a disgusting mess last week and I had to be the one to find her like that with her urine all over the place," I wailed. I tried not to cry, but remembering my furious sense of obligation unsettled me.

"I can't stop wanting out, Bob."
He nodded.

"I hate that old lady. I hate what she's doing to me. I patronise her. And I don't go gladly. I'll never go gladly again."

Later I had a vivid dream. Lydia invaded my sleep. I saw her walk down the long corridor of The

Home, dressed in a black and white striped dress. She went into one of the washrooms and someone there shaved her head and gave her a bar of soap with her name stamped on it. Then she was suddenly young again, and gleaming out at me from a photograph of herself and Richard Burton. The dream must have disturbed me. I awoke to find Bob holding and comforting me like I was a frightened child in the middle of a terrible storm.

I'd gone down to the beach again early on Friday. While there I found a ladybird on a stone, among other stones, no foliage, no green stuff, no sap rising, no aphids, no nourishment, nothing but this utterly misguided, lost little ladybird. I took it and placed it on the back of my hand, blowing at it gently, hoping it would fly off to a more promising place. It hovered for a few seconds and then landed on another, similar stone.

During my journey to The Home I was tense. As I drove slowly along through a mile or so of loose chippings I became increasingly frustrated. Now that I'd made a definite decision I wanted to get on with it. I turned on the radio. It was a cello solo. Ironic. It was at a musical event that I had first met Lydia. We'd sat together for the greater part of the evening discussing the various instruments of the orchestra. The cello was her instrument. I had 'fiddled around' on the violin while at school and grew to love classical music. I especially loved orchestral concerts. I even listened before they began, to all those stray notes floating in the air, the delicate flutter of melody during the preparations, the tuning up. I suppose that's why Lydia stuck to me like glue. She recognised a kindred spirit.

"Did you see the master-class on TV last night?" she asked in between Mendelssohn and Bruch.

"No, No. I was out last night."

"It was the cello, you know, dear," she said, non-plussed. "That was my instrument. But my nephew took mine to Australia years ago."

"Was it a good programme?' I asked. I was loath to enquire why a nephew should have taken her cello out to Australia. Maybe she could no longer play.

"Oh, it was splendid, dear. It was Paul Tortelier, you know, the French Master. So sensitive. He even stopped one of the young cellists in the middle of a piece and asked him to play it again. "You should fly like a bird," he told him, "and not like a Boeing." She mimicked the Frenchman so well that I dissolved into instant laughter. In that laughter and pleasure were planted the seeds of our future relationship.

As I made my way to Lydia's room I noticed that the Sister-in-Charge regarded me coldly. This struck me as rather odd. Generally she was very friendly, glad to see one of 'her ladies' receive a visit. It occurred to me almost immediately that she might be annoyed that I did not report Lydia's behaviour last week. That certainly would have irritated her. She was in a huff. But I was appalled to find Lydia in an adult cot with the sides firmly secured. She was propped up on three huge pillows and her hair had just been brushed. Someone had placed a piece of crystal near her cot and she had become preoccupied with the little clusters of colour skating across the walls. She was obviously pleased to see me.

"Janet, dear, I'm so glad you've come. I've been thinking all week about what you said."

"Which part of what I said," I asked. I was wary. I wondered how I would tell her I was pulling out.

"The little river and the sea," she said. This seemed a safe topic. I encouraged her.

"Well, my dear, you said you thought the sea was greedy and devoured the little river."

"I did."

"But don't you see – you must see – that's what it's all about!" Lydia was quite frail and this last speech was delivered with a sudden burst of energy which startled me. It was as if her voice was a sharp pencil scratching out her deepest thoughts.

"Where does the river rise?" she wanted to know. I told her it began in the mountains about twenty miles away.

"What happens then?"

"It flows out of the ground and over the land."

"I know that. Go on. Go on."

"Well," I hesitated. I wasn't sure what she was after. "Well, it flows down the mountain towards the..." She cut in on me. "Towards the sea. That's what you were going to say, my dear. Towards the sea." It was a long time since I had seen her so animated. "It's what the river wants, you see? It flows down the mountain and then it pans out." Her voice slowed down and softened. She became hoarse. "Towards the end of it's journey it spreads out effortlessly and allows the sea to take it. That's what a river is all about, Janet. That's the whole story."

"Well, did you tell her?" Bob came home expecting to find me full of my new freedom. Instead he found me dealing with the tail-end of a fit of tears.

"No, I didn't get to tell her at all. She wanted to talk about the river and the sea."

"But why didn't you bring up the matter yourself?"

"I couldn't."

'Why on earth not? And what's this about the river and the sea?'

"I don't know, Bob. I really don't know. She just went on and on about the little river needing to be absorbed by the sea."

"And you didn't even try to…"

"No. It was weird. She was talking in riddles but it was all very compelling. And it made me sad."

I began to cry again. Bob tried to comfort me. I love it when he comes up behind me and dislodges my hands from my work and kisses my neck and my ears like that.

"It was as if I had to hold back today," I told him. "As if she had all this stuff prepared." I was trying to figure out the dynamics of the afternoon. "I think I felt I had to honour her efforts by simply paying attention. Do you understand that?"

He gave me a tight squeeze.

On Friday the bin men were late and they made a mess in the driveway. I had to clean it up before I left for the home. Lydia had been on my mind all week. I hadn't understood what she was getting at last time I was there. I'd listened, but I'd not really understood. Neither had I been able to disengage from her. Perhaps I'd get a little further today. I also had a present for Lydia. It was a painting of a river. I thought she might like to put it on the wall beside her bed. I was deep in thought when Sister suddenly rounded a corner and whisked me off to her office.

"Mrs Irvine," she said slowly, "I'm afraid I've some bad news for you."

Immediately I thought Lydia had made herself worse

by not taking her treatment.

"What's the matter?" I asked.

"Sit down please, Mrs Irvine and I'll ask Nurse to bring you some tea."

"Is she bad? Have you moved her?" I pushed the chair away.

"No," Sister said emphatically. "No, I'm afraid Lydia is dead."

"But she wasn't that ill," I blurted out, "and only last week she had…"

"She left here last Wednesday night," Sister said calmly. "She dressed herself in the middle of the night and somehow slipped out."

"Slipped out? Slipped out where?" I demanded.

"She walked for about a mile and a half through the wooded area at the back of us here."

I shivered. I could feel Lydia goosepimpling in the cold night air.

"She got as far as the river. That's where we found her, lying along the bank, head first in the water."

I gasped.

"We're not saying it was suicide, Mrs Irvine. We're not sure of that. It could be that she became dizzy and fell. We simply don't know."

There's a picture on the wall of my bedroom. It depicts a river in full spate, the brown water trampling through tall ferns. It's a bit like the one I visit in the hills behind the home. I don't go there very often – certainly not every week – and definitely not on bin day. On bin days I read or listen to music or sew. But in the winter, I sometimes make my way to the place where Lydia died. It is, I find, the perfect place in which to be alone.

PLASTICS AND PAINT

See the man with the pink hands and the black hair sitting behind the oak desk? The phone rings and immediately he pushes me aside and answers it. The conversation is about plastics and paint. Mergers. Take-over bids. Doesn't matter that it is Sunday and that he has promised to take me for a ride on the new miniature railway in the park. This deal has been in the pipeline for several months. In plastics and paint nothing happens in an afternoon. But the denouement - the wrap-it-all-up bit - can be accomplished almost immediately. Picture me there by his side, seven-year-old eyes anxiously monitoring my daddy's every movement.

"Don't cry," he says as he sweeps past. "I'll be back soon."

"But you said you'd take me to ...," I begin to protest, but as I speak the door is slammed in my face and the big man hurries away.

At the school's Christmas concert there is a gaping hole in the audience where my daddy should be. Mother is there, of course, smiling her thin smile at everyone, acutely conscious of her husband's absence.

"Your Caroline is so like her Daddy, isn't she?" Mrs Sloan offers as the two women sip tea together during the interval.

"Yes, she is."

"That black hair is very dramatic - and she's so pretty too."

"I suppose that's true," my mother replies.

"Isn't your husband coming tonight?" Mrs Sloan at last musters the courage to enquire.

"I'm afraid not. Robert's got a meeting that can't be missed."

These are the childhood scenes I see as I slip into sleep. And I remember how he treated Peter when I first brought him to our house. I was sixteen. Our friendship was new and enchanting and I desperately wanted it to last forever.

"I will not permit my daughter to laze about," my father told an astonished Peter. "She has her study to do. I expect her to take over the business from me." He sighed, no doubt weighing up the effort he anticipated in making me over into a successful businesswoman, the kind he could be proud of in his old age. Peter left the house without even a backward glance, and never asked me out again. There were three others, but each time my father discovered I was dating someone he insisted that the boy be brought home for afternoon tea, and each time he'd lay into him, sending him away without hope. I was eighteen when Matthew, the last of these three, left. He rang me afterwards and I heard my father tell him that I had "absolutely no wish to speak to him."

That was over ten years ago. Physically I've grown more and more like him. If I were male I'd be his double - long nose, spherical eyes, pale skin and, of course, the black hair. I made an early escape from my childhood home and there was little incentive for making visits after my mother died. Father continually asked that I do so, even sent me a special pleading invitation for my birthday, but I no longer responded to that kind of emotional blackmail. Last August Steven and I spent a forthright in the

Caribbean and I relented – I posted my father a card from our hotel. When I returned he claimed he was quite ill. I contacted his doctor and it was confirmed that he had about six months to live. Cancer of the liver, the doctor said, even though his patient had been a most abstemious man. I requested indefinite leave from school and as soon as they had arranged a replacement teacher I was on my way.

The first function of a dutiful daughter nursing a dying father is to be honest. But he'd have none of it.

"I'll soon be right as rain," he'd say, "and you can get back to those charming pupils of yours." He'd never forgiven me for rejecting plastics and paint in favour of a career in teaching.

"Would you like to talk?" I invited.

"Save your 'talk' for Steven," he replied, pushing away his breakfast tray. It was obvious that he wanted me in the house, but only on his terms. Hardly surprising, since it was on his terms alone that he had been a father and tolerated me as his child.

During his illness I went for long walks along the river. I admired the serenity of swans. Slender-necked and strong, they arched their broad wings elegantly until they were airborne and free. I envied them. Once I saw a kingfisher dart from bank to bank, its small and gleaming body a surprising light slicing through the evening mist. It made me wonder if kingfishers were entirely different to each other, or if this one resembled its parents absolutely, was perhaps a replica of its father or its mother.

"Black people all look the same," I once heard a girl

say as she sat in an airport in Capetown. She was naive, of course, or ignorant, or both. But human beings can resemble each other in extraordinary ways and each day I remained with my dying father I saw his face stare out at me from the bathroom mirror. Younger, healthier, female, but the undoubted image of my father. I watched him closely for signs of sorrow or regret or shame but he displayed none of these emotions. If I were brave enough, I told myself, I might have confronted him. But his masked expression held me at arms length until the moment he died.

A nurse came from the other side of town and washed his shrunken body. I noticed how carefully she combed his black hair so that the partial baldness would not be seen. How appropriate, I thought, that I should see him down like this, his best striped suit, his favourite Italian shirt, his hair combed to the usual smart style.

Steven was furious when I first mentioned the 'nose' job.

"Couldn't you think of something better to do with your inheritance?" he demanded.

"Father was finished financially," I replied. "It's only £150.000. Hardly an inheritance."

"Your father went to great lengths to set that money aside for you," Steven reminded me.

"So he did," I agreed.

"It would go some way towards buying us a nice city apartment," he continued. "Along with what I've got. If you put a dint in it we never will."

"Perhaps not."

"Don't you care?" he demanded, frustrated now.

"I want ... no ... need to make this change," I insisted, "and that comes first."

Even though I was able to put my cash on the table the rules were strict. I was interrogated about my desire and where it was born and how it grew. Did I realise the risks? they demanded. Did I understand that a general anaesthetic would be required? Was I absolutely sure? I never mentioned my likeness to my father, but I was able to convince the medical panel that I was a suitable candidate. Within three weeks I was admitted to the clinic and the operation was carried out. They shortened my nose and, about a month afterwards, when the pain eased I had my hair cut, dyed ash brown and then streaked with a delicate blond. I returned to school for the first week of the spring term.

There was accommodation on campus, and as Steven was a junior lecturer we had a flat there. It was cold. The heating system was about a hundred years old but few complained. It was a prestigious college and there were others queuing up to take all the available space.

"If you could see your way to contributing towards a deposit on an apartment," Kevin sneered, "then we might possibly be warm again one day."

"I told you I need to hold on to the rest of the money ...," I began.

"Jesus, Caroline, don't you think you've done enough?"

"I'm not sure, really I'm not."

"You're not sure. You've dyed your hair and had half your nose chopped off and you're not sure.

When will you be sure, may I ask?"

"I wish I knew."

"God Almighty, Caroline," he screamed, "you are screwed up." He grabbed a raincoat from the hall. I watched as he walked across the compound and out into the busy street.

We had a party on Saturday night. Steven had forgotten his huff and was in a great mood. Alex came, and his girlfriend Sara. They were mature students, both doing Politics and Russian. Steven had this fascination with all things Russian. He had studied the language for quite a while until pressure of work forced him to give it up. But in the night he'd whisper its love language to me and I'd succumb. I think I loved Steven then, but love is such an ambiguous entity, isn't it, and I'm not entirely sure. There was, however, no mistaking the love light in Alex and Sara's eyes. Alex told us that when he was seventeen he'd had a miniature of Sara's face painted on his eyelids. Such exotic obsession. Whether their relationship will last or not is another matter.

On Sunday morning we slept in and it was Steven who volunteered to do up our breakfast fry. He whistled as he worked, and then I heard him drift into song, the familiar Beetle words sounding old fashioned and dull. I had a headache, and longed for that first, special coffee of the day. But soon I heard crockery shatter on the kitchen floor and Steven howling with rage as he burst into the bedroom.

"I found this," he roared, holding aloft a letter I though I had carefully hidden. It was another estimate from the clinic. "You are a stupid bitch."

"What would you know?" I demanded, "what

would you know about anything, hidden away in that ivory tower of yours? I don't think you've any idea of the kind of pain families ..."

But he interrupted. "Families," he yelled. "What about families? As far as I'm concerned "families" are tentative things - organic - like atoms gathering together into clusters and then dispersing - you make the most of them when you're in."

"I was talking about the effect of indifference on ...."

"On you?" he demanded. "On poor Caroline?" He opened my wardrobe and began to pull the clothes from their hangers, flinging them in a raging heap on the floor.

"You can do what you like from now on," he announced. "You can get your ears pinned back if you like, or your chin wired, or your teeth extracted; you can have your face lifted or your bum lifted, I don't care."

"But I wouldn't want a bum lift," I pleaded, "it's just my face - it's so like his."

"You're insane, Caroline," he hissed. "And I want you out. When I return this evening you are to be gone from here."

In Emer's bedsit I bawled my eyes out. She gave me some gin. I don't think she understood why I wanted to have my cheekbones rearranged, but it's because of these sloe eyes. If they can alter the shape of my cheekbones they can change the setting of my eyes. I can spare enough cash from my 'inheritance' to do that. And have enough for a little holiday in Greece when I have recovered. I was hoping Steven would come along too, but he has refused all my calls, and when I went to the lecture block his colleagues looked at me funnily and said he wasn't there.

The surgery is due for next Tuesday. I can't wait to go walkabout back home when it's all done and see old Mrs. Hutton's face when she meets me again. After the nose job and the dyed hair I was shocked to find that she still recognised me.

"You're Robert's daughter all right," she insisted when I met her at the bus stop in the town, "his absolute spitting image."
When next I visit I'll bet she won't say that. No one will ever again say that I look like my father. If I have to use every penny he left me I'll see to that.

ALONG THE ESTUARY

Orla Dowling left the classroom and got sick in a corner of the yard.

"What's wrong with you?" Katie asked as a pale-faced Orla shuffled back inside.

"I think I ate a dodgy burger."

"You should tell the teacher," her friend suggested. "She might let you go home early."

"Tell Miss Prickly Pear? No way! There's no one at home anyway, so I'd rather be here"

Five o'clock. Orla has her atlas spread out on the dining room table. When her mother phones she is on a magical tour of the Greek Islands. She is going to live there eventually, and paint, and paint and paint. She is going to be a famous artist.

"There's a pizza in the freezer," her mother tells her. "And you can warm up some soup."

"But I wanted to talk to you about ..." Orla begins.

"Tomorrow," her mother interrupts, "It can wait until then, can't it? I promise we'll have a good old chinwag tomorrow. Ok?"

"Ok, Mum."

"And listen, darling, don't wait up for me tonight. I'll be a little late."

Mark arrived at seven. Orla unhooked the chain on the front door and slid back the bolt. He was smiling as he stepped inside, his blond hair trailing across a casually creased forehead. Orla persuaded herself that he looked like Hugh Grant.

"A little birdie told me you might have the place to yourself," he murmured as he kissed her. "Great."
In the kitchen he opened a can of beer.

"Want some?" He held the brimming glass towards her. She shook her head.

"Have it your own way then," he scolded, "but it'll be your fault if I have to drink this stuff all by myself. He sauntered into the sitting room, Orla trailing closely behind him. "Boy, am I tired," he drawled as he stretched along the length of the calf-hide couch. "I've had lousy day. Didn't sell a single thing."

"Would you like some pizza?" Orla asked.

"Yes, if it's absolutely covered in cheese."

"It is. And there's lots. I'll get some plates."

They watched a video. Orla had planned to see "Titanic'' but Mark brought "Gladiator' along and they watched that instead. He also downed the remains of the six-pack.

"My mother will be mad at me," she told him as he stuffed the empty cans into the kitchen bin.

"Why is that?"

"That was her beer. She'll think I've taken it."

"You can tell her it was me."

"You're not supposed to be here. She'd go ballistic if she knew you'd been here."

"But you want me here, don't you, pet?" He flicked an index finger under Orla's chin. "And you want me in your bed too, you little whore."

Mark left at midnight without hearing Orla's news. There was no point in telling him, she had decided. It would make no difference. And she would not tell her mother yet. That woman lived in cloud cuckoo land most of the time, with her charity dinners and her concerts and her days at the races. She also had this new man on the go – well, newish anyway since she'd had a bit of a fling with him years earlier. His name was Emmet. Orla liked him a lot, and wished he had become her daddy. But it didn't happen. She was about eight years old at the time, and spent a whole summer wishing and wishing. She learned then that wishing was a waste of time.

During the fifth month Orla decided that she would call her little baby Jamie. He would be exactly like her father. She'd never met her father, of course, but she was certain that the tiny infant taking shape inside of her would resemble him. Better than the black and white photograph she always kept in her diary, the baby would come in full colour. She'd be able to touch him. And she'd hear him laugh and cry.

"Did you ever think of – of getting rid of me?" she'd once asked her mother.

"Heavens no, darling. What do you think I am? I love you. I loved you even before you were born. I'd never have done that."

"But weren't you afraid .....?"

"Of what? Never. I knew I could manage on my own. And I was right? You've turned out just fine."

Orla wondered what her mother would say if she knew about Jamie. She would be angry – she was sure of that. She wanted Orla to get eight straight A's in her Leaving Certificate and to go to University. A baby was definitely not part of that plan.

'My daughter, Orla intends to be an architect'.

Orla could see her out there bragging to her friends.

'My daughter is studying medicine at college'.

'My Orla is a brilliant engineer'.

At seven months Orla bought a size 12 to replace the size 10 trousers she wore to school. They fitted fine.

She felt frequent movement deep inside her body. Jamie was waving his arms about. Jamie was preparing to break into the world. And his mother also had plans. About ten days before the baby was due she would go to Dublin. She would check into a maternity hospital. They'd look after her there. When the baby was born a social worker would find a flat for her. Orla would have her own place then, and her own money. She and Jamie would be fine.

Katie phoned. "I haven't laid eyes on you since the holidays. Where are you hiding yourself?"

"I've been busy."

"Are you coming to the Community Centre? They're having a disco tonight."

"Katie, I can't. Some fellow's due to call and fix the tele."

"I'll drop in tomorrow morning then. Let you know how things went."

"Sorry, I won't be in." Orla lied. "Look, I'll ring you later, ok?"

She went for a walk along the dunes. It was her favourite place in all the world. Here countless tracks needled through soft turf, and she followed one of these to a place where everything was sand, grains piled high and loosely ridged, and endlessly shifting and heaving and whispering like the sleepless Sahara. Orla shuddered. Something squeezed so hard around the middle of her stomach that she had to hold her breath. The spasm soon passed however, and she walked on to where the river lost itself inside an eager ocean. Birds skimmed across green water to their homes along the cliffs. From across the estuary Orla heard their endless chatter. It must be nice to really belong like that, she thought. She'd never had any contact with her grandparents or with an aunt or uncle. Her mother refused to speak about it, but Orla had the distinct impression that they'd cut her out of their lives. Would that happen again, the past insidiously folding itself into the present so that life had only one particular shape? She could not live with that kind of isolation. But surely her mother would not repeat those terrible sins. She'd welcome Jamie. Maybe even help to rear him? Orla would return home eventually and Jamie would have the two of them to fuss over and to love him.

She rested on an old wall that had once been part of a harbour. It was lightly covered with a filigree of seaweed, reminding her of the thin-haired heads of the old ladies she saw at the local nursing home. She shivered. It was getting cold, and a fine mist clung to the edge of the sea. She moved on. At one point she thought she was lost, seeing only scutch grass and sand on every horizon. The old boathouse should be near, though. When she reached that she could rest up again before returning home. Ten minutes later Orla crawled through the boathouse doorway. Her breath came in short, awkward gasps. Pain raced through her body. She cried out, but only the raucous screeching of seagulls answered her. She tore into her sweater with her teeth until it became a tattered rag. She bit her tongue, tasting her own blood. There was blood on the ground too, slowly seeping into the pebbled earth. Eventually the baby came, his head all damp and floppy as he landed softly on the ground. He cried briefly before lapsing into silence. Orla drifted away.

A sliver of late evening light lit the place where the baby lay. When she woke Orla lifted him. He was terribly cold, but she would warm him. She began to rub his body all over, legs, arms, head, hands, feet, finishing with his tiny trunk. She took off her jacket and wrapped him carefully so that she would be able to carry him home. Swaying wildly at first, she quickly steadied herself before moving from the building and along the estuary. She could hear music in the distance. It was 'Prelude a L'apres Midi du'n Faune', her mother's favourite piano piece. It was a sign. Orla stumbled on, certain now that her mother would welcome little Jamie. It was all she needed to know.

As the man drew close to the hawthorn hedgerow there was a sudden burst of awkward, whirring flight, and a pheasant rose into the air, its glittering green head pointing eastwards towards the woods. He passed quickly so as not to disturb the hen that was nearby, sitting on her nest. Though it was May it was still cold, high cirrus coasting in from the ocean, the outline of the church steeple flecked in snow. He walked rapidly, his arms swaying wildly, his boots splintering the silence. Soon he was crossing 'Archer's Acre' where his brother grazed some cattle during autumn time. It was empty now, new grass on the way, many thistles. Towards the centre of the field was a high ridge with several trees. It was said that one of those trees had been used for target practice since the middle ages. Now someone had dragged a dead fox across its lower branches and it hung there, slowly disintegrating. The man shivered, wondering where Una might be right now.

His brother waited at the farmhouse door.
"That bloody wife of yours has been on the phone again," he said. "As if I could do anything about her precious 'Polly'."
The man stamped the damp out of his feet.
"Couldn't you talk sense into her?" his brother demanded. "Tell her I'm not going to divulge the beast's whereabouts. Let her know we've enough here to worry about?"
"She's reared that lamb from birth. She's afraid she might lose it."
"Daft idea anyway making a pet of a lamb. If she had a few kids trailing out of her it'd soon put a stop

to that nonsense."

The man struggled with his reply before swallowing it, whole. It wasn't a time to argue. His brother had always wanted to work on the land, and had saved for his farm since he was eighteen. He achieved his goal when he was thirty-four.

"Where's the jeep?" he said instead. "We'd better get started."

They brought the cattle in from outlying areas, field by field, until they were all penned. The old jeep moved slowly at first, pitching awkwardly through mud, but it shifted more easily in the first open field and there was a stampede as the cattle moved to either side and a way opened up before them. For one glorious moment the man felt the exhilaration he had experienced when he watched cowboy movies as a child. Big country. Big men. Big beasts. The wide open skies. Nothing narrow or stifling in that celluloid world, like a Civil Service career, a personal life that had become utterly confused, or days that carried the smell of burning flesh on every breeze. He jumped from the jeep when it reached the top of the field, and began to drive the first cattle down towards the yard. It was four in the evening before they were all in, hooves stamping on wet concrete, impatient, wary.

"The department men'll be here in the morning - early," his brother said.

"I'm sorry. And sorry you're being hassled about Polly. It's just that she ....."

"I know. I had no right to .... when you can't ..... no right at all."

The man rested a hand on his brother's shoulder.

"We're both tired," he said. "The whole country's tired. I think I'll go home."

Polly was in her pen when he arrived.

"They're not going to kill her. She's not sick. They can't," his wife said, defiantly placing her frail body between the lamb and their front gate.

"Maybe not," the man sighed. "Maybe there'll be a miracle and all this slaughter of the innocents will end immediately."

"You won't let those department people go near her?" she insisted. "Tell me you won't."

He smiled weakly. "I promise I'll defend her to the bitter end."

"You know what Polly means to me," she said as she followed him into the house.

"I do."

Even the bedroom, its windows closed against the world, was saturated in the sickly sweet smell that was now a routine part of life in the area. The man remained awake, thinking of Una, of how, for months now they lay together, so close that they thought no one could ever come between them.

"I feel strange when I'm with you," he'd whispered. "Possibly even a different person."

She laughed.

"No, I mean it."

"Then you must be more than a little lost."

"Lost? Me lost?"

"Yes, lost. They say that when you 'find yourself' you're the same for all people."

He sighed.

"You have to tell her," Una said.

"I can't."

"No?"

"She wouldn't be able to take it. She's not strong - like you."

She turned her back to him. "It might look like I'm strong," she said. "But I'm not. And I can't take this deceit for much longer."

Last week, Sunday, twelve o'clock she'd phoned him at home.

"I need to talk to you," she whispered, as though his wife might hear her.

"What's wrong? Why are you ringing here?"

"Meet me in O'Neills. Half two. I'll expect you to be there."

He stood holding the phone to his ear for several seconds after she'd rung off. The sky was blue. A cold wind blustered in from the north east. The Angelus bell shrilled in the distance.

The man knew he could not tell his wife about Una. Their disappointing marriage, with its implacable childlessness, had wrecked her spirit. And he knew that the lies he told her were more humane than the truth would ever be. Una also knew that. She'd stormed out in the drizzle dark of their last night together, sheets unruffled, drinks untouched. But deep down she knew that. Perhaps she wanted to end it between them. That was probably why he'd received this rather decisive summons to O'Neills. He wouldn't blame her if she wanted out, though he'd fight hard to dissuade her.

The coast road was clear of traffic as he motored towards the city. At first the sea was a blue, flat glaze only a few fields away from the road he travelled. Later the land rose upwards and he could see the three islands called 'Ladies in Waiting'. Una and he had gone on a day trip there once, while his wife was in Lourdes with her sister. The boatman put them ashore on the largest island and came back in the evening to collect them. For hours they wandered the humps and hollows of the place, sometimes lying close to the cliff edge to watch the bustle of kitti-wake, tern, guillemot and puffin. In the ancient monastic ruins they opened their picnic basket and ate, Italian breads, salads, cheese, fruit, and some lemon cake that Una had made. There was also that special white wine. They were quiet afterwards, lying in the short grass that grew like a carpet where the altar had been. That's where they first made love, framed by hawksbeard and dandelion.

Lying in his bed now his wife's breathing became a faint backdrop as he relived the panic of that meeting in O'Neills. Una was edgy, nervous, chiding him for being five minutes late. And she had obviously rehearsed her opening.

"I had a visit from a pin-stripped young man yesterday," she began.

"Yes?"

"Before I had time to open my mouth he made an announcement."

"About what?"

"About what he was doing. "Hello," he said, "its nothing serious or anything. I'm not a Mormon or anything and I'm not after your money. What I'm doing is I'm in the area talking to people with young children. Have you any yourself?"

"That was a bit of a mouthful," the man remarked. He was puzzled. What was he expected to do this information?

"I didn't invite him in," Una continued. "I told him he was a few months early - that I hadn't any children - yet."

The man laughed. She stared at him. "I wasn't joking," she told him, "our baby is due in seven months time."

The man's wife called out in her sleep, a pitifully soft sound that quickly faded. Its roots were totally inaccessible to him, as were those of her daytime thoughts and actions. He wasn't sure if it was she who had first moved apart from him or if he had already began to slide away. "You've a smile to die for," she'd said when they first met.

"I know," he'd answered, "and so have you."

Six o'clock. He left her sleeping in the unhappy room with the closed windows. He dressed and walked quickly towards the end of the village. The street light beside the public telephone was broken and he had to fumble in the half-dark, selecting the coins he'd need to ring Una. He'd speak with her again, tell her he'd leave his wife and come to live with her, plead that she should not destroy their child. He dialled her number carefully and let it ring for about ten minutes before hanging up. Then he tried her mobile and was delighted and surprised to hear her answer it.

"Una, it's me," he said, "I need to talk to you."

"We've done all our talking," she said.

"Where are you? Please tell me where you are?"

"I'm at the airport. I decided to get an earlier flight. I'll be in London by eight."

"I'll leave her," he said.

"No you won't. You think you will but you won't."

"It's over between me and her."

"Look, I'm off now," she said. " I won't be back again so I'll say 'goodbye'."

Before he had time to respond the phone went dead.

He wandered out of the village towards his brother's farm. When he reached the hill he saw the funeral pyre, the black and white and fawn bodies of the cattle crumpled together, the railway sleepers doused in petrol beginning to flame, the air wretched with smoke and sadness. In the yard his brother, unshaven, eyes deeply sunk in their sockets, stood alone. The curtains of the farmhouse twitched briefly and the man heard his two young nephews sobbing and their mother begging them not to watch out any more.

"What the hell's up with you?" his brother asked, startled. "Why are you here?"

"It's nothing."

"You didn't have to come, you know."

"I'd nowhere else to go right now - nowhere else I wanted to be, that is."

Even in the half-dark of an unnaturally smoky dawn it was obvious that both were crying.

"That's my life's work out there - burning," the farmer said.

The man nodded. "I know."

"Polly should be all right, I think. They've no idea there's a pet lamb in the area. Just keep her locked inside."

"Una's ditched me."

"Well, didn't you tell her you wouldn't chuck your marriage to set up a place with her."

"I did. But I made the wrong decision. There is no marriage any more. And Una is on a flight to London to rid herself of our child."

The flames leapt high into the air now, and the

smoke grew thicker, and the man could almost see and hear a frenzied mob shout out like the people did at a medieval witches' burning. It was all too hot and too chokingly painful for any mortal soul to bear.

"I should have gone after her," he said to his brother.

"It wouldn't have done much good. Nothing will. Things are out of control now. It'll take a long time to ...."

"A long time?" the man interrupted. "It'll take forever."

The farmer shrugged. "I'm tired," he said. "Let's go inside. I'll make us some tea."

DINNER FOR FIVE

I'm sixty-five today and I can hear my arteries hardening. In spite of the fact that this unique 'Sonata of Mortality' has been playing and replaying itself in my head for several months now I agreed to Miriam's suggestion of a little dinner party "just to mark the occasion". We invited Sally and Andrew, whom we have known over fifteen years, and a divorced colleague of mine called Ray. A birthday celebration for five in leafy Dublin 18. Good food, the best wine, and some civilised conversation to pass the time until we each went our separate ways again. Any other kind of party would probably have been too strenuous, I suppose. After all, I'm sixty-five years old and heading, full steam ahead, towards 'the abyss'.

Sally did not like it when I used that word. We were discussing the ultimate of existential questions and, as usual, I put my foot in it.

"Maybe there is no meaning to life after all," I said, "maybe this entire 'search for meaning' stuff is, in itself, quite meaningless. Did you ever stop to consider that?"

She was spooning prawns from her glass into her husband's mouth, but braked in mid-air, leaving Andrew to retrieve the stranded prawn.

"You don't mean that. It's impossible to imagine all this ... this aggravation amounting to absolutely nothing in the end."

"He only said maybe," Andrew reminded her.

"But it was a definite maybe, wasn't it, Tony?" Ray prompted. Miriam had begun to gather up the used glasses and to take them to the kitchen. She frowned at Ray and me as she retreated. Sally looked pained.

"Tony," she said, "I thought you, of all people, would take this matter seriously. I mean you. ..." She stopped, looking both offended and embarrassed, and quickly dodged into her glass of Sancerre. She'd wanted to say that because I was one of those people who once went away to be a priest I'd be expected to take these matters seriously for the rest of my life. And she'd wanted to say that she craved someone like that to draw alongside her from time to time.

"I do take it seriously," I told her. "That's why I said what I said. It's because I do."

I joined Miriam in the kitchen. She was finishing off the Marsala sauce and its rich smell filtered into every corner of the room. I laid out five warm plates on the worktop and served out the Beef Tournedos, settling each crouton carefully before spreading the pate, and topping each off with its filet steak. When they were ready Miriam took a deep breath before dribbling the sauce over each portion.

"It looks great, doesn't it?" I said. "I'll bring these out now."

"Before you go...," she said, blocking my way.

"Yes, what it is?"

"Sally - try not to irritate her. She seems to be having a real hard time right now."

Before I had time to reply she gave me a gentle push towards the door and followed me in with dishes of potatoes and other vegetables. Ray had just opened a bottle of Amarone and was pouring the wine.

"It isn't as if...," he began, but stopped in mid sentence to help with the food.

"As if what?" Sally prodded.

"As if we could do anything about it one way or the other," he finished, filling Sally's glass to the brim. "Now try that."

She sipped the strong wine briefly and set the glass down, lifting it again as Andrew proposed a toast.

"To Tony," he said, "and to the consolations of old age and to ......"

"To the mystery of things," Ray added, smiling.

"To the mystery and adventure of life."

Five glasses clicked briefly together, mine, my wife's and those of these three people whom we really cared about. We made some flawed music together at that moment. Afterwards we continued to eat.

Andrew was only fifty-two. It was easy for him to toast "the consolations of old age" when he did not have to sample them right now, I thought. But he was a decent sort. A salesman. Away from home a lot but mad keen for home life and the company of his wife, Sally. She was ten years younger - but the age gap didn't really show. And they had a son of twenty-four, living in London, an IT whiz kid, or so they said, of whom they were extremely proud. At one stage Andrew used to look longingly at our brood and wish that he and Sally had at least two children. "But that's life," he'd eventually shrug. "No guarantees."

"Try dishing up home-made burgers and chips for six twice a week," I'd say. "You'd soon get pissed off with that."

Miriam and I relaxed while Ray organised dessert. He did a great Tiamasu. I realised that, in Miriam's head, this sixty-five thing was really special as I had been close to death in my forties. Car crash.

Intensive care for a week. Hospitalised for two months. But I made a good recovery. She has a formal family gathering arranged for next Saturday in the Cualinn Hotel. It's supposed to be a surprise but Donal, our eldest, who is working as a translator in Prague, let it slip. I assured him that when the time came I'd act suprised.

"Come and get your just desserts," Ray called from the kitchen door. Like the children in the Oliver Twist advertisement approaching Mr. Bumble, we all trooped in on cue. We giggled our way back to the dining room, settling down again with the food and a bottle of Madeira.

Sally was disinclined to eat.

"Watching the figure?" I joked.

"Not really," she snapped.

"Would you like some fruit instead?" Miriam asked her. "I have some peaches and some melon."

"No. No. I'm sorry. I'll just sip my wine."

Ray and Andrew launched into a discussion about a t.v. show they had both seen the previous night. A documentary about prison. One ex-prisoner had said that, for years, he had dreamed of a soft bed to lie on at night, but when the time came he found no comfort in the bed he had dreamed about. After years of incarceration he could only sleep on a hard bed.

"I wondered," said Andrew, "if it was the body or the mind that refused to enjoy a good bed."

"The body surely," Ray offered. "The mind had wanted precisely that for years, hadn't it?"

"So it seems. So it seems," Andrew persisted. "But is it true? That's what I want to know."

"How do we know if anything is true," Ray said, "except by testing it out in the real world?"

"Then it's our experience that determines what's true and untrue?"

"To a certain extent - yes."

"Then there's no such thing as objective truth?"

"Probably not."

Sally had dribbled some wine down the front of her yellow blouse. She tried to rub it away but only made things worse. She stopped when she spotted me watching her. We were all a little merry now, even Miriam, who was busy clearing away the dishes to the kitchen.

"I'll go and help Miriam," Sally said, but when she stood up she swayed on her feet. Andrew coaxed her back into her chair.

"There's a king-sized dishwasher in there," I told her. Miriam'll stuff everything in and be back in here in a jiffy."

Sally turned her attention to Ray.

"What you said there - about truth, I mean, do you really believe what you said - that there's no such thing as truth?"

Ray frowned. He was smoking now, drawing hard down on his slender, home-rolled cigarette.

"No, Sally. No. That's not what I mean. I just mean that truth is much too big a word for anything we can know."

"I see," Sally told him, but it was patently obvious that she did not. Miriam had joined us and we were all sitting in the conservatory, watching the sun sink behind the oak tree at the end of our back garden. Andrew sighed, a slow tortured sigh that swirled around us and would not settle.

"If there's no truth then there's no right and wrong," Sally continued, painstakingly articulating each word. "There's no truth and there's no right and there's no sin because there's no damm wrong." She was shivering now, pulling her thin blouse tight around her shoulders.

"He didn't say that," Andrew said quickly. "He only ..."

"No Andrew. She has a point. If there's no right absolute truth there can't be a 'right and wrong' in the way we learned at school. It's impossible."
Miriam leaned across to Sally.

"They're playing games, Sally. Word games. Take no notice. Tomorrow they'll both be back to normal."

We had coffee in the kitchen. A strong Colombian. Ray and Andrew were driving and wanted to sober up. Miriam and I had made up a few guest beds the day before, but Ray had an appointment next morning and Sally and Andrew seemed very uncomfortable with the idea of stopping over. He kept rapping the table with a spoon as he drank. In spite of the coffee Ray was almost asleep in his chair, and Miriam and I were beginning to flag when suddenly, without warning, Sally began to cry, great shuddering sobs that rocked the entire room. No one moved. She eased off for a few seconds, then started over. The sun disappeared. All that remained of its warm promise was a jagged red streak in the sky. Ray lit up again, his hands shaking. Andrew stared into space.

"More coffee anybody?" Miriam invited in that mock cheerful voice she used when offering our children unpleasant medicines when they were small. It was strange to hear it now, on this, my sixty fifth birthday. There was no response. Instead Sally turned to Andrew.

"I had to be straight with you," she said. "Don't you realise that? I didn't want this baby - not after twenty-four years - no woman would want that - but....."

Andrew's lower lip quivered. Hope briefly shone in his eyes.

"But I can't now. Not even if I wanted to," Sally shrieked. "Not now that the doctors have told me what to expect. So I'm going away next week. And it won't be wrong, I tell you. It won't be a sin. It won't be a huge, God-Almighty bloody waste."

She was crying again, and beating out an invisible pattern in the air. Ray moved across to Andrew and put a hand on his shoulder, making a frail effort to mitigate the horror of what he had heard. Andrew stood still in the only space where daylight still lingered. Miriam and I remained seated.

BETWEEN TWO NOTES THAT FALL

Donal is coming again to visit me. He thinks I need the company. He has not yet discovered that every living creature is always and forever alone and that only in death is there some small semblance of togetherness. If we could manage to see it, a famous scientist once said, the sub-atomic world would reveal itself in "a web of connections". I like that pronouncement and the idea that when I die my bleached and scattered particles will connect with the entire universe, may even blend at last with those of Peggy. She is long gone, of course, and she went another route. Burning was not for her, she said, and I buried her in her father's tomb as she had wished.

When Donal comes he'll bring cigarettes and smoke one with me as he always does. He'll light both, his hand shaking as the match flickers between his breath and mine. He is never fully relaxed with me.

"You should come to the west," he advised me after Peggy died. "You'll know when you see Esther praying. You'll just know."

"Do we have to chatter endlessly with God to know?" I demanded. I had pleaded with that God of his to restore Peggy to me and remembered how thoroughly my pleas had been ignored. She was alive at that time, physically very well, walking the lanes and fields about our home but she was absent in a most fundamental way.

"I realise how you feel," Donal began. "I know .."

"Peggy left me seven years before she died," I interrupted. "How could someone like you possibly know anything about that kind of absence?"

He smiled at me as though I were a wayward child.

"You're angry now," he said. "But if you were to become sure of things, really sure, that anger would disappear. You'd rest easy in life - and in death."

Peggy would look in the mirror sometimes, with a red lipsticked grin on her face, and wearing that blue, broad-brimmed hat she'd worn once at a wedding. Sometimes I'd come behind her and smile sideways at the image. Sheer confusion always registered on her face, and fright at this stranger who had appeared from out of nowhere into her fractured world. I wanted to reach out and haul her back from whatever dark space it was she occupied, but her expression invariably hardened and hysteria took hold again.

"Who are you?" she'd demand. "Keep away from me. This is my house. You don't belong here."
Occasionally I tried playing music for her, but her face remained impassive and only her left foot recorded the fact that there was any rhythm there at all. And once, just once, desperation drove me to believe that I could kiss the malady away. She was in the kitchen, drawing with a crayon, when I grabbed her and kissed her hard and long. There was no response, neither sweetness nor struggle, but when I released her she staggered from the house.

"I'll fetch some water from the well," she hissed at me as she hurried away.
It was many decades since anyone needed to carry water from the old well but if it pleased her to think she was engaged in some useful task then I thought, so be it. Maybe I should have followed her, but I was too disgusted by my own raw desire to do that. A neighbour came by later and I knew by his expression that something awful had happened out

there in the arid space between my wife and me. Together we hurried to the well and I saw her lying beside it, her facing resting in the shallow brown water, her hands entwined around tall ferns — and she was dead. I latched onto one image, the ferns in her grasping hands as though she were overcome by weakness and were trying to save herself. But in the early morning hours I was snatched from sleep by the insistence of my heart that I had sent her out to her death.

Only now that I am ready to go, can I explain to Donal the conditions under which I stay. But he's a priest, and he'll resist me to the bitter end.

"Why all the impossible questions?" he once exclaimed. We were walking the lower slopes the mountain together and I'd asked about Redemption, Atonement, the idea of Jesus buying us back.

"The lilies of the fields, the mountain deer - they don't question the minutiae of their existence and they get by," he said.

"They 'get by'. You can't be serious?" I remember laughing. "You want to do more than get by," don't you? Isn't that what your church's drama is about? Your stories. Your stratagems. Your hope. Isn't that why you bought into the system?"

Donal frowned. My words had drilled right through the soft evening air and grievously wounded him.

"What's your problem?" he flared. He looked like a small, bullied little boy. This was not the time for further argument, I decided. Donal was my cousin. I had no right to try to demolish him with my own painful cynicism, or with savage words. I shrugged and smiled, a graceful loser's standard gestures, and we both walked in silence into the lavender-tinted evening.

Esther thought she had removed the terror of life by exploiting it. She claimed she saw the Virgin in a grotto from which the statue had been removed. Donal had become an enthusiastic follower of hers.

"Esther knows the truth," he told me a few months after we had buried Peggy.

"You can't be serious," I said. "Surely 'truth' is much too complete a word for anything we may know?"

On this occasion Donal was relaxed. He understood Esther. He could wait for me. "I do see what you're getting at," he said. "And you have a point. But Esther listens to Our Lady. She's been told what way the world is going. And she knows the end."

"What is that then?" I asked. I wondered how Esther could laugh and sing each day, knowing the terrible, predicted final outcome to the existence of life on earth.

Donal shrugged. "It's all in the Good Book. In the Old Testament. And the New. Hell is for sinners. Eternal life is there for those who know and love God. It's up to us."

Spring? Summer? Autumn? Winter? Which was the season in which I might best see? Which part of the year could carry me through to better things? For a while I really wanted to believe that I could believe.

"Allow yourself to listen," Donal pleaded, "just for a few short days allow yourself to listen." I'd finally agreed to 'go west' with him to see Esther in action. We arrived on a Friday evening in late May. The grotto was lit up by a tracery of blue and white lights and the erotic scent of hawthorn saturated the air. About fifty people stood with bowed heads behind an old woman who faced the grotto. She was kneeling, gazing upwards, her face creased with age, yet somehow bright and young. Donal motioned me to stand beside him at the back of the crowd. Not a sound could be heard but only the rattle of rosary beads, and the soft breathing of many tensed bodies. It was warm. No breeze stirred. Night was easing itself gently in. A spring holiday came to mind, one which Peggy and I had spent in Seville, away from everything that had hitherto marred or scarred our lives. I thought of the way she'd wrapped her arms tight around me there and declared that she didn't mind if I didn't, that we could never have our own child. I thought of her green eyes and her copper hair, and how seductively she'd danced the Flamenco. I was busy remembering these beautiful and sad things when a hushed exclamation from the assembled crowd brought me right back to the grotto. A sudden wind whispered through the trees, unsettling everything that had hitherto been absolutely still.

"She's coming',' the crowd chorused, "look at the trees."

Donal whispered in my ear. "The Blessed Virgin always moves through the trees as she comes down."

People began to sing the 'Ave Maria' and by the time the hymn was finished Esther had moved behind the grotto railings and was conversing with a 'Lady' no one else could see. Gradually the old woman's bright and smiling face altered into something far more sinister as she began to relay the messages she had received, messages of despair and doom, the imminent coming of the anti-Christ, the calamitous destruction of our world. It was obvious that Esther relished these predictions, and the crowd listened in awe as she spoke, breaking into applause when she announced that the 'Lady' had finally left.

"She levitates too," Donal confided. "She may do so soon."

"I don't want to see her levitate," I told him. "I've seen just about enough to want to leave."

He grabbed my arm. "Don't close your heart now," he urged. "Let God take hold. Look what happens here. These people have real faith, can't you see that?" His gravelly voice hovered on the edge of exasperation.

"I don't see that," I said. "Belief clings - like this madness - but surely faith lets go."

All that Esther stuff happened years ago. Donal has, of course, come again many times and we skirt around the subject like two lovers unable to declare. In the meantime I've learned to stop wanting to know how or why Peggy went away from me, why our lives had been ordered like that. Donal had a point about the lilies of the field and the mountain deer. They accept life. They accept death. Why should I look for a reasons for my suffering and not for theirs? Why should I demand explanations only for suffering if both joy and suffering are part of the whole pattern? And is not the fledgling poised for first flight and the tired bird folded over in death the same creature? Life is entire and complete in each precious instant. It is we who maim the moment by expectation — and by too much inspection. If I tell Donal that I'm now ready to die he'll say that I've become morose again. But there is no secure plan - and there really is no problem to be solved. I can watch stars as they creep into the night sky and rejoice, yet know that the pebbles on the beach or even the dust settling on my upswept floor are as mysterious as the stars. And truthfully it was Esther who taught me how to let go. It was the ugliness on her face as she reported the affliction that would befall those who were not as certain as she was — it was this sight which turned me away from the desire to be certain of anything at all.

I've fought it for years, I'll tell Donal, and I've finally won. I'll sit at the piano and play. He'll probably light some cigarettes, hand me mine before drawing at length on his while formulating a reply. I'll stop the music suddenly, just after a strong, dramatic sound, and in the silence I'll meet his eye. Later, I'll breach that silence with a smaller, more plaintive note.

I am the pause between two notes that fall, I'll say then, and sit before him, still and waiting. That's how I plan it anyway, for my own amusement, in my craziest dreams. But really such plans are senseless. There is no sure way to prepare, for anything – anything at all can happen in that trembling hesitation between two notes that fall.

———

"I am the pause between two notes that fall into a real accordance scarce at all:
for Death's note tends to dominate –
Both, though, are reconciled in the dark interval, tremblingly
And the song remains immaculate."

Rilke, The Book Hours, I

I did not notice the beginning, how the spark softly fell, how it grew in a dry place away from the clutch of the sea. Neither did I see a tiny breeze enter the scene. But it did. A furtive breeze entered in and increased the spark to a tiny flame. And that flame quickly grew, forcing its orange tongue into the early evening air. I saw the sun out over the western horizon, in partial hiding, not yet ready to go down. I saw the flames leap over the hot ground. Theirs was an evil dance. Later I saw the devils die, each one decreasing, emptied of energy. When I approached the spot there was a foul smell in the air and a black wound scorched the earth. To the north geese rose in precise formation and flew inland from the edge of the sea. I went home

My mother shivered by the sitting-room window. She was watching out. When she saw me she opened up the door and let me in. Then she carefully closed it over and went back to the cold, shivering window again.

"Dad's not home?" I asked, knowing the answer. His noise was not yet in the house nor his silence. He was still away.

"You get to bed before he comes," she said. She spoke abruptly. In my memory it is how she always spoke, that clipped, mechanical enunciation, as though she were afraid to let the language flow.

"But I've got to ...." I began, remembering all that I had planned to do.
She forestalled me. She was determined. She spoke as though I were still a child.

"I said get straight to bed."

In the morning I crept out as softly as bare feet would allow, fearing she would hear me. I did not want to see him at all. His piercing glance was more awful than himself and I was afraid of it. If my exit drew him out of hiding he would scatter me. My soul would try to love him and my mind attempt to please him but my body would not obey. I'd drop his flask. Or burn his toast. Or bring him the wrong cigarettes from the desk. It always happened like that, as if I was drawn in all directions when he was near. And I had my tongue out, childishly waiting for little titbits of praise, something to nourish me. Once, when he looked at a painting I'd entered for the school competition, he said a half-nice thing. I remember.

"That's as good as your mothers," he said, grinning. She was there too, watching him palpate the multi-coloured lumpiness of my small canvas, and listening.

"You should take a few lessons from the boy here," he added, addressing her. "You might learn something useful, dear."

"What's it called?" she asked, sidestepping him.

"It's sheep on a mountain," I said, "but I don't have a name for it yet."

"Are they sheep?" he asked, peering at it. It was how he asked that troubled me.

"You've got to stand away from it, Daddy," I urged, resenting his trespass, "you're standing too close."

"Yes," he said, laughing, addressing my mother again. "You could learn a thing or two from this lad here."

I wondered why he laughed while my mother was on the verge of tears.

But then my father was very funny. In those days I saw him make laughter everywhere. He would whisper to his friends, people in the town, men he worked with, and instantly they'd begin to smile. They would draw themselves inside the circumference of his pronouncements and he'd whisper again and again, and suddenly the circle wold explode into fragments of fun, laughter all over the place, like a sun drenched rain puddle splashed by the boot of a playful boy.

She rarely laughed. But when I was twelve and first took my place on the school soccer team I made her smile.

"Gerard," she urged me one day, "tell me something about the game."

"What's there to tell?"

"How many players, for instance?"

"On the field at any one time about eleven," I told her, "but there are lots of subs too."

"And what position do you play?" she continued.
I hesitated

"I'm not sure," I replied, for the experience was quite new to me, "but I think I'm a drawback."
Her amusement spread, ripening into a broad smile. I remember being disturbed to see the strangeness of my mother's smile.

He put her out one night. He stampeded her into the darkness. He sent her out into the raw cold with only a light dress on. She'd come home at half past ten, the sound of a car crunching in the driveway alerting him.

"Where were you?" he demanded.

"Out with Eva."

"Where?"

"At the library."

"Library," he snapped. "And what was my dear wife doing at the library until now when she might be at home with her own precious books or her precious piano or her paints?"

"I was with Eva," she said.

I could see the lump rise in her throat. She tugged and twisted the green pendant that hung clumsily around her neck.

"Go on," he taunted.

"We were just at the library."

"Reading more books, is that it?" he scoffed. "Reading books until half past ten?" He made the association between books and the library seem absurd.

"No," she said, "it was a lecture. Archaeology. A talk on the ancient monuments of this area."

He turned to me. "Now there's a sensible lie, my lad, a very sensible lie. She's claiming she's after more culture. Education and culture, mind you. Isn't that nice?"

I wished I was strong enough to be afraid only for her. And I struggled for a long time for anger like his so that I could shout. It never came.

"Now, my dear," he continued, "perhaps you could sit down here and instruct us, the ignorant." He pushed her into the fireside chair opposite him. She landed awkwardly and hurt her thumb. She winced.

"I don't know where to begin, Alan," she faltered, groping around in her mind for a healthy way forward.

"Just begin. Pick any nearby archaeological gem and begin."

"It's not that simple," she stammered.

"Simple?" The word sounded sinister on his lips.

"Are we too simple to grasp your high-falutin' gibberish? Is that it?"

He moved towards her. She began to rise from the chair.

"It's just that the terminology is new to me," she explained as she moved towards the door. He smiled. He seemed to understand.

"Complicated?" He stood in front of her.

"Yes," she said, "that's it. It's a bit complicated at first."

"I assure you," he said evenly, "that we'll make every effort to fathom it." He pushed her into the chair again and imprisoned her there with his long arms and his huge hands.

"I want to go to bed now, Alan. I'm tired." She struggled sideways and quickly slipped under and out of his arms.

"Open the door for your poor mother," he ordered me.

I ran in front of her and pushed open the bedroom door.

"Not that door," he said calmly, "the other door."

I hesitated.

"I said the other door."

Slowly I moved away from the bedroom and along the corridor towards the front door. I opened it. I saw him pull her by the hair. She made a grab for a coat on the hall stand but he intervened.

"You're a stuck-up bitch," he said, deliberately enunciating each word clearly. "You bloody stuck-up bitch, you can get out now. Out now and stay out." He pushed her away from him then and she tripped on the steps and fell. Inside again he bolted the door. That was thee years ago. She was ill for a while. But she got better, so well, in fact, that she never cried again.

In the hospital they questioned her.
  "Why are you angry?"
  "Do you always cry?"
  "Are you anxious?"
  "Do you love your son more than your husband?"
  "Does it satisfy you to have him beat you?"
  "Do you think you are neglected?"
  "Do you like drama?"
  "Do you like to be in the centre of a fuss?"
She wrote all the questions down, the spoken and the unspoken. I know. She showed me. She showed me her old diary. There were no observations recorded, no descriptions of events, no emotions expressed, no longings catalogued, no ambitions, no answers at all, just the interminable questions.

I was sixteen then. They finally cured my mother when I was sixteen. She came home from the hospital with a smile stamped on her face. She was well. Very well. They had cured her of her desires. They had applied salve to her soul. They had disguised her confusion and she was well. The books disappeared. She sold them. One day I arrived home from school to the shock of several empty bookcases.
  "Where are they gone?" I asked, understanding a little but not a lot.
  "To a bookshop in Dublin," she said flatly.
  "But why? Why all your books?" I could countenance the loss of some but not the entire collection. After all, she might be bored with some of them. She might want to move on. But a few hundred books?

"Never mind," she told me, "never mind. It's better that way."

The piano was sold to a scrap dealer. She dismissed its loss with the emphatic statement that it was riddled with woodworm. We were better without it, she said. And soon afterwards the canvas collection and the oils went too. She flung them on top of the rubbish heap at the far corner of our one acre garden. I retrieved a few tubes of paint before they were covered over with more debris. I have them still.

My mother saw the fire last spring. Shivering there by her cold window she saw the flames leap along the edge of the cliff. She betrayed no emotion. She said nothing. I suppose the fire did not offend her. But I went back there next day. The ground was cold. I laid the palms of my hands out over the scorched earth and it was cold as ice. I saw a black beetle track across its ugliness, finally entering the jungle of weeds and grass at the edges where the fire had only partially flamed.

I painted last spring's fire as it flushed the edge of the cliff. It is a large canvas. I used her oils. Soon I'll go again to the same spot and make a new painting. It's covered over now with fine, lush, long grass. It seems that the spot is cured. It looks well. If I stand some distance away not a trace of the wound can be seen. The place fits in with the surrounding land-scape. But recently I dug into the earth with my heels and could still see the blackness of that awful day. Under the excellence of the new pale green grass is the evidence. The scar is there. I'll paint that too. I'll use a flashback technique. I'll show all. With my brushes I'll show exactly how the grass grew.

When I'd finished speaking, my father turned away from me.

"Just as well your mother's gone to her rest," he said softly, as though to himself. The muscles of his back and shoulders quivered under his light cotton shirt. I knew he was struggling, holding back the tears. I longed to comfort him but there was no comfort at all to be found between us in that cramped house.

"I'll go then," I said, moving slowly towards the door.

"Go," he told me, his voice painfully edged with grievance, "please go."

As I walked away I was still certain of my father's love. But at that moment I did not need so much to be loved as to be understood. I needed him to see how hollow my life was, how empty the 'success' lauded by many. I had earned a reputation for great efficiency, but that was slipping away from me. I forgot appointments, avoided meetings, left my mail unanswered. It hardly seemed to matter any more. It is easy to be efficient when you are single-minded, I told myself, when you desire only one thing. That was no longer the case.

There was an hour to fill before I began my journey back to the city. I walked the beach. I picked a flat stone from the sand and saw in it the outline of Sadie's face. Strange, I thought, how we search for the human even in the most inanimate things. I knew I could not eradicate my feelings by telling myself that I should not have them, though this 'solution' to my dilemma had been offered on several occasions. No matter which way I looked at it I saw that my lifestyle, far from offering glorious freedom, set unacceptable limits to who and what I might be. I ached for the company of people who did not see me only at a distance – for people who could see me right down low – on the ground – for people who could see me as I really am. A glance out to sea brought the surprise of seals swimming a few dozen yards from where I walked. As a boy I used to watch them haul out onto the rocks and bask in the summer sun. The world seemed an orderly place in those days, season predictably following season, school work to be done, goals to be achieved.

"This landscape, this town, this family is the frame of your life," my mother used to say to me, "but what you put into it is up to you."
I made my decision early, and up to about three years ago had not looked back.

The train throbbed with life. Shankill, Dun Laoghaire, Blackrock, right into Westland Row I was surrounded by the everyday and the mundane. Old men and women travelling to visit their friends. Housewives shopping. Children coming from the seaside. Teenagers talking tough. Sometimes the young people would catch me watching them and they'd blush, or they'd light cigarettes and allow the smoke to curl into my face before stubbing them out. When they looked at me I suppose they saw a despised authority and not a man longing to be ordinary – like them. I was already growing weary of piety, holiness, call it what you will, when fate stepped in. It seemed to me that the word 'holy' imposed a despotic hierarchy on everything, that we were forced to measure effort, meaning, learning, all sorts of things, by that unnatural yardstick. 'Blessed are the meek', the New Testament taught – but is aggression always wrong? And is passion invariably a sin and not perhaps occasionally a strength? I argued endlessly with myself until I could no longer rest. I swallowed tablets to invite sleep and staggered to the altar in the morning, drowsy and dull. When I led the people in the recital of the creed I was more conscious than ever that belief was a very special mixture of knowing and not knowing. But when I tried to pray - I mean real prayer, dogged, savage howling out at God for assistance - echoes alone answered me. I attempted to follow in His footsteps, and they became smudged or simply disappeared. I leaned on Him for support and found that I was leaning on a filigree of dust and air.

I would have stood at that cross-roads for a long time if Sadie had not come striding in. 'Trespassed' is the correct word really. She was a gate-crasher a trespasser onto the defended territory of my heart. On the first occasion I'd been roped into chairing a Parent/Teacher meeting because a colleague was ill. A dispute arose between several persons as to whether or not a teacher should ever hug a child. The consensus seemed to be that it was no longer safe to do so. But then this woman, five foot five-ish, flaxen-haired, about thirty five, stood up.

"Do you know what a hug is?" she demanded. 'Have you any idea at all? A hug is a protection against the awful ravages of the world. All the tigers are out there scratching but they can't come in. That's what a hug is. It's keeping the tigers at bay." There was a titter of amusement among the crowd. I called the meeting to order as the woman sat down.

Later she touched my arm as the others were filing out.

"I suppose you think that what I said is nonsense?" she asked.

"Oh no," I stammered, "not at all."

"I know what it is like not to be hugged," she said. "My husband died five years ago. He was a young man. We were a lively couple. But it is the hugs I miss most. The feeling of being cared for, defended. The feeling that his arms around me kept out the badness of the world."

Before I could reply she walked away. I wished I'd had the opportunity to tell her I understood the deprivation she described.

Afterwards I frequently thought about her and wondered if she'd ever brave a P.T.A. meeting again, and if I'd be fortunate enough to be facilitating it. I speculated about her young dead husband. How great a thing it must have been to love someone so much that the whole of life was coloured by that love. She'd never love like that again, I thought, and was immediately overtaken by a jealousy that shocked me to the core. I cared. I cared for – about a woman I hardly knew. I was, perhaps, in love for the very first time.

These early details were dissected by my superiors when I spoke to them. The Parish Priest – and later the Parish Priest and the Bishop together - pointed out that the woman was lonely and vulnerable. They insisted that I was drawn to her loneliness. It was difficult for them to appreciate the delight I experienced when I was with her, how nourished we both were by our emerging love. I tried to explain that I could no longer accept that holiness had to be achieved by the subtraction of such a natural part of life. I spoke of the puritan streak in Catholicism that asked us to admire women, put them on safe pedestals while forbidding us to love them. The Parish Priest shuffled from one foot to the another before offering me a brandy. The Bishop frowned, advised me to 'consider' the situation and to come back to him in three months. At the second meeting he acted as though my friendship with Sadie was over. He was willing to overlook my 'indiscretion', he said, and to assign me to the post of Diocesan Administrator. He knew this was the type of work I had looked forward to for several years.

My father used less bravado at our meeting. I'd written a short note forewarning him, but he seemed defeated almost as soon as he opened the front door. In deference to his feelings about what was proper I always wore my black suit and my collar when I visited him. I did this on that last visit home and instantly regretted it. It became apparent quite rapidly that in his eyes I no longer had the right to wear those 'sacred' garments. I had lain with a woman. I had soiled my special life.

"Dad, she'd love to meet you," I pleaded.
He spat into the sink.
"You'd like her," I told him. "She's spirited. Afraid sometimes but aware that she's afraid. In tune with life."
He grunted.
"Dad, I'd be a priest and a husband if they'd let me," I explained, "do you understand that?"
"Have your cake and eat it," he said savagely. "I know."

"Won't you at least let us come and visit you when the baby is born?" I asked.

"That child," he said steadily, "will be no grand-child of mine."

The walk by the sea cleared my head. I was confident that there would be no going back. When she'd first told me of the baby I was dismayed, the enormity of what I'd done finally brought home to me. But in the context of a world full of people living and attempting to love my sin seemed small indeed. Sadie drew back a little after I'd proposed. I knew she was afraid that I would be mortally unhappy without my work and would regret my decision. I tried to convince her that, although I'd miss the priesthood, is was a price I was more than willing to pay.

"We could leave Ireland," she said then, though it was obvious this was an option she did not care to face.

"No, we'll stay. I'll get work. I know I will."

About a week after my visit to my father I moved in with Sadie. I started job hunting and got work within a month. It was my experience in administra-tion that did the trick. We ate breakfast each day before I left home, and strange as it may seem, this was one of the most beautiful experiences for me. Company in the morning was an absolute counter-point to the empty presbytery kitchen. Sometimes Sadie worked late and I was there when the little boy came home from school. Later she and I would cook dinner together and sit eating before the telly. For me there was a sense of drama to it all – almost as though I did not trust the reality of this new life – as though I might wake up one morning and discover that Sadie had been turned into a Wicked Witch – or worse still, disappeared. But we'd find each other after even the hardest of days – as on the day, only seven months after my visit home, that the phone call came through from my ex-Parish Priest telling that my father had been found dead in his bed. Sadie stood back while I thanked the priest for his condolences. Her arms were tight around me as I sobbed. And when the weeping eased off she was still there, hugging me, keeping the tigers at bay.

ELECTRIC STORM

It was lovely, fire all gobbledy up the sea, like it was hungry, like it was starving, like me. I couldn't pull away from its tongue. It shot down from the sky and into the water, long, yellow, slinky tongue licking the sea. I said come taste me, me, me. I taste nice, like ice cream, flavour of strawberry.

It's quiet now. Everything is full of sky and sea. Blackness. Blackness everywhere. I see nothings all around me. And I smell salt. Sea salt. Taste. I open my mouth. Lick the salt from the air. Smell all the oceans in every place with one nose like it's my nose, like I can smell secrets and whatever and they don't know. Nothing. They know nothing. Books. And pictures. Pictures moving in the corner of the room. In my room more pictures. Big moving pictures. Put me in my room and say "there, you can watch your own TV. Now, dear."

  "Robbie! What did you do that for? Why did you put the Tele under the bed?"
Laugh. No why like they know why.
  "Tony. Come here. Robbie has broken the plug. Tony!"
Woman who sometimes kisses me is cross now. Eyes hit me across the face. I'm screaming. No, it's not me, it's the no place inside of me that screams. I don't like it when she hits me. It takes away my own pictures. It makes me head a no place.
  "Give him a cup of cocoa, Florence. It'll calm him. He'll soon get himself off to sleep. Hurry up now."
Man who tried to make another him looks at me. Looks like he almost knows I've got my own

pictures, big pictures, not like pictures in the box but mine. Call him back. Sit down and I'll show you, only you, just you, sit down, don't go, sit down where I can show — you.

"Florence. Florence. He's getting agitated. Is his drink ready yet?"
Woman gives him drink to give to me but I've got pictures, real pictures not like pictures I throw under my bed.

"Drink that up son. You're tired. You need to rest now."

Black on the top of the sea goes away 'cos the tongue slides down again from the sky. Ears move. Ears hear the long hiss of that snake in the grass. Long grass. Rabbit in the long grass. See him in the long, yellow grass? I do, when the snake bites into the ground and that "I'm not here at all' look is in the rabbit's eyes. Go away, away, away and leave me alone. He says you here beside me but you no use at all. He says go away, I want to hide. I sing. Song for the rabbit so it won't be afraid and hiding. Come to me soft, moving thing so that I can hold you close, your noise thumping beside mine, thump, thump, thump, thumping together, thump. Close eyes and open all else and the noise he makes is near, and small, like a feather brushing against another feather. I feel something on my face, no, not slap like hers but a little fluff of air and it covers me with a new song and l sing.

"Robbie? Where are you? Are you down there?"
"It's pitch dark down there. What on earth took him out in a storm like this? Oh God, where will this all end?"

Fire rides across the sky to another place. Sea still sizzling. Rain comes. I eat it. Rain tastes good. Rabbit sleeping now and I put on the night like it's my new coat. And I go in to the wet place. Little, wet place especially for me. Lie there and the pictures will come back. Wall is sticky. Fingers slip along the sticky. Floor is sticky. I pull a piece of the sticky and it comes away. Sneaks up my nose. Smells all sea, like it crawled up from the bottom of the ocean. Rabbit is awake. He smiles at me. He doesn't like the sticky and he wants to go away. I blow a little wind over his fur and he goes – away. Down I lie, like it's my bed, only stones are big and full of sticky. I stay still and sea-swish makes music, and the new music dances in and out of my ear and I want to sing my song too.

"Down here, Florence, bring your torch down here."

Stab in the eyes. Light comes. The sticky is green now that I see.

"He's here. He's huddled up in here."

Arms and hands of the man lift me away. Go with him now but no pictures in a box. Put them under the bed.

"Is he alright, Tony? Is he all right?"

"Stay calm, Florence, he's fine. He's just become a bit excited by the storm."

"Excited? Is that what you call it? Excited."

Her voice crying and I'm sore inside. Touch the cry. But she'll push me away. Touch. Do it like the sea only small and you can taste the cry.

"Did you see that, Tony? He kissed me. He's kissed my face. He understands – something – he understands, Tony."

Big whistle noise all over and him and me and her

face and her everywhere.

"Tony. He's said something. He's spoken."

The midwife claimed it was one of nature's most capricious tricks, the way my brother and I came into the world. She said that years later, I learned, when it was obvious how badly nature had behaved. In the beginning there was only delight, and a mixture of awe and anticipation lodged in my mother's heart. Two babies together after years of childlessness, two small bald boys. They called me Tom and he was John. I was the firstborn, the one who blazed a trail from warmth to the cold outside - or the one who was pushed into this icy world by the other - whichever version you favour shall be yours. I have my own truth. I know that I had, even then, made the decision. But it was John who was first to school.   In fact he had a head start of two years. The initial intention was to send us both together but the trauma of my first day hurled me tearfully back into my mother's arms.

"Come along now, children," I remember the teacher urging when several small boys hung back in the yard, "and we'll make a start."
John and I held hands and faced the classroom together.

"How old are you John Quirke?" she asked as soon as we were all sitting in our seats. She knew our ages, I thought, because this information was written with a black-inked pen in the old roll book on her desk. But still she asked the same question of each boy.

"Four and three quarters, Miss," John answered confidently.

"And your brother?   Tom, how old are you?"

"Four and three quarters, Miss."

"I didn't hear that," the teacher said, "stand up so that I can see you and please speak up."

"I am standing, Miss," I told her, straining on tippy toes so that she could see. Laughter rippled through the classroom as I spoke. "And I'm four and three quarters, Miss, same as John," I added, close to tears. Nobody had ever laughed at me like that before. My mother told me years later that afterwards she spent many days kissing the dismay away from me.

I 'started school' again two years later. A man with a long face and horn-rimmed glasses took me by the hand and led me in. A diffuse whisper faded to utter silence as we two stood together framed in the classroom doorway.

"Tom Quirke here is nearly seven," the man announced, eyeing the assembly for signs of mischief or insubordination. "Due to an unfortunate set of circumstances he is only now beginning his school career. I have been assured from many quarters that this is a very bright boy and I intend to place him in the First Form."

John's winked at me as I caught his eye. Nobody seemed to notice.

"Go and sit over there," the man told me, indicating a seat by the window, "and keep your eyes and your ears open to everything I say and do - I repeat, to everything I say and do."

Mr. Hutton called me aside at the end of my first month. "How goes it, boy?" he asked.

I told him it went well. Nobody, you see, had laughed at me.

"Do you like school?"

"Yes."

"Why?"

"I don't know," I shrugged, knowing, but not knowing how to say that it enlarged me.

"Tomeen," he enquired then, "would you like to try some extra lessons?"

He held out the invitation like a precious gift. I saw it glitter in the evening sun, a prism scattering colour and light in all directions. My tongue bent itself in two and I was unable to utter an adequate reply.

"You can go home now," he said, spotting my struggle, "and if you wish we'll begin next Wednesday ten minutes after the others leave for home. Later on, if it goes well we'll see what else can be done."

I remember the day I began my supplementary lessons with Mr. Hutton. It was the same day my brother stopped carrying me on his shoulders across the stream near our home. We were with a crowd of other boys and it was time to wade through at a spot where the brown water rushed headlong over many stones. Because I was much smaller John usually allowed me to ride on his back and my feet never got wet. On that day however, he waded in alone and when I called out after him he stopped in mid stream and frowned at me.

"Surely teacher's pet can manage on his own from now on?" he said, as much for the others' benefit as for mine. He ran ahead with them and I had to struggle alone with the slime and moss and the strength of the water as it hurried to the sea.

I was nearly ten before I began to question the logic of my life. By that time John had grown tall while I remained fastened to the earth. Indeed, children born years after me outgrew me one by one, and the little ones played with and around me for a while until they discovered I was different, and those of my own age abandoned me for exploits and adventures they believed beyond me. Among strangers too I would find eyes briefly fixed on me and instantly averted. At such times I longed to hide from scrutiny but concluded that no safe place existed. It was Mr. Hutton who attempted to make the world mine. I remember my introduction to William Blake. He asked me to sit still and listen, and as I did a jungle emerged before me and from the words he uttered the large and splendid shape of a wild animal shimmered in the trees. I did not fully understand the 'Tiger' poem of course, but the clear memory of my teacher's reverence for words remains with me. He handled language in a way no other person did, not even the minister at church who also appeared to be dazzled by drama and story, legend and song.

The silences between us also nourished me. Sometimes, during my tuition time, Mr. Hutton would leave the classroom abruptly and I would follow, to the woods, or along the shore, or we might accompany the River Cuala for a mile or so as it twisted towards the sea. Occasionally he'd step out from his silence long enough to make a remark or to explain something that was puzzling me.

"Tomeen, would you go over to that ditch and pull a buttercup for me," he instructed one day.
I did as I was told, but I was unable to resist the comment that it was far more beautiful rooted among its companions than in Mr. Hutton's hand.

"We'll put it down here," he said, ignoring my criticism, "and I'll slice it through and we'll see what's there."

With delicate precision Mr. Hutton cut through the bloom with a sharp penknife and magically the details emerged, the structure of the stalk, of sepals, petals, carpels, ovary, all the many small and hidden pieces of the flower revealed to me. We did the same with daisies and dandelions and with many other wild and flowering things. This one is pollinated by the wind, he'd say, and this one is designed to attract insects and is pollinated by the bees.

"I've sacrificed a few flowers," he said to me one day, "so that you can better understand all the flowers you love. You see that, don't you?"

I did not, of course, not for a long time. Nor did I see the necessary connection between understanding and love.

They say that everyone ultimately loses their innocence and I lost mine the day I spotted my brother stealing from my mother's purse. She was working in the garden, planting lettuces and cabbages, when he pulled her handbag from the kitchen press, spread the contents of the purse on the table and selected a five pound note which he pocketed before putting everything back in order again. When he turned to leave he saw me standing at the door.

"You don't go running with tales to mother," he said, startled, "just because she's all over you all the time."

I did not reply.

"Do you hear me, titch?" he demanded, "don't you go telling tales."

There was little I could say. His theft immediately

become an insignificant thing compared to the harsh way he had confronted me. In an instant the distance between us radically increased and the small five-letter word he had used bored into my heart.

John died when we were fourteen. On a mid August morning we sat side by side with our parents in church, the sun streaming through stained glass trapping wayward pieces of the cosmos in its light, the other children impatiently waiting for the final closing hymn. John was quiet and withdrawn. We had grown apart, he and I, both conscious of the enormous divide between us. Occasionally we would reach out to each other, hoping again for the closeness of the cradle or the womb, but the effort of doing so seemed to accentuate the tension between us. My father had great hopes for John and fed him with extravagant ideas of what might happen when he 'grew up', and how his 'career' might develop. He had no plans at all for me. But on the Friday after that sun-sprinkled Sunday morning John was in church again, and he was coffined and still. We were not certain how he died - the doctors speculated about an undetected heart defect which he might have had since birth - but they also suspected that he harboured a rare viral infection. During the service my father mounted the pulpit and read one of the lessons while my mother sobbed. I had an idea I'd like to place a little bouquet of wild flowers - like the ones Mr. Hutton and I often saw when we walked in the countryside - on top of his coffin. Before the pallbearers took up their positions I left my seat, flowers in my hand. It was only when I stood beside the coffin, which rested on a trestle in the centre of the aisle, that I realised that it was far too high and I had to carry them back with me to the pew. From behind a marble pillar I saw the midwife scrutinise me, her eyes tired and bloodshot under a grey/brown hat. Later, in the churchyard, I stood within earshot as she gossiped with the woman who had taken over her duties since she had retired.

"That's a cruel trick Mother Nature played," she whispered.

The other agreed, her rich auburn hair bouncing about with every movement of her nodding head.

"Fancy now, preparing those two in the womb like that, the one getting all the growth only to die on the threshold of manhood and the other barely three feet tall."

The companion nodded with even greater vigour.

"Do you suppose," she asked, "that wee Tom'll grow any more?"

"I hardly think he'll grow more than another inch," the old midwife said, "perhaps not even that much at all."

Mr. Hutton remained my special teacher. He came to me with renewed effort after John's death, as though he felt it his duty to restore the balance of my world. When I was fifteen he offered me an Emily Dickinson poem, I'm not sure why, but perhaps it was to inform, or maybe even to challenge me.

Apparently with no surprise
To any happy flower,
The frost beheads it at its play
In accidental power.

The blond assassin passes on,
The sun proceeds unmoved

To measure off another day
For an approving God.

Very nice, I thought, but my brother had been
snatched away before I had a chance to learn to love
him again and I could not tolerate a God who would
do a thing like that.

By the time I was seventeen Mr. Hutton and I had
covered an immense territory together, history, art,
geography, literature, three languages, mathematics
and the sciences.

"What's a recessive gene?" I asked one day,
surprising him. I'd charged ahead in my biology
studies and had come across something crucial.

"You want to do genetics?" he enquired.

"Yes, I do."

"Now?"

"Now is the best time, I think. I've got to understand my life, Mr. Hutton. I've got to make sense of
it. I've got to know."

We soon began 'my genetics'. And in that world the
phrase that rang out most repeatedly was the one
"dominant mutation".

"You understand what that is?" Mr. Hutton
asked.

I said I did.

"Science doesn't tell the complete truth," Mr
Hutton told me. "It's just one way of examining the
world. It's useful. But you've also got to learn to
look with the heart."

I dismissed his advice as a nonsense.

Strange then, but in the weeks that followed

messages came to me in several dreams which told the same story over and over. I had grown wings. I rose effortlessly into the sky, gliding over mountains, hovering over lakes, coasting along the edges of the sea, gazing into the hearts of cities, spotting the secret pulsating energy in the buried centre of the earth. At first I battled with the wings that would enlarge me. Stupid, I told myself, to attempt to discover what dreams might have to say. They were of the same fabric as fairy tales, tantalising, but unable to deliver anything real.

"You're very distant these days, Thomas," said Mr. Hutton. He'd taken to calling me 'Thomas' since I'd turned seventeen.

"I - I've got a lot on my mind, Sir."

"Such as?"

"You'll think it silly."

"No. No, I won't."

"Mr. Hutton, I've had dreams - no, just one dream really - for several weeks now, and in it I'm a bird making many journeys and marvellously free."

"Hmmmn."

"The dream won't go away," I complained.

"Why should it," he responded, "when it's not yet achieved a result."

This remark focussed me. I was accustomed to regarding dreams as anarchic fantasies which ought to be scrubbed clean away with the light of day. And here he was, my special teacher since I was seven years old, hinting that I was obliged to make my dream come true.

The winter of my nineteenth year spread, sly and gleaming, across the countryside. It tightened its grip. The dream went away. As soon as I began to imagine my greatness it disappeared, leaving behind an afterglow, a vague exuberance squatting in my soul. On the day I left for college I said my 'good-byes' to my parents at our home and it Mr. Hutton who drove me to the railway station.

"You'll probably forget your old teacher," he said as soon as I'd collected my ticket.

"Sir, I won't ever."

A barely perceptible smile crept slowly across his face. "You'll do brilliantly in science," he said then in a matter-of-fact way, "but always remember to feed the spirit." He stuffed a volume of poems into my hand.

"Do you really believe what that dream of mine said?" I asked. He was standing on the platform and the train was about to leave.

"You can't run away from who you really are," he replied. "There was a time when it seemed you would accept the world's estimate of you - 'poor little Tomeen Quirke' - but I'm confident that time has passed." He pushed me quickly from him and into the nearest carriage. In less than five minutes I was kneeling on my seat and watching him dissolve into the grey distance. For the first time in my life I was going somewhere alone.

The college was old, a collection of granite and lime-stone buildings built at various times during the eighteenth and nineteenth centuries around an oval area of open ground. A small stream wandered through this park, flanked by woodland to one side and scutch grass and gorse to the other. The water was home to a few otters, the occasional pair of swans and many ducks. In the northwest, beside the main entrance gate, was the science block and it, together with the library and C-Block, where I had a room, became my home. I wrote home, of course, long wandering letters to my parents, giving details of my routine at college, of my various activities and of the friends I had made, shorter, factual ones to Mr. Hutton. I'd tell him how my studies were progressing and he'd write back after a few weeks wanting to know more. I'd share the delight of discovery with him just as he had done with me. He was retired now, and reading even more than he had done when he was tutoring me. I'd like to have studied Astro Physics myself, he confided in one letter. But it would have taken too long. My parents didn't have the money. And in those days it was hard to see where it might lead. My mother's letters were always bright and cheery, but with a layer of desolation below the surface. I know that she, and even more so my father, thought that John should have been at college too, studying to be a lawyer or a doctor. He should have been there ahead of me - or at least by my side.

I had been at college for three years when the fire began in a back section of one of the dormitories. By the time I woke up smoke billowed from many windows and a jagged cacophony of voices spread around in exited and nervous anticipation. Sirens screamed out in the distance.

"It's the Ferguson dorm," a fellow beside me said, "for first years and foreign exchange students."

"Oh God. Are they still in there?"

"Seems so."

I moved a little closer to where the fire was and through the smoke I saw some of the college staff try to release a side door. It was jammed or locked from the inside.

"If we could get that door open we could direct them down from the back stairs." someone said.

"Get them down anyway."

"They won't come unless they can see a way out."

"But there's no way in from here. How can we open the door? We can't get it open if it's locked from the inside?"

"There's a toilet window open over there," one man pointed out.

"Too small," his companion said, "only a child would get through there. And it's dangerous. There's a burning beam directly overhead."

I measured the size of the window against my body, conscious for the first time of its advantages. A rush of acid spread from my diaphragm into my throat and my heart thumped in my chest. In a second I climbed the four or five feet upward towards the window. There was a surprised "aahh" from the crowd around me, but the sound dimmed as I disappeared inside and jumped to the ground. The fire raced somewhere above me and thick smoke seeped inside my chest as I left the toilet block and searched for the door. Others obviously relayed my progress to the staff for, within seconds, I heard the megaphoned voice of an official advising the students to come down to the side door in an orderly fashion, one by one. I discovered the huge bolt and pulled it back into a cavity in the wall just as the students appeared, a large, howling mass, which quickly trampled me. A heel kicked my head and a foot stamped my face and when I tried to call out no sound came. There was searing pain and then silence as white wings lifted me and lashed me against the full and brutal force of a winter storm.

I'd like to tell Mr. Hutton what I saw then. Someday, perhaps I will. He came to the hospital soon after the accident and stood at the side of my bed. I knew he was weeping. I longed to reach out and touch him, but I was powerless to do so. It seemed that my body was encased in iron. There was no movement but the beating of white wings dipping downward towards the earth.

A WINDOW FACING NORTH

Oh Mary, don't you weep, don't you weep,
Oh Mary, don't you weep, don't you weep,
Oh Mary, don't you weep, don't you weep,
Pharaohs' army is drown-ded.

It's her song and I sing for her alone - or so I tell myself each time that jaunty tune wanders into my head. My once-weeping Mary should no longer weep. If she were here now, a toddler on her father's knee, I'd neutralize all those regrettable tears. I'd scrub everything clean so that my darling Mary would no longer be hurt by the way the world was. We'd talk. We'd say what we thought of each other and of her mother and of how things were all those years ago - and why everything was shaped like that.

Mary went away when she was eighteen. I didn't want her to go, of course, but instead of gently nudging my way into her soul in order to uncover her reasons, I exploded.

"It makes no difference Father," she said calmly, after I'd barely stemmed the tide of angry words which I'd unleashed about her, 'I'm going anyway."

"You know we had plans for you here," I said then. "We've money saved to give you a good start."

"You have?" she shot back at me.

"Yes," I continued, "we've been putting it by for quite a while now — ever since John went off to Hamburg, in fact." John was our youngest but one and he had left when Mary was eleven and he was twenty-two. He'd been home once since.

Mary stared at me silently.

"As you can imagine," I continued, "it's grown into quite a tidy sum now. With only you left it was easy to put by. You can be anything you wish, Mary. The money's there."

"I'll go," she said simply. "I'll go. She doesn't want me here."

Next morning, when the trees were hardly awake, Mary left. She wanted to do the driving. I sat beside her in the front and her mother, awkward and tightlipped, sat behind us, surrounded by packages, bags, suitcases and things. I had to shout at Mary to slow down when she'd rushed through three consecutive sets of red lights.

"It's dangerous," I told her.

"It's not dangerous at five in the morning" she asserted. "Nothing is dangerous at five in the morning." Again there was raw ice in the voice, a hard, dead silvery surface like cold steel. The boat left at half past six. Sheila and I had nothing at all to say to each other on the return journey. Long ago we had learned not to trespass on each other's thoughts.

It's a whole year now since Sheila died, and only lately have I begun to tackle the clutter about the place. My eldest children came home for the funeral but neither John nor Mary made it. John was away at sea and wrote me a long letter saying how sorry he was, how it might be for the best anyway and how he would get to see me real soon. Mary did not respond to the many urgent messages I had sent her.

Two weeks ago I had a dream. It was warm. Detail soon fled but the sensation it offered was of exquisite music filtering through my spirit, bubbling, caressing me from head to toe. Nothing lasts, of course, and an urgent waking clipped the dream in two and the hot, pulsing umbilical to the unconscious was immediately severed. Straightaway I drank hot chocolate and hurried back in search of the dream again. I wandered into a few wrong houses along the way but when I came to the place of special warmth I recognized it instantly. Trouble was Mary strode into that place and chilled me to the bone. In the dream her mother had given her a birthday present of perfume but it was not to Mary's taste.

"Wouldn't you use it at all?" her mother asked.

"It would have to be for a very special occasion,"our daughter replied, "like my funeral or something."

I emerged, cold and shivering, from that sought-after second episode.

That was the day I began to clear out Sheila's things. Mrs. Adwin next door had called several times and offered to do the job for me.

"It's often difficult," she told me in her shrill, high-pitched Lancashire accent, "for a man to do such things. Needs a woman's touch, it does, especially when it's a woman as has passed over."

I was able to evade that offer by promising that she could deliver Sheila's best 'things' to the Oxfam shop as soon as I had done the initial sorting out. And it was because of that rash promise that I began the task next day.

I woke early. I had to trust the day not to deceive me. Even without love there is grief and pain. I'd allow those two wander where they will. To give them voice was an effective way to dispel the demons. That's what I'd do, I told myself. I'd get on with it. Sheila's clothes, shoes and mementos were gathered into several heavy-duty plastic sacks so that when Mrs. Adwin called I was able to fill up the boot of her car.

"Sorry Jim," she said as she was leaving. "But it's best over and done with. You'll feel much better now."

I'll never fully understand what prompted me to do Mary's room as soon as I'd finished Sheilas' but I could no longer stay away. Truthfully I must admit that I'd never liked her room. She chose it herself when she was nine or ten and loved the forest sloping away across several acres, and the birds in spring, she said, and all the pretty colours of the trees and the shapes of their long fingers in winter. It was a room facing north and though it was decorated in several shades of pinks and amber I always considered it a dismal place. The heavy wooden shutters, which Sheila routinely closed over before the child went to bed, made it even darker and colder. I'd tried to tempt Mary away.

"Move to the front of the house," I urged. "It's much warmer. And you can see the town and the railway from there."
She shrugged.

"I'll put in new matching curtains and carpet," I continued. "I was thinking of doing that anyway."

"No thanks, Daddy," she decided quietly, "I like my own room best."
There was no further discussion. She occupied that room until she left for London at 5.am. on a summer morning when she was barely eighteen years old.

There was no disorder at all in my youngest daughter's bedroom. Blankets and sheets were folded in neat piles and stored away in a wall closet. No clothes hung in the wardrobes, no rejected garment, no school beret. Nothing at all remained to indicate how large a space she had occupied in our hearts while she had lived here. Mary came late into our lives, of course, and that was a shock. Sheila was ill at first and was often exhausted and nervy, but I believed she finally grew to accept this new little person and was as committed to loving her as much as I did. My wife was reserved, and did not find her way easily into other people's hearts. But I was sure she had been won over entirely by our Mary.

"Come and see her dance," I said proudly one day.

"No."

"Ah Sheila, would you leave that for a moment and come and see our daughter dance."

Sheila was polishing the fine-grained wood of our sitting-room floor. When I invited her to creep out with me and to spy on our little daughter as she danced and performed for her friends my wife became more vigorously occupied than ever. Her apathy and downright indifference to Mary hurt and puzzled me. But I continued to convince myself that the child was doubly loved.

The phone shrilled in the kitchen. I'd forgotten to switch it upstairs to my study and I lost the call in the time it took me to reach the receiver. I always hoped it would be Mary on the line. You see, after all those years of tears there had been the silence. And after the silence the departure. And then nothing - nothing at all.

The wooden shutters in Mary's bedroom half covered the glass. I decided to fold back the shutters so as to let in more light. The right hand shutter folded away easily. The other one was quite stiff and I struggled with it for quite a while. When it finally yielded I spotted something hidden at the back of the recess. I pulled out a jotter with Mary's name written in an unformed hand on the cover. I opened the jotter and read a few details.

Mary was nine. It was her birthday. On that occasion she two-wheeled on a bicycle for the first time. Another day the teacher praised her for her recitation of a favourite poem. And there was the time the cat died. She was devastated. She was eleven. Other tiny details were recorded, not systematically but sporadically, whenever Mary was sufficiently moved or excited about something new. A blackbird's eggs hatched in her secret hide-away place in the woods. Something about that girl, Emer, who was her friend until she said something about Mary's daddy. What's that? About Mary's daddy? About me? Within a week of the entry on Emer's remark the jotter received one final confidence and was then stored away so carefully that no one, not even the child who spoke her thoughts through it, would read it again - until it lay before me now.

I asked my Mammy if my Daddy was not my real Daddy, it read. She said to stop talking nonsense and to go out and play. I told her what Emer had said. Emer said that definitely my Daddy was not my real Daddy - that my Mummy knew – that someone else was my real Daddy and he had gone far away. My Mammy was very cross, she screamed at me. She said to get out of her sight and stay out of her sight 'cos she didn't like to have to look at me, and that I was her big mistake.

As our mothers made us, so we are, it seems. I knew now why Mary turned her heart away from the world when she was thirteen. I knew why her young soul had seized up. Two factors, two hard and extraordinary pieces of information had been hurled at her at that most crucial time. She was not her daddy's daughter and her mother could not bear to look upon her face. Strange. Strange. I should be angry now on my own behalf. My wife had taken a lover. My wife had allowed me to believe that this late and lovely child was mine, flesh of my flesh, my own blood coursing through her veins. But if this small piece of schoolwork jotter had told it as it was Mary was no more of me than the child of my neighbour a mile down the road. What a savage deceit. But it was Mary's trouble that troubled me. I now realized what was on the other side of her strange teenage silence. Truth, without grace, can be a brutal thing and the child was too young, trusting and innocent to absorb such a brutality. It was left to me now, standing in her bedroom beside a window facing north, to cry. I cried so much that ten years of dryness was washed away. I saw the wind shudder in the leaves. I watched the evening thicken into darkness. Oh Mary, don't you weep, don't you weep, I thought - oh Mary, don't you weep alone anymore.

Two days ago she rang. If I were to call it telepathy I'd break the habit of a lifetime of logical skepticism but out of the years of silence her still-girlish voice whispered down the line.

"Daddy, can I come home?"

"Come home? Come home? Of course you can come home."

I was so excited the words skated across my tongue

and fell in all directions. "Of course you can come home, Mary. You don't even have to ask."

"I thought you'd say no," she said.

"Come home. Please come home."

"I've been a long time away," she ventured.

"I know that."

"I've been far away."

There was a hint of something wretched in her voice, of another place - of a place not of the body but of the mind. I said nothing, knowing she had more to say.

"Daddy, I've done things, been with people. I've been in trouble. I've ...."

"That's all right, Mary," I said calmly, sensing there were further revelations to come before she could trust my love.

"Daddy?"

"Yes?"

"Daddy, I've got to tell you something. It's a secret. You never knew. Mother did. And I did – eventually – but you never knew."

"Then tell me Mary," I said. "What's the secret you want me know?"

The receiver trembled in my hand and my head ached, but I held my own fragment of new knowledge in check.

"Daddy, you're not my biological father," she said flatly. And before I could reply she continued. "My father was an actor. He and my mother had an affair. When she got pregnant he promised to take her away with him. But instead he ran away without her."

Pictures of the child dancing and acting for her friends filled my mind. And Sheila would not watch her youngest daughter perform. And Sheila was scared to see her daughter act. And Sheila dare not risk seeing me watch and admire and discover the talent of another man's child.

"Mary," I told her, "a few weeks ago I began to do over your old room. I've put fresh paints on the walls and I've added several hooks so that you can hang your own prints. There's a new gas fire and I've asked Mrs. Adwin to buy a duvet and matching drapes."

I could hear her weep at time other end of the line. All those tears. All those most necessary tears. My face was moist because I too was crying.

"Mary, do come home," I croaked.

"Daddy," she said eventually, "can you meet me at the airport 5.am. Friday?"

"Of course I can, child."

She came back at me, doubting the validity of my words. "It 's not too much trouble for you?"

"No. No, it's not."

"But it's very early", she insisted, "five in the morning."

"Mary," I told her, "nothing's too difficult at five in the morning. Remember that."

FLYING HOME

This is the time I like best when flying, those first tentative minutes after takeoff before the plane establishes its path, when the world is skewed and topsy-turvy, clouds and wing tips and earth and sky a crazy pattern which may be absorbed without being rationally accepted. All too soon the world settles down into the banality of unclipped safety belts, on-board bar service and three minute three course meals. So I savour the chaos now. As the gigantic wing beside me angles towards the heavens I close my eyes and allow myself to become limp. In a split second of space and time the universe has irrevocably changed.

When Shannon left - I mean when she radically, finally left - I began to think I might go home again. Previously, when we both took that step back in 1990, it was a disaster, my wife loathing the small, everydayness of life in Ireland, so much so that I lost patience and was often cross with her. But when she cried in her sleep, with homesickness, I felt sorry for her. Torn between pity and anger, I finally agreed to return to Toronto. Peace, you see, was not an option - it was a necessity.

Back in Canada once more - in the beginning - I was touched by the way she used the word 'we'. It seemed as if all her terrible whining 'I' ness had been sucked clean away between the straining skyscrapers of her native city. It was as if she accepted that the notion of her Irishness - her paternal grandmother was a Breen from County Clare - had finally been disproved. She even gave up going to the Irish Club, acknowledging at last that her adopted ethnicity did not fit. But she avoided the angry disappointment of Cinderella's big-footed sisters by encouraging me.

"It fits you," she said, "like a glove."

"It ought to fit me," I said, puzzled. "I am Irish." She laughed. "The club scene, I mean," she explained. "The Irishman abroad sort of thing." She was back in her downtown job in the Women's College Hospital, and I was working from home, receiving as many commissions as I wanted or needed. But I'd never been mad about the Irish Club, tolerating it only in so far as it allowed Shannon the latitude she reckoned she needed in order to "dig down deep into her roots". Why she thought it a place that I would naturally be drawn to remains a mystery to me.

In 1994, Shannon's sister, Keri, was married in Montreal. It was an unusual affair - a whirlwind romance and, after only four months, a full white wedding for two thirty-nine-year olds. When I voiced my misgivings, saying I thought they might have lived together for a while beforehand, Shannon huff-puffed my concerns away. It was obvious that she desperately wanted to be happy in their romance. It became increasingly apparent that she was not happy with me.

I guess she began to discover, soon after our return to Canada, that I was not the unsophisticated country boy she thought I was - that she was missing, in fact, the things she was sure she was attracted to when he both met in U.C.G. all those years ago - my "brogue" - my resolutely freckled face - and what she dubbed "the quaint, Darby O'Gillish" quality of my life.

"I just love you Irish," she said back then. "cute clowns, every one of you."

Hardly true, but I did make her laugh, you see. She assembled a daisy chain that day, sitting on the grass in Eyre Square, knitting the tiny snub-nosed flowers together and placing the green, white and gold garland around my neck. It is that time, beyond anything else, which now comes back to me, when all was sweet and dewy and innocent, as we, Paul O'Connor and Shannon Tomlinson savoured the newness of each other during our student days.

Keri and Pierre came to visit at Christmas, driving down through a storm and arriving about three hours later than expected. The four of us had dinner a few hours afterwards, our plates balanced on our knees as we sat in front of the fire, the snap and crackle of pine logs, and their perfume, easing away all the tensions of the day. I found myself wondering aloud about our lives.

"When we came back here I though you'd be jumping over the moon," I told Shannon, "but you're not jumping over the moon. As a matter of fact you've done no damn jumping at all."

I knew later that it was the wine that spoke.

"And that surprises you," she drawled, raking the ashes over, piling up some fresh fuel on the fire.

"I can't figure it out," I told her. "You wanted us to come back. Now we're back, but it isn't working."

Keri and Pierre exchanged alarmed glances, and I was suddenly annoyed that I had spoken, concerned that all the benevolence of the evening would instantly disappear. Keri rescued me.

"May we give you our gifts now?" she asked, all child-like and breathless. Before we had time to reply she ran to her suitcase and produced two, perfectly wrapped parcels.

"That's for you," she said to me. "we thought you'd like it - and this is for you." She handed Shannon her gift and kissed her lightly on the cheek.

"Go on," Pierre said. "Open them."

Shannon's was a fabulous green evening gown - "you can wear it to the St Patrick's Day Ball" Keri said - and mine was a collection of poems. For our part, we handed over the household items Keri and Pierre had hinted they would like for their new home, before retiring to bed. I believe that uncomfortable, desperate, tired hope I had still entertained that somehow Shannon and I would make a go of it died during that night. But Christmas itself has a way of making people terribly lonely. There were, however, small alleviations. We went skiing together, all four of us, and the white earth and the fresh air calmed my spirit and enlivened Shannons. I hate to use a cliche, but Keri and Pierre seemed to be blissfully happy with each other and gave the lie to the idea that the only fun love is young love. Once you discover pleasure of that sort, I thought, it's very hard ever to turn your back on it again. I hoped it would last with those two, just as, I suppose, I had once hoped it would last with Shannon and me. Even though they were older than we were, I saw Keri and Pierre as two adventurous children, carefree   and innocent in a threatening world.

Cold at the beginning of winter is very different to cold at the end of spring. By May the earth had still not thawed out and everyone ached for warm sun and green earth and blue skies. Shannon flew up north for a fortnight, and I was as glad as she was of the break. Alone in my own space I might identify the disease which was afflicting Shannon and me, find a remedy, and know at last what was possible. And, I convinced myself, I would come to rest in the possible. But Shannon cut right through my carefully cultivated hope by ringing the day before she was due back in Toronto with the news that she was not returning home at all.

"I'm going to look for work here," she said. "Keri said it shouldn't be too difficult for me."

"But you don't speak French," I blabbered, instantly recognizing the absurdity of my response. She laughed uneasily. "I have good school French. And I can learn."

"What's the matter with us?" I asked her then. She hesitated, the raw rasp of her rapidly drawn breath advancing at me down the line. "I don't know, Paul," she said, "maybe it's just me. I don't know, I've been unsettled ever since we came back from Ireland ... I just don't know."

There are times in life when you have to trust what comes into your head.

"Do you, by any chance, miss Ireland?" I asked.

"I suppose I do - a bit. In the beginning it seemed to be at the edge of things - if you know what I mean and I like - I thought I liked - living at the edge of things." She was rambling on, almost incoherent, tears evident in her voice.

"You're right in the middle of things here," I told her. "Isn't that what you decided you needed when you discovered "the edge of things" wasn't what you wanted after all?"

"Maybe. But there's something else. I'm not sure what it is but there's something else."

"What do you mean?" I demanded angrily. And I

immediately relented. "Come home, Shannon, and we'll sort it out. I know we will."

She sighed. "I'm going to hang up now," she said.

"And I'm not coming back. I'm sorry, Paul."

Once the plane settled on a steady course I began to see the past again, and how I had, even as far back as those college days, a distaste for dangerously fanatical commitments. No 'Red' revolution for me. No 'Labour Left', no 'Youth with a Mission', no politics at all. No 'Save the Language' group or 'Save the Otter' group, absolutely no gathering together with others to mould the world. Shannon's upbringing was different Her father was an 'Irish' fanatic. She had to be Irish, dance Irish dances, sing Irish songs, be a perfect Irish specimen in a flawed North American world. It was easy to see how she gravitated towards me. And I knew how flattered I was, back then, to be part of her vision of a true homeland on the other side of the Atlantic Ocean. If they did not exactly coincide, then our disparate worlds certainly overlapped. But ... and it finally hit me right between the eyes - I was no more comfortable with the 'Complete Irish Package' than she was. The Irish end of my life had been modified - some would say tainted - by my North American experience. I too, was radically unsettled, no longer at home in either place.

We are winging in over Arranmore Island now, beginning the descent for our landing in Dublin. Inland the country is shrouded, cloud upon cloud spread over the earth. I know that there is beauty and friendship down there, which I love and treasure. There is a history too. Mine is a land in which the very stones have voices. But it also has a way of life that I feel I can barely tolerate. Is this what the "something else" is? Did Shannon sense my unease and go on to distrust her own senses? Was I now coming home to a place which was no longer home?

We approach Dublin Airport from the north. When we break through the cloud I look down and instantly recognize the megalithic tomb at Newgrange and the soft plains of County Meath, colonised by visitors who, whatever it meant in those days, must have become Irish. Identity. That's it. The question of our marriage - mine and Shannons - was contained in the question of who or what we are. And since neither of us appeared to be able to answer that question satisfactorily, the marriage had died.

We glide over the hangars now, and we touch down. As instructed, I have my seatbelt fastened. But I am not safe. The roar of the airplane's reverse thrust drowns out the screaming in my heart.

PURCHASED FROM THE EARTH

The fun we had in those days! Discos. Drink. Midnight binges. Girls in the back of the big blue van. By the way, Mr. Leslie says it's all right for me to call it 'fun'. Initially I was surprised at this, but he explained that it doesn't do at all to reconstruct the past. Better to appropriate the present and pray ourselves into an everlasting future, he says. So now I can say it was fun and not sin, and I'm glad of that. You see, it wouldn't do for me to be too pious and high-sounding when I speak with Alec. He is beginning to see me as a friend and I want things to continue that way. When 'it' happens - and it will happen soon - I want him to be called with me. I suppose it would be better if all my friends and my sister and parents were taken too, but that seems highly unlikely. And Alec is, after all, my special responsibility.

The fun times began when I was about sixteen. There was no shortage of readies in our house and the odd few quid was always available to me. I had a good social life and everything I did seemed to have a gigantic buzz about it. Indeed, I believed myself to be the unique centre of a wonderful world. But things changed. After a few months studying philosophy in college I had relinquished that idea. It seemed that not alone was I not the centre, but that that there was no centre at all. It was then that I fell apart. Not dramatically like Sue, or as tragically as Hughie did, but bit by relentless bit my belief in the permanence of the world and my importance in it was critically eroded. There was this guy called Craig. He argued me away from every certainty I had. Coming down the central stairs in the Arts Block one day he tripped over my foot and tumbled noisily down several steps.

"Are you ok?" I shouted, noting that he had made no effort to rise.

"Sure," he replied, but still he did not move.

"Lean on me," I invited, and when he did I pulled him back into a standing position. He winced.

"Where does it hurt?" I asked anxiously.

"Hurt?" he frowned. "Hurt? Nothing hurts."

"But you look like you've injured something," I insisted, though I was hoping that he would continue to assure me that all was well.

"Berkeley didn't hurt his foot when he stubbed his toe on a stone, now did he?" he asked.

"I suppose not," I faltered, a little overwhelmed.

"Neither did I hurt myself falling over your dammed foot because there is no such thing as pain."

Initially I suspected that Craig was a poser, anxious only to impress. But I got to know him quite well. He lived it. He didn't merely spout out rhetoric. He was as autonomous and unyielding as stone, managing to hold the universe at arms' length simply by declaring its non-existence. He and I were insubstantial entities in an arbitarily constructed universe and of no cosmic consequence at all.

"If you think you have found truth," he said to me one day, "then kiss it lightly and let it go free for evermore."

"Craig," I protested, "that's daft. Truth needs to be nurtured. It needs to be handled with kid gloves. It deserves to be molly-coddled."

"That's your trouble, Vincent," he retorted, "you don't know how to be innocent."

"Innocent?"

"Yes, innocent." He savoured the word on his tongue for a few seconds before expanding on his idea. "Innocent, like you know nothing, like there is nothing to know, like there is no you to know anything anyway. Get my drift?"

"Are you sure you don't mean 'ignorant?'" I asked, not merely to be smart but also out of genuine concern for the matter in hand.

"No, I don't," he said emphatically. "To be ignorant is to think you can know damn well everything. That's not what I mean at all. Innocence comes after knowledge. It creeps in when you acknowledge that you can know nothing in a fixed and final way." He spilled the words over me like a benediction, smiling, determined to be honest. Right then there was nobody I trusted more in the entire world. His refusal to be complacent was the noblest kind of action I had ever encountered. We became close friends.

Craig went away when we had known each other less than two years.

"The East," he said, "somewhere where things are less pronounced, if you know what I mean."
I remember him now, the pale, thin face, the fine blond hair flicked back into deep blue eyes, the half smile. Craig going away and talking, as usual, about the impossibility of going anywhere at all.

"Do you have to mope?" my mother demanded.

"No," I said, thinking all would be fine if I could summon Craig back again and we, two nothings in a know-nothing world could discuss, define, conjecture, debate, endure. My mother had great patience in those days, as concerned and tender as ever, but Craig, the bastard, had left me alone to wander in this wilderness, and I was not equal to the task. Dispossessed of his convincing support, I floundered. Drink came to my rescue. It made me happy again, singing, carefree, and easy about town, in love with life.

The exams in May were inconclusive. I was not weak enough to be thrown out nor strong enough to proceed any further without repeating. And my grant had run dry and the bank manager had called me in and my world was in shreds. Three whole days into total abstinence, and I found myself walking the city streets, cold, hungry, mortally wounded by my failure and afraid to go home. Craig was a few thousand miles away, I had to remind myself, when a chap who resembled him passed close to me near Stephen's Green and I almost ran, crying, into his arms. Later that afternoon I saw a man standing on a box, shouting into the wind. He wore a white, homemade knitted sweater with the words 'Jesus Loves Me' worked in red on the back.

"Do you know why you're here?" he called out, his eyes trawling the gathering crowd for a response. There was no reply.

"Do you know where you're going?" he asked then.

"To Kenilworth Square," someone said.

"And do you know how to get there?" the man continued, ignoring the heckler.

"On the number fifteen bus."

"It's very simple," the preacher persisted, you're here because God has brought you here. You're going back to God. You can get there by accepting Jesus Christ as your Lord and Saviour."

A young woman with a guitar began to play and

sing. Two or three people shouted an occasional 'Alleluia', and when it was all over the white and red Jesus man made straight for me.

"Are you saved, brother?" he demanded, "are you saved?"

Of course we can be cynical about life, as Craig was, but it does no good. Pretending that there is no reality does not obliterate the terrible truth that unless we accept Jesus as our Lord and Saviour we are headed for hell. On the day Luke Leslie noticed me I was filthy with sin. Now my slate has been wiped clean. To celebrate that fact his wife knitted me a pullover something like his, but my lettering is in green. I've accepted Jesus and I'm saved. I'm going to heaven. And I've got my own personal 'shepherd' leading me all the way. His name is Tom.

They saw my surprise when a 'shepherd' was first mooted.

"It's just like a big brother, really," Luke Leslie explained.

I nodded and he continued. "You remember in the gospels Jesus emphasised the importance of the shepherd in leading the sheep safely home?"

"Yes," I answered. "Yes, I remember."

"Well, from now on Tom is to be your shepherd. And remember Tom himself has a shepherd and so have I. We all have, except for the women of course, because they are in the charge of their husbands or their fathers or the men in the church."

At first I was a little uneasy with this arrangement, but after some time I realised that it was a highly satisfactory one. Tom teaches me. And he's like a confessor only he's not one, if you know what I mean. He makes me go over everything with him so that he can keep me on the straight and narrow.

I was a bit upset when he asked me to stop seeing Ursula. But I accept that his reasons were good ones. She is one of those women's libbers, you see, and their philosophy is clearly against God's law. He says he'll find me a suitable girl when I'm ready. His daughter, Rachel, always brings me tea when I visit him, and she sits by me at the meetings. She told me her daddy did not approve of University. He considered such places to be hot beds of pride. But I've more or less dropped out of university anyway. I'm in training for more important work. Time is moving on because the world, as we know it, is about to end. And I've a duty to warn people that we're living in the end times. I've spoken to my parents about that. I told them I was concerned about them and about my sister, Tammy. When I explained why this was my mother's eyes misted over. And then the tears began to flow, gently at first, a mere trickle, but swiftly gathering momentum as they grew into an angry stream. I decided to concentrate on Dad. He was less emotional, I reasoned, and would surely see that I was right to be concerned about their souls. After all, they were going to hell, nothing was more certain than that. My father listened. He whispered the mandatory yes son, no son, I understand son, but when I asked if he was ready to accept the free gift of salvation he merely said, we'll see, we'll see.

I had to leave home shortly after that. Tom said I should. My parents refused my help and had the temerity to bring O'Grady around to lecture me. He's their priest, and they insisted he was also mine.

But I denounced him in no uncertain terms. He's also on the road to hell. Oh, I've done my best with him too, but I've not succeeded. Alec is altogether different and maybe that's why Tom has asked me to take care of him. He's hesitating, but he's open, and I think he's nearly there. His is an unusual story. He and his twin brother and their sister, Linda never did take to the message as their parents did, but then Linda got a fright one day and converted straight away. She's heard the bible read a lot, of course, as had her brothers Alec and Andy. But it must have sunk in with Linda. One day she came home from school and found both her parents unaccountably absent - and she freaked. She remembered 'The Rapture', how the Lord's anointed would be taken up into heaven without the terrible transition of death, and how the 'unsaved', remaining behind, would suffer famines and pestilences without respite. She was convinced that her parents had been 'taken up'. Funny that, because they had, in fact, just been called unexpectedly to the airport. They returned later to find their distraught daughter on her knees in front of Mr. Leslie. This pleased them immensely. But Andy took off to Australia soon after that, declaring them all mad, and since then Alec has hovered on the brink, his immortal soul struggling between life and death.

One of the first things Tom emphasised was that we could not afford the luxury of feelings. You didn't feel love of God, he explained. In fact you couldn't depend on a feeling at all. Love was and had to be a decision. He knew how much I thought I had loved my friend Craig and he helped me to surrender that obsession. And as for Alec, it was up to me to ensure that no sentiment crept into our relationship. He was a lost soul needing to be saved. If this happened he would be my 'brother' in Christ.

I showed Alec a passage in scripture that means a lot to me. Actually, it was the one I used in my farewell letter to my parents.

> "And they sang a new song before the throne and before the four living creatures and the elders, and no one could learn the song except the one hundred and forty four thousand who had been purchased from the earth."

When I first encountered that piece of writing I wondered how Tom managed to apply it to himself and the other people in the group. You see, there were one hundred and forty four thousand people singing the new and exclusive song, but weren't they described as "the celibates". Tom took time out to explain things to me. He demonstrated that the word 'celibate' had been used metaphorically to denote all those who had refrained from intercourse with a fallen world.

When they discovered I had left my parents rang Tom. Naturally he refused to speak with them. They then contacted the police, but as I'm over eighteen there was nothing they could do to force me back. When I left I packed everything of spiritual value and discarded the rest. In my bedroom they would find only my bed, my hi-fi, my video machine, my tele, and most importantly, the letter in a blue envelope which I had propped on top of it. Tom told me about my parent's phone calls, but not immediately. It was almost eight months later, in fact. I understand the delay was necessary because many new brethren are dragged back to their unsaved families as a direct result of hysterical and emotional intervention. I appreciated Tom's discretion. My mother rang again several times and pleaded that I speak with her. But I can't. She understands nothing of the lives of those who are to be purchased from the earth. However, she'll know soon enough. Mr. Leslie is out every day preaching that the time is almost upon us, and I'm with him on that one. I know it will come soon, and I want to be ready. I want Alec to be fully prepared too. My parents and Tammy will be left behind, but I can't help that. They refused to listen to me. They huffed and they puffed and they blew my words down. But in my new life their fate will not concern me. They had the same opportunity as I had. If they had listened they too would be saved. Like me they would be purchased from the earth.

DREAMS AND OTHER OCCURENCES

The Morgans are going to die. In a dream last night I saw their thin bodies spread out flat on mortuary slabs, as close together in death as they had been in life. Ronnie, the eldest, was once a mate of mine in school. We even hung around together for a while afterwards, until he began to work as a lorry driver and I took up an appointment in the local bank. His bookish brother, Liam, kept his learning largely to himself, that is until he began to meet up with Adelaide as she was coming home from school. I saw the two of them together several times on the canal bridge. Once I hid under the bridge so that when they met I could hear what was going on. He read poetry to her from one of his books. I warned my parents that Adelaide was dating Liam Morgan, and naturally they forbade her to see him again. She did see him, however, but Ronnie was there too and she convinced my parents that it was not a 'real' date because the older brother was included. I hated the way Ronnie looked at my little sister's breasts and legs. I asked him nicely not to meet up with her again but he laughed at me. I thought of getting him into trouble with his boss so that he'd lose his job and leave the town, but I couldn't come up with a viable plan. Often I had to suffer the sight of him and Liam talking to our Adelaide on the bridge, or walking the canal bank, or visiting the only cinema in town.

My parents are dead these two years now and there's just my little sister and me. I remember the day she was born as if it were yesterday. I was nearly eleven years old and had got quite used to being an only child when they told me that my mother was "in the family way". On the day Adelaide arrived my old-man-Daddy laughed and joked like a young guy. He was on the phone for half the day, telling his friends and the various members of our scattered family his good news. However, he was awkward with me, as though this evidence of his continuing sexual prowess might somehow corrupt our relationship. My mother was different. When she arrived home from the hospital she allowed me to take the baby in my arms for a little while. Her tiny face was all screwed up into a funny kind of grin. My mother said it was just wind, but I knew that the baby was smiling at me. When she opened up her eyes and looked directly into mine I vowed that I would do anything for Adelaide, that she was my absolute favourite human being in the entire world.

I hated my parents for packing me off to boarding school two years later. But I managed to get myself expelled after only three months and my father had to plead with the local Christian Brothers to take me in. The blokes in that school sometimes jeered me about Adelaide.

"Here's Daddy Connor with his baby in his arms," they'd shout. Or "who's a good dada then?"
Ronnie Morgan did not involve himself in any of these slagging sessions and I suppose that's one of the reasons why we two became friends. Adelaide and I also grew very close. The eleven-year age gap made no difference. My parents never had to worry about taking her to school, or to the beach in summer, or into the town. I did all these things and more. If she wanted someone to tell her secrets to, I was there. If she was excited about something at school I was the one who was first told the good news. But things

began to change when she started hanging about with Liam Morgan. There was a new attraction – poetry on the canal bridge. I bought a book of poems by a woman called Emily Dickinson and surprised her by going into her room one night with the blue and white covered volume in my hands.

"Adelaide, listen, what do you think of this?" I asked and began to read.

"Exultation is the going
of an inland soul to sea,
past the houses –
past the headlands –
into deep infinity"

"Connor," she shouted, "would you get out of here."

"Bred as we are,
among the mountains,
can the sailor understand
the divine intoxication
of the first league out from land,"

I continued in a rush.

"Are you crazy or something?" she asked angrily. "What exactly do you think you're at?"

"Poetry. The American poet Emily Dickinson," I announced, holding up the book with the portrait of a solemn faced young woman on the cover.

"Poetry?" she echoed.

"I know Liam Morgan reads poetry to you," I told her.

"That's different," she choked, a look of astonishment creeping across her face.

"No, it's not," I countered.

"Look, I won't argue with you, Connor," she said. "Just take your stupid Emily what's-her-name and get out of here. And another thing," she added as I left, "don't ever come into my bedroom again."

It was obvious that the Morgans were bad news from the beginning, with Liam constantly spouting poetry to my sister and big-boy Ronnie sniffing around, brimming with sex. Things were reaching a critical point, and I felt strongly that something needed to be done. As my parents were no longer around I saw it as my solemn duty to protect my little sister. But she wasn't as close to me as she used to be, and whenever I warned her off the Morgans she either laughed or told me to go and get my own 'effin' woman and not to be bothering her. I blame myself really. I should have made it clear to Adelaide at the outset that relationships of that sort were simply not on.

Her twenty first birthday was coming up in July. I'd planned to drive her to Dublin for the day, bringing her shopping in Grafton Street, taking in a theatre show and finishing off the evening in grand style with a meal out in one of those up-market sea food restaurants in the city. She laughed when I told her of my plans. She laughed a lot lately, especially when we argued about the Morgans. Her laugh irritated me.

"Liam and Ronnie are throwing a bit of a bash for me," she said as she dismissed my plans for her birthday.

"Are they now?" I felt my tongue curl and my fists tighten every time she mentioned them.

"They are," she said. "You're welcome to come along if you like. It'll be in 'Fitzers' to start with and afterwards at their house."

"Their house?" I choked. "You're going to drink yourself silly in the pub and then go to the Morgan house?"

"I did say you were invited," she said crossly.

"Adelaide, I forbid you to have anything to do with that party," I said in my sternest voice. "I absolutely forbid it."
She merely grinned at me.

Yesterday was packed with antagonism when it should have been an occasion of special joy. July 15th. Her twenty first birthday. A grown woman now and a stunner. She went to work as usual but came home early and started to doll herself up, scarlet lipstick plastered across her face and her auburn hair all streaked with yellow. Disgusting. In the end I had to lock her into her bedroom so that she couldn't go to them. It wasn't exactly what I'd hoped for, but there was no way I could allow her to go boozing with those two on this most important occasion. I ignored her screaming and the way she swore at me. After a while her screaming turned to sobbing and soon afterwards her sobbing eased. She must have gone to bed eventually and fallen asleep.

I went for a long walk and finally ended up at the far end of town. I saw the lights on in the Morgan place and heard loud music. I felt like going in and announcing that they could close their party down, that Adelaide had decided to give their little gig a miss. The front door was slightly ajar, and I opened it. There was nobody in the hall. From there I peeped into the sitting room and wasn't at all surprised to find several couples kissing and snogging around the place. The Morgans were as busy as the other blokes. I couldn't see the girls but only flashes of leg and thigh. The one with Liam was completely hidden. He kept stroking her and murmuring Addie, Addie.

Dirty bastard – couldn't even remember which woman he was with.

It was at this stage that the pain in my forehead began. Within seconds my head began to crack open, as if someone had drawn a clever though my skull. Immediately afterwards everything went blank. When I came to I was sitting on the roadside about a mile away. I managed to stumble back home and into my bed. That's where I dreamed my dream. Liam and Ronnie Morgan were dead. The dream showed me what had happened. There was a fire in their house, lots of smoke, panic, injury – and death.

Adelaide must have slept well after all her howling. I had to have breakfast alone. Afterwards I decided I'd better go and wake her. I was determined to make it up to her, you see. I'd get round her like I used to when she was little and we'd have a proper celebration in a week or two. For the moment I'd do the chivalrous thing and bring her breakfast in bed. Poor Sis – it was the least I could do. I made some light brown toast, which she liked, and coffee and a boiled egg. I laid out the tray neatly, coffee to the right, toast, egg and marmalade to the left, and a white rose, fresh from our garden, across the top. I carried the tray very carefully, hoping I wouldn't make a noise and wake her until I entered the room. Then it'd be a real surprise. But when I got to the landing I noticed that there was a sheet of paper laid across the door saddle and that the door was partly open. I realised immediately that she'd remembered the games of gaol we used to play as kids, when escape was the object of the exercise. If the key was left in the locked door it was relatively easy for the prisoner to pull it through on the paper and to free themselves, provided there was a reasonable gap underneath. Adelaide must have pretended to be asleep and absconded just as soon as I'd left the house. But she'd have gone directly to the Morgan place. And the fire? Oh Adelaide, my precious Adelaide!

The tray fell to the bedroom floor just as the sound of a siren echoed down the long avenue to our house. I went out to meet the police. I'd made up my mind that I'd tell them about Adelaide and the birthday celebration. They had a right to know that. But they'd hardly need to be privy to my dreams.

DEALING WITH THE ANGLERS

Sometimes, when I go down to the river, I see the anglers. There are usually three or four of them along the bank, crouched under big oilskins, watching the water. They never speak. Hardly move. Never smile. Anglers. I pass by on the other bank but do not look in their direction. I glance at the water instead, at the silver twirls and swirls of it, admiring its raw power as it rushes over the low weir. I won't shout across to them, even if they could hear me. Instead I count. I count my footsteps carefully on the first journey and make sure I place my feet inside the very same steps as I return home. I feel slightly safer walking like that. Right now it's easy because the weather is wet.

I like wet winters best when the anglers gather along the river and I can watch them in secret from behind the bushes that grow along my bank. Behind me is a new golf course, but the golfers never bother me and I don't care about them. It is how the anglers sit in silence that interests me, and the way they thread their hooks with worms and cast out into the water and wait for hours for the fish to bite. There's something shivery about it all, the wriggling earthworm down there in the water waiting to be taken into the mouth of a doomed fish. I wonder if the anglers eat the fish later on, dipped in batter and cooked in a deep fat fryer the way my mother does them. Or lightly poached, perhaps, and sprinkled with lemon. But I doubt it. I've seen them, on more than one occasion, throwing buckets of dead fish away. I never eat fish. I tried once, but all I could see was a plate of angry eyes devouring me. I made an attempt to swim with them later, when we were on holidays in Clare, but I couldn't hold my breath long enough to stay under. And when I tried to gather up the water with my hands it evaded me. I try to gather up to my thoughts too, but often they get lost in a swirling, twirling waltz like the dancing waters which leap over my weir. In my room - on my tele - I have a video where I see men with black wetsuits and tanks on their backs swimming with fish coloured like flowers and spice. They never get lost.

I keep having this dream. I'm in a foreign country. I enter buildings with other tourists, but each time I come out and look back at the building I've just been in it has changed into another. At that stage the pounding of my heart awakens me and the images of unfamiliar buildings soon fade. I tried to tell my mother about it but she said it wasn't important, that dreams don't count at all in the overall scheme of things. Easy for her, though. She sleeps tight at night. For me sleep is always hard to achieve, and often full of disturbance. Sometimes I give up on sleep entirely, leave my bed, take a torch and walk along the river. Months ago I saw an otter. It moved across my path and just blended into the river, like it had been made of water all along. I hoped it would leak back out onto the bank later on, but that didn't hap-pen. I waited until dawn crept in over the eastern sky but I never saw it again.

Once I saw a film about this man and woman in Scotland who got close to some otters. But that never happened along my river, and I don't know why. My mother said it was all nonsense anyway, this looking out for wild animals like those two in the film had done. She said most animals were perfectly capable of looking out for themselves, and that the people involved should have better things to do with their lives. She became agitated when she spoke like that. She was always complaining too about the muck I brought in after my trips along the river, but she wasn't really serious because I saw her smiling to herself sometimes as she housewifed the dirt and dust away.

Last week the librarian took some of the books I was reading away from me. She said I should only have five in front of me at any one time and that there were other people there who also needed to use the library's 'services'. I never saw anybody else reading about fish, only me, so why that woman took the books I chose away from me is a mystery I just cannot fathom. I wanted to tell her about the anglers fishing along the river, and my concerns, but she didn't seem to me to be the kind of person who would be genuinely interested and I never speak to anyone just for speaking's sake.

There is a fish sanctuary a mile or so upstream from where the anglers sit. It is a small deep stretch beside a bridge and sometimes people stand there and watch the fish swim freely about as though they knew they were safe. It works, I suppose, but the price is too high because they become careless and easy there, and when they swim outside that place they let their guard down. I wished that they would swim so tightly together that nothing at all could pass between them, nor even a drop of water, so that, compacted like that, they might not be so easily spotted. But they never seemed to develop such a strategy. I saw a polar bear swimming on her back once, so relaxed and content that she did not know that the zoo keeper had arrived with her fish. What if he had arrived with a gun in his hand? Living creatures ought always to be vigilant while about their business in this world.

I like being alone - I mean really alone. Being alone alone is not as painful as being alone in a crowd. It's difficult in the library sometimes, especially when all those students come in after college closes for the day and they're all over the place chatting and pointing out bits of information to each other. I stay quiet and try hard to keep out of their way. But it's those who make the most noise and fuss who get their way in the end, isn't it? I know that because the librarians are always attending to them and they can take as many books as they like from the shelves and they never get hassled to "put things back where they got them" like I do.

Yesterday I saw a shark being hoisted out of the water off the coast of Australia so that Olympic contestants could swim where he had been. And the commentator on television seemed to suggest that it was outrageous that he should have been there in the first place, and that it was perfectly all right to wrench him from his liquid home and to cart him away. Where human and other animal worlds overlap it's always like that. The human race is one giant appetite which has to be satisfied. It's that 'for man's use and benefit' verse in the Old Testament which is responsible for that, and the 'increase and multiply and fill the earth' bit. The Bible has a lot to answer for, I believe. All along its language has been lying to us. Our original sin was not a fear of ignorance at all, but a strong inclination towards arrogance.

It's true. I admit it. I don't know how to stop wanting things to be different. On the table near the kitchen window there is a vase of roses and beside it a pair of binoculars in a black leather case. I try to take pleasure in the roses and to resist what the binoculars have to offer. But my mind won't allow me to do that. It makes it impossible. I compromise. I quickly sniff the roses before picking up the binoculars and focussing upriver. It is obvious to me now that this is where my life's work is. All the other places that I might occupy - shopping centres, city street, garages, armies, offices, make me feel ill. The river is my domain. I feel at home here and I feel my work is here and all I have done really, in refusing to join any other activity, is to surrender to the reality of my life. After all, there isn't one right way of being a person and all others wrong. I had to argue that one out with my mother for a long time, but she's accepted it now. She still can't see what I see, but she realizes that the river has wound its way through my soul. Knowing where you fit in has its advantages, I suppose, just as surely as knowing what to believe. In my case I've found the perfect fit, but my beliefs, if I were to speak them out loud, would trouble many people.

But the time has come. I'll soon have to speak out. They say they know - that the truth of the Bible is clear - that humankind is in charge of the world. But the truth is that we need a word of infinitesimally smaller scope. And people can not be left hiding in that safe, dark place called 'certainty' any longer. It is my task, I believe, to turn things around, to revolutionise the world, to send man right down to the back of the class. Up to now I've probably not had an adequate sense of outrage about the way things are, but watching how the anglers behave has changed all that. I may fail, of course. I have a talent for failure. But I also have a talent for risk, and the two together, risk and failure, might see me through. It will be a small beginning, but there is, after all, only one me and I have a few thousand years of misinformation and malpractice to deal with.

I'm not exactly sure how I'll launch my campaign. But, since he died five years ago my father's shotgun has been lying in a box under his bed, and I suppose I should check that out anyway, so that when the time comes I can make a small beginning by frightening the anglers away.

OUR ORDINARY WORLD

We had a special name for him. We called him 'Hug Harold' because he was a member of a new religious movement whose members demonstrated great affection for each other on all possible occasions. For a while he tried to bring us with him, but his touchy-feely behaviour put us right off, and we told him so in no uncertain terms. He moved out after six months of unsuccessful efforts at evangelisation, and we started to keep a weather eye out for a replacement to house share with us. Bernard wanted to try for a girl - to bring a touch of feminine refinement into our bachelor lives, he argued - but a democratic vote with a majority of two to one prevailed in favour of maintaining our single-sex status.

"Life is not a computer," Hug Harold told us on the morning he moved out. "You can't go back and delete, you know. Decisions have to be made now. The right decisions, understand that?"
Andrew yawned. I smiled a thoroughly placatory smile and Bernard abandoned his personal computer long enough to bid the 'preacher' a fond farewell.
"Ok. Ok." he told Harold "we'll have ourselves a good think about what you've said, won't we lads? Now look, you'd better hurry, that taxi is burning up juice outside."

The man who sets the exams papers always knows the answers, of course, and we knew exactly what we wanted in a fellow tenant - someone who was not at all like the late departed Hug Harold. Dermot was quiet, self-effacing - the "you wouldn't even see me on an x-ray" type - and we wasted no time at all in making the decision to invite him to join us in our suburban home. He cheerfully did his share of the cleaning, paid his expenses within a few days of being asked, and seemed, in fact, the ideal tenant. In his essential aloofness he also promised to be a soothing successor to Hug.

We settled down, the four of us together, Bernard, Andrew and I anticipating calm and happy days ahead. But things did not go according to plan. It was two months before we heard Dermot raise his voice at all, but when it happened it was as if an explosive force had been held in check for a very long time. I was in the kitchen fixing myself a stir-fry when the commotion broke out above me. I heard Dermot before I heard Bernard.

"Don't do that," he screamed, "just lift it and put it into a dark corner. Don't do that."

"You bloody eejet,' Bernard yelled back, "I want to have a shower now, not after I've gone through your daft insect rescue routine."

"It won't take a second," Dermot urged. His voice was calmer, gentle, pleading.

"Will you get out of here," Bernard shouted. "I'm showering now and to hell with any creature who's stupid enough to trespass anywhere near me."
He slammed the door in Dermot's face, and water cascading carelessly from Bernard's freckled skin onto the cold grey tiles at his feet was the only sound to be heard as Dermot retreated.

"Spiders have a right to life too," Dermot roared in my ear as he reached the bottom of the stairs.

Andrew worked "in the community". His sharp wit and easy smile were challenged on a daily basis by what he saw and heard in the murky corners of our ordinary world. Dermot declared himself "fascinated" by the stuff Andrew did. He was a writer, he said, a "critical observer of life", and the more help- less and sordid people were the better he liked it, it seemed. But we never saw him do anything to earn a crust. We enquired once if the great novel of the decade was incubating.

"I have some more living to do before I tackle that," he told us.

Did he favour poetry then?

"Occasionally a sonnet suggests itself to me," he said carefully, "but you must know that true poetry is written only for oneself."

Exasperated, Bernard was careless enough to float the idea of regular articles on subjects of public concern for a magazine or a weekly newspaper.

"Like an opinion column!" Dermot exclaimed, "now that's one daft idea. Don't you realise that I hold my opinions lightly? An 'opinion' column is the last thing - the very last thing - I'd be likely to write."

Bernard sighed. There were times, he told me later, when he longed for the relatively uncomplicated company of Hug Harold again.

With the aid of a grant from the Department of Education and a twice-yearly sub from my parents I was studying science. I was the only student member of our little coterie and I was also the youngest of the foursome. Dermot often tried to pull rank and to treat me like a child. When this failed he criticised my studies.

"You scientists are always chasing after 'order'," he complained one day. "You must be insecure, wanting things to be entirely predictable and explicable."

"That's not true," I told him. "We simply want to push out the frontiers. Certainty doesn't come in to it - at least not in the way you seem to think."

Dermot threw a log on the fire. "Imagine if that didn't burn," he invited. "Imagine it exploding instead. That's what I enjoy, the possibility of things going wrong, of the whole show falling madly to pieces."

I held my tongue. Accepting that possibility was, as I understood it, part and parcel of all science. But this fellow's grim determination to be top of the pile in a totally irregular and pitiful world irritated me. I was alarmed then when he suggested that Andrew "write up" a daily diary from which he, Dermot, might gain further "experience."

"Don't worry about it," Andrew said when I expressed my reservations, "there's material and there's material, if you know what I mean."

"But confidentiality," I pointed out, "what about your client's rights to confidentiality?"

Andrew looked at me as though I were a dribbling infant on his first day at school.

"You can take it from me, Peter," he said, "that knowledge of my client's sorrows and sins is safe with me."

A late autumn day. We were in the garden. The landlord had agreed a reduced rent if we took care of it, and we had been happy to agree. I was raking up leaves and Andrew was burning them when Dermot arrived.

"Imagine if that tree owned itself," he said, pointing to an ash tree at the end of the garden. We ignored him.

"There's this oak tree," he continued, "somewhere down the country, that actually owns itself."

"Yeah." Andrew tossed another pile of leaves onto the bonfire and defied him to explain himself.

"It was Bernard who told me," Dermot said. "He said that this farmer left the land around an oak tree - I think it was supposed to be a sacred oak tree - to the oak tree itself, so that when he died the oak tree owned itself, if you know what I mean."

He slowed down as the explanation progressed, conscious for the first time perhaps, of the absurdity of the statement. Andrew pointed to an ash tree.

"That one does own itself. Did you not know that?"

"How come?" Dermot eagerly enquired.

"I don't understand either how it owns itself," I said to Andrew. "After all this is a suburban garden. The other one - the oak tree - was on a large farm."

"It's something to do with the lease," Andrew offered. "Wouldn't that be it, Dermot? You're the expert on these things. You tell us."

But Dermot was edging away from him now, his eyes as wary as those of a cornered animal.

"I only mentioned it because ..." he began to say.

"Because you're a shit-head,' Andrew interrupted, and far too stupid to know when Bernard is having you on."

Soon after that Dermot went away for a month - to do a course on Astral Travel, he said, and when he returned he was as quiet and withdrawn as he'd been when he first came to us. He also seemed to have developed an interest in sculpture and tried to make a papier-mâché model of Rodin's 'Clenched Hand'. We, that is Andrew, Bernard and myself, were dead curious about this but agreed that it would be better not to question him too closely in case we might get ourselves into something awkward. It was Dermot who came to us when he eventually succeeded in making a model that remained intact.

"What colour do you think I should paint it?" he asked one morning as we ate breakfast. The famous hand lay on the table between us, knuckles pointing towards Bernard.

"Silver, I think," Bernard suggested tentatively, intimidated, I think by those protruding knuckles.

"You couldn't paint it silver," Andrew countered, "it's a hand, a human hand, so it has to be flesh-coloured."

Dermot turned to me. "I don't fancy silver or flesh-coloured," he told me. "What do you think?"

"Sea-green," I said. It was the first thing that came into my head. "Sea-green is a natural colour but not the natural colour of a human hand. You could say a lot with sea-green."

Dermot nodded. "Not bad. Not bad at all. But I was thinking more of some shade of red."

Bernard stood up. "I'll be late for work if I don't push off now," he said, "but if I were you Dermot I'd definitely avoid red."

"Why is that?" Dermot wanted to know.

"Because of Ulster and the Red Hand." Bernard answered. He closed the door behind him as he left, so that only Andrew and I witnessed the momentary confusion which registered on Dermot's face before he began to scream.

The border disappeared that day, that thin, ambiguous line between the intact ego and the terrors of insanity. We were thoroughly unsettled by

Dermot's collapse, feeling guilty, and dreading the thought that something like that might happen to us. Andrew convened our first 'case conference' after our initial visit to Dermot in the hospital. We'd found him sitting in the day room, listlessly thumbing through a copy of Roget's Thesaurus.

"I'm looking for a word," he explained, "a word that will make all other words superfluous for all time."

"In what way?" I dared to ask. It seemed to me that a writer, of all people, should treasure a multitude of words. Andrew kicked my shins under the table. "Sure, Dermot," he said, "I know what you mean. Words have a nasty habit of getting in the way sometimes, don't they?"
Dermot brought a furious fist down on the table.

"That's it," he yelled. "Do it again - like you've done before - like you've all done - refuse to admit that I know what I'm talking about - that I'm right. A prophet in his own country - that's what I am. Can't you see?"

"I see that it's difficult sometimes to be under-stood," Andrew answered calmly. "We talk and people listen - they really do - and they respond as best they can, but it's simply not enough. There's no genuine connection."
Andrew looked as though he meant it, but then his work must have thrown up all kinds of situations in which the deficiencies of human language were
clearly revealed. During this exchange Bernard twisted his evening paper into an unreadable shape, gazing through a bay window into a windswept yard. Eventually he focussed on Dermot.

"We're sorry if you feel we've let you down," he announced.

Dermot swept a casual hand across imaginary space. His tone had altered, no longer confrontational but calm, almost confessional. "It's ok," he said, "it's not you, it's the whole world. The entire universe, in fact. We're not made for closeness, you know, though we desperately persuade ourselves we need it."

Bernard sighed, and we each settled down into the bleakness of that statement, drawing jerky breaths, struggling hard to discover if there was anything else we might usefully say. We must have been holed up in that awkward limbo for several minutes before the door of the day room opened and a woman came creeping in as though mortally afraid to enter such a perilous place. Dermot glanced at her and immediately looked away.

"I'd like to speak to my son," she whispered to us from behind a gloved hand, "on his own if you don't mind, please."

Long after Andrew and I had wearied of the twice-weekly visiting regime Bernard hung on in there with Dermot. Exam-time was approaching and I persuaded myself that I needed to get in as much revision as I possibly could. I'd phone sometimes, and speak briefly to Dermot, or be told by a member of the staff that he was "making good progress". During this time Andrew was away in The Netherlands - at an international conference on some social work theme - and I envied him his perfectly valid excuse for not visiting. It was nearly three months since the day Dermot had been admitted, and though he'd moved from building to building inside the hospital and from ward to ward, there was no sign of his coming home. Bernard insisted that these moves represented 'progress', and in the absence of first hand evidence I had to be content with his assessment of the situation. On Andrew's first evening back with us I mentioned my misgivings to him, but he merely shook his head.

Soon after that Bernard confided that Dermot had stopped asking about us. Human beings tend to remember selectively the things that interest them, I suppose, and I accepted that Dermot was no longer interested in what was happening in my little world. But even Andrew's complicated comings and goings no longer appealed. Only the future, Bernard reported, occupied any significant part of Dermot's thoughts and plans. He wanted to be ready for what would happen in the year 2012, a momentous event which, he claimed, would alter us all for ever. I was astonished at this apparent volte face in Dermot's thinking, remembering clearly how he had faulted science for "wanting certainty", and how he once boasted that he liked the thought of "the whole show falling to pieces". But strangely, Bernard seemed convinced of the rightness of what Dermot was proposing and believed that astral travel and a wordless world would be part of a new order. Dermot was speaking very little now, he told us. He refused to talk to the staff at the hospital and used a minimum of non-verbal communication to get his message across. Mental contact happened mostly at a subliminal level, Bernard claimed, and for this reason came through uncorrupted by ideology or flawed rhetoric. As a result of these 'communications' Bernard too decided to go away to "learn more" so that he would be ready in advance for what he called "the big heave".

Two weeks later he set off, his I.T. career casually abandoned behind him. It was raining softly on the evening we drove him to Dunlaoghaire on the first leg of the journey, which, as he put it, would supply answers to questions he had not yet dared to ask. As we drove to the ferry terminal the wipers of Andrew's car came into action at regular intervals, and I watched them compulsively until I was almost hypnotised, the odd nature of the journey unsettling me. Bernard was silent, flushed with a quiet excitement, and unable, it seemed, to wait for the moment when the boat would pull anchor and move off. Afterwards Andrew and I hung around the terminal, waiting for the boat's huge bulk to fade into the swirling mists of the horizon. We were each absorbed in our own thoughts, the distance between us seeming to widen as rapidly as the distance between the shore and the departing boat. Eventually I thought I heard Andrew sigh. I was just about to break the silence when a hand fell on my shoulder and I turned around to confront a smiling Dermot. He looked terrific, far more rounded than the stick-thin Dermot we had previously known, and with a better colour. Andrew pulled himself together more quickly than I did.

"You've just missed Bernard," he said, in as casual a tone as he could muster. "He's off on a journey of discovery, it seems."

Dermot frowned, but it was obviously a feigned surprise.

"Didn't you know?" I asked him. "Didn't you have a hand in - in this business yourself?" My words tumbled out clumsily, conscious as I was of Dermot's skewed smile and of his eyes mocking me. We were outside the terminal building and the street lamps glowed yellow and a pale moon glazed the cold black water of the bay. Dermot looked directly out towards the point where we had, only a few minutes beforehand, seen Bernard's ferry drop below the horizon.

"I like the sea," he said softly. "It takes what it wants in the end."

ISBN 141202095-6

9 781412 020954